"You got any idea what you're so scared of?"

Tears bit at Carly's eyes. "All of this. The town…my options. You."

Sam's eyes flashed as he quietly said, "I don't suppose you'd care to explain that."

"I don't know that I can. It's just that this all seems so real. And I'm—" she met his gaze, sadly shaking her head "—not."

Sam's face hardened. "That's crap, Carly."

He withdrew his hands from his pockets, then took three or four slow, deliberate steps toward her. "Funny thing," he said, "but I think I've got a pretty good handle on the difference between illusion and reality, And as far as I'm concerned, you are one of the most real women I've ever met. So deal with it."

He headed for the door, only to turn back and say, "By the way, I'll be picking you up for the dance tomorrow night around seven. I'd appreciate it if you'd wear something to make every male in the room regret not being me."

Dear Reader,

Let April shower you with the most thrilling romances around—from Silhouette Intimate Moments, of course. We love Karen Templeton's engaging characters and page-turning prose. In her latest story, *Swept Away* (#1357), from her miniseries THE MEN OF MAYES COUNTY, a big-city heroine goes on a road trip and gets stranded in tiny Haven, Oklahoma…with a very handsome cowboy and his six kids. Can this rollicking group become a family? *New York Times* bestselling author Ana Leigh returns with another BISHOP'S HEROES romance, *Reconcilable Differences* (#1358), in which two lovers reunite as they play a deadly game to fight international terror.

You will love the action and heavy emotion of *Midnight Hero* (#1359) in Diana Duncan's new FOREVER IN A DAY miniseries. Here, a SWAT cop has to convince his sweetheart to marry him—while trying to survive a hostage situation! And get ready for Suzanne McMinn to take you by storm in *Cole Dempsey's Back in Town* (#1360), in which a rakish hero must clear his name and face the woman he's never forgotten.

Catch feverish passion and high stakes in Nina Bruhns's *Blue Jeans and a Badge* (#1361). This tale features a female bounty hunter who arrests a very exasperating—very sexy—chief of police! Can these two get along long enough to catch a dangerous criminal? And please join me in welcoming new author Beth Cornelison to the line. In *To Love, Honor and Defend* (#1362), a tormented beauty enters a marriage of convenience with an old flame…and hopes that he'll keep her safe from a stalker. Will their relationship deepen into true love? Don't miss this touching and gripping romance!

So, sit back, prop up your feet and enjoy the ride with Silhouette Intimate Moments. And be sure to join us next month for another stellar lineup.

Happy reading!

Patience Smith
Associate Senior Editor

Please address questions and book requests to:
Silhouette Reader Service
U.S.: 3010 Walden Ave., P.O. Box 1325, Buffalo, NY 14269
Canadian: P.O. Box 609, Fort Erie, Ont. L2A 5X3

KAREN
templeton

Swept away

Silhouette

INTIMATE MOMENTS™

Published by Silhouette Books

America's Publisher of Contemporary Romance

SILHOUETTE BOOKS

ISBN 0-373-27427-0

SWEPT AWAY

This edition published by arrangement with Harlequin Books S.A.

® and TM are trademarks of Harlequin Books S.A., used under license. Trademarks indicated with ® are registered in the United States Patent and Trademark Office, the Canadian Trade Marks Office and in other countries.

Visit Silhouette Books at www.eHarlequin.com

Printed in U.S.A.

Books by Karen Templeton

Silhouette Intimate Moments

Anything for His Children #978
Anything for Her Marriage #1006
Everything but a Husband #1050
Runaway Bridesmaid #1066
†*Plain-Jane Princess* #1096
†*Honky-Tonk Cinderella* #1120
What a Man's Gotta Do #1195
Saving Dr. Ryan #1207
Fathers and Other Strangers #1244
Staking His Claim #1267
****Everybody's Hero* #1328
****Swept Away* #1357

Silhouette Yours Truly

*Wedding Daze
*Wedding Belle
*Wedding? Impossible!

†How To Marry a Monarch
*Weddings, Inc.
**The Men of Mayes County

KAREN TEMPLETON,

a Waldenbooks bestselling author and RITA® Award nominee,
is the mother of five sons and living proof that romance and
dirty diapers are not mutually exclusive terms. An Easterner
transplanted to Albuquerque, New Mexico, she spends far too
much time trying to coax her garden to yield roses and produce something resembling a lawn, all the while fantasizing
about a weekend alone with her husband. Or at least an unin-
terrupted conversation.

She loves to hear from readers, who may reach her by
writing c/o Silhouette Books, 233 Broadway, Suite 1001,
New York, NY 10279, or online at www.karentempleton.com.

Thanks to Debra Cowan, Pam Martin, Teresa Harrison, Kari Dell and Leta Wellman, who patiently answered all my farming questions—I trust I gave you guys a good laugh or two along the way. Trust me, I'll never look at bacon the same way again!

Chapter 1

In the three years since his wife's death, Sam Frazier had prided himself on not tumbling into the abyss of helplessness common to many widowers, especially those with young children. Whether his refusal to let chaos gain a toehold stemmed from his wanting to do Jeannie proud or just plain stubbornness, he had no idea, but he thought he'd been doing okay. Until this bright and sunny September morning when his teenage daughter tried to sneak past him wearing more makeup than a Las Vegas showgirl and not a whole lot more clothes, and he realized he had one foot in that abyss, anyway.

Not that Libby was having a good morning, either, having attempted her little maneuver when the kitchen was filled with her five younger brothers, several of whom thought girls had cooties as it was. Girls who were related to you *and* who had suddenly taken to looking like *women* were clearly the embodiment of evil and hence to be thwarted at every opportunity. Or at the very least greeted by a chorus of disgusted gagging sounds, which even Sam—inured as he generally was to such noises—would be hard put to ignore.

Sam caught Libby's hand and spun her around on her army-tank shoes, the ends of her long, dark hair stinging his bare arm. Silence shuddered in the room, broken only by one of the dogs lapping at his water dish, as something damn close to terror shot through him, that his little girl—especially in that skimpy, mid-riff-baring top and dark lipstick—was no longer "little" in any sense of the word. And he knew damn well exactly how every teenage boy in the county was going to react to that fact.

"More fabric, less makeup," Sam said calmly, his gaze riveted to Libby's defensive light brown one. He felt a twinge in his left leg, an old ache trying to reassert itself. "Go change."

"No time, Sean's already here—"

"He can wait." Sam dropped her hand, nodding toward her room, an old sunroom off the kitchen he'd converted so she'd have more privacy and because five boys in two small bedrooms upstairs was no longer working.

"I'm not changing," she said, chin out, arms crossed, in a pose that would have been the picture of defiance but for the slightly trembling lower lip. Sam felt for her, he really did: teenage angst was bad enough without the added indignity of being the only girl in a houseful of males. "All the other girls wear makeup, everybody'll think I'm a total loser if I don't."

"First off, baby girl, *all* the other girls don't wear makeup. Or wear clothes that look like they outgrew them four years ago." Since Sam substituted up at the high school on a regular basis, Libby knew better than to argue with him. "And anyway," he added before she could load her next round of ammunition, "I didn't say you couldn't wear any makeup. Just not enough for three other girls besides you. And you know the school dress code won't allow a top like that—"

"Well, duh, I've got a shirt in my backpack to put on over it when I'm in school. This is just for, you know, before and after."

"And this is, you know, not open for discussion. Go change. Or," he added as the black-cherry mouth dropped and an indignant squawk popped out of it, "Sean goes on to school and you take the bus. Or better yet, I'll drive you."

A fate worse than death, Sam knew. "This is so unfair!" she yelled, then stomped away, only to whirl around and lob across the kitchen, "You're only on my case because you don't like Sean!"

"Has nothing to do with whether I like him or not," Sam said mildly, even though hormones poured off the boy like sweat off a long-distance runner. Locking Libby away in a tower somewhere for ten years or so was becoming more appealing by the second. "I don't trust him," he said, just so there'd be no mistake.

Eyes flashed, hands landed on hips. "What you mean is, you don't trust *me!*" Four-year-old Travis snuggled up to Sam's flank and asked to be picked up; behind him, he could hear muted clanks and clunks as Mike and Matt, his oldest boys, went about making sandwiches for lunch. "God!" Libby said on a wail. "I wish you'd find a girlfriend or get married again or…or *something* so you'd stop obsessing about us all the *freaking* time!"

Five sets of eyes veered to Sam as he idly wondered where the sweet little girl who used to live here had got to, even as he tamped down a flash of irritation that would do nobody any good to let loose. Smelling of Cheerios, Travis wrapped his arms around Sam's neck, while eight-year-old Wade and first-grader Frankie, still at the breakfast table, silently chewed and gawked.

"You're entitled to your opinion, Libby," Sam said levelly. "But you're upsettin' your brothers, you're keeping Sean waiting, and you're gonna be late for school. So I suggest you keep those thoughts to yourself until a more appropriate time. Now get moving, baby girl."

"Don't *call* me that!" she shrieked, then clomped out of the room.

Letting Travis slide back down to the floor, Sam turned to the boys and said, "It's gettin' late. Time to get a move on. Wade, is it my imagination, or is that the same shirt you had on yesterday?" He frowned. "And the day before that?" At the kid's sheepish shrug, Sam swallowed back a smile. "Go change before your teacher makes you sit outside, okay?"

The eight-year-old trooped off as, with a time-honed precision that was truly a thing of beauty, breakfast dishes were cleared, lunches distributed, assorted arms shoved into jacket or sweatshirt sleeves, and Sam felt a little of his hard-won peace return. Farming was a challenge, no doubt about it; raising six kids by himself even more so. But it was amazing how smoothly things could run—or at least, had run up until the Attack of the Killer Hormones—by simply establishing, and enforcing, some basic parameters, making sure everybody did their fair share.

As all the boys except Travis filed out to catch the school bus, Sam shifted his weight off his complaining leg, deciding there was no reason at all why the method that had stood him in good stead since Jeannie's passing shouldn't continue to do so. Not that it hadn't been hard at first. Lord, he'd missed her so much those first few months he'd thought he'd go crazy, both with grief and unfulfilled longing. But the pain had passed, or at least dulled, as had the collective ineptitude. Jeannie hadn't meant to make them all dependent on her, Sam knew that, but it had simply been in her nature to do for them. She hadn't wanted anyone else messing in her kitchen; there was no reason for the kids, or Sam, for that matter, to remember where anything was because Jeannie had a photographic memory. But when she died, of a freak aneurism that nobody could've predicted, let alone prevented, and it became clear exactly how useless they all were in the house….

Well. Never again, was all Sam had to say. And now that everything was running more or less smoothly, he saw no need to go mucking it all up by introducing another human being into the mix. He'd had his one true love. Maybe it hadn't lasted as long as he'd hoped, but there'd be no replacing Jeannie, and he had no intention of trying. No matter how much Libby thought otherwise.

No matter how bad the loneliness tried to suffocate him from time to time.

His daughter clomped past again, her midriff now covered, her makeup more in keeping with what Sam considered appropriate for a girl who didn't turn fifteen for another month. He grabbed her again, this time to inflict a one-armed hug, which she patiently suffered for a moment or two before grabbing her backpack and sailing out the back door. Now alone in the kitchen, except for a dog or two and a cat who must've slipped inside when everybody left, he silently reassured his wits it was okay to come out of hiding.

Like his mother used to say, it was a great life if you didn't weaken.

He found Travis in the living room, on his stomach in front of the TV, watching a faded Grover through a scrim of wiggly lines. One of these days he was gonna have to break down and get a satellite dish, he supposed, except he couldn't work up a whole lot of enthusiasm for making TV even more appealing to a houseful of kids.

"Hey, big stuff—you make your bed?"

"Uh-huh."

"Then go pee and get your jacket, we've got supplies to buy, fences to fix."

A half minute later, the little boy returned to the living room, trying to walk and straighten out his elastic-waisted jeans at the same time and not having a whole lot of success. Underneath a pale blond buzz cut, big blue eyes the exact color of his mother's met Sam's as he squatted to fix the boy's twisted waistband. "C'n Radar come, too?"

Sam glanced over at their most recent acquisition, who looked to be part Heeler, part jackrabbit. Biggest damn ears he'd ever seen on a dog. Mutt had shown up during a thunderstorm a month or so back and didn't seem much interested in leaving. Despite Sam's regular declarations of "No more animals," every homeless cat or dog in Mayes County seemed destined to land on their doorstep, although Sam told himself this was not because he was a pushover.

"Don't see why not," Sam said, and boy and dog practically

tripped over each other on their way out the door. Seconds later, they were all in the pickup, headed into Haven and Sutter's Hardware. Granted, you could find bigger, fancier, and probably cheaper home improvement centers in Claremore and Tulsa. But what with gas prices being what they were these days, and the fact that Abe Sutter carried only what the local farmers needed and not a whole lot of stuff they didn't, thus drastically reducing the temptation to spend money they didn't have to begin with, most folks found Abe's more of a bargain than you might think.

The sun had pretty much burned off the morning chill, leaving behind one of those nice Indian Summer days that could make a man feel in charge again, even of headstrong teenagers who craved their freedom right when they needed the most watching. Never mind that the thousands of black-eyed Susans bobbing in the breeze on either side of the road seemed to be laughing at him, that the golden fields falling away as they crested each rolling hill stirred up memories of another teenage girl, her face flushed with newly discovered sexual passion during some hot and heavy necking sessions with a certain teenage boy who'd ached to take them both to places they'd never been, even as he knew the time hadn't been right for either of them, not yet.

Sam had respected Jeannie's wish to remain a virgin until marriage, but waiting had nearly killed both of them. Especially as "waiting" had meant until after they'd both finished college and Sam was sure he could support a family. Was it any wonder that Jeannie had gotten pregnant on their wedding night? Or that Libby was the way she was, being the product of all that pent-up passion?

Considering how good his and Jeannie's sex life had been, doing without all this time hadn't been nearly the struggle he'd thought. The farm, though, was in better shape than it had ever been, leaving Sam to consider, as he crested a hill to find himself trailing a camper-shelled pickup with an Ohio plate, that he probably was the only farmer in existence who actually liked repairing fences.

His musings disintegrated, however, when, with a great deal of squealing, the truck suddenly swerved like a spooked elephant, lurched off the road into the shallow, weed-tangled ditch, then shuddered to a stop as if grateful the ordeal was over. Adrenaline spiked through Sam as he pulled up behind the listing vehicle, squinting in the glare of sun flashing off white metal.

"You stay put while I make sure everybody's all right," he said to Travis, unbuckling his belt and climbing out just in time to hear a female voice let loose with a very succinct cussword, followed immediately by a man's admonition to watch her language. Which in turn resulted in an even *more* succinct cussword.

The driver's side door popped open, slammed back shut— which resulted in a loud "Dammit!"—then opened again, this time to stay put long enough for the skinniest woman he'd ever seen to push herself up and out of the truck like a frantic, if emaciated, butterfly emerging from its cocoon. Pinpricks of light flashed from a series of earrings marching up her ear.

"You okay?" Sam asked, not realizing she hadn't seen him. She jumped back with a startled "Oh," one hand pressed to her flat chest, her long fingers weighted down with so many rings Sam wasn't sure how she could lift her hand. Especially considering her wrist looked like it would snap in two if a person breathed on it hard.

"Yeah, I'm fine," she said on a pushed-out breath, swiping one hand over dark hair yanked back from her face to explode into a surprisingly exuberant, curly ponytail on the back of her head. "Just pissed." Startlingly silver-blue eyes glanced off Sam's for a split second before, her forehead creased, she returned her attention to the still-open truck door. "Dad? Can you get out?"

Forget the butterfly image. The set to her mouth, the way her nut-colored skin stretched across her bones, brought to mind the kinds of insects that cheerfully devoured their mates after sex.

Sam moved closer to lend a hand, if needed, just as a pair of chinoed legs in lace-up walking shoes emerged from the truck, followed by a white head and wide shoulders. With a grunt, the tall man levered himself out onto his feet.

"Yes, yes, I'm fine," he said to the gal, then turned back to glare at the listing truck. "Although my state of mind pretty much echoes my daughter's."

Reassured that nobody was hurt, Sam chuckled, then extended his hand. "Sam Frazier. I've got a farm a couple miles up the road." The older man's grasp was firm, his ramrod posture bespeaking a military background. As did his direct, blue gaze, only a degree or two warmer than his daughter's.

"Lane Stewart," he said, then nodded toward the woman, his expression a blend of exasperation and amusement with which Sam was all too well acquainted. "My daughter, Carly. To whom a certain squirrel owes its life."

That got an indignant roll of those clear blue eyes, the gesture not unlike Libby's. Her outfit, too, was straight out of the Young and Reckless catalogue, complete with baggy, low-riding drawstring pants—revealing a small tattoo above her left hip—the filmy overshirt billowing out behind her in the breeze doing little to hide the expanse of midriff visible underneath her cropped tank top. But this gal was no teenager: telltale age lines fanned from the corners of her eyes, had begun to dig in on either side of a full mouth glistening in one of those no-color lipsticks. And whereas most teenagers seemed to think good posture somehow violated their right to free expression, Carly stood as though tied to a ladder, shoulders back, practically nonexistent—and unconfined—breasts thrust forward. Her feet—knobby, used-up looking things in lime-green, ridiculously high-heeled sandals—pointed simultaneously to the north-east and south-east, as if undecided which way to head. And yet, pissed though she was, bony though she was, she moved with an almost hypnotic grace that had Sam thinking things not normally associated with helping out strangers with car problems.

Right. Car problems.

"Think you can move your truck?" he asked Carly's father, as Travis and Radar hopped out of Sam's, the dog bounding off into the weeds to chase something or other. That squirrel, most likely.

"Have no idea," Lane said, which Sam took as an invitation to join the older man in the ditch to check underneath the vehicle. A minute later, having agreed that, yep, the axle was bent, all right, Lane called Triple A on his cell phone as Sam took in Carly and Travis standing four feet apart, sizing each other up. Neither one seemed quite sure what to make of the other.

Since apparently nobody'd yet answered, and to distract himself from staring at the man's daughter as much as anything, Sam said, "Mostly likely, they'll send out Darryl Andrews. Since he's the only mechanic in town."

"And what town might that be?"

"Haven. Oklahoma," he added, since you could never be too sure with tourists. Then Lane said "Hello, yeah, I've got a broken down vehicle here, I need a tow" into the phone and Sam went back to watching Carly and his son, who appeared to have started up something resembling a conversation.

The kid was kind of cute, Carly supposed, if you were into that sort of thing. Like the way the sun glinted off his hair, fine and white blond like peach fuzz, the pudgy little tummy pooching out his sweatshirt, his scuffed Spiderman sneakers. He was subdued but not shy, which she found nearly as disconcerting in the preschooler—when did kids start losing their baby teeth, anyway?—as she did in grown men.

Like the lanky one with the honeyed gaze currently talking to her father.

"That's my daddy," the child said, and Carly forced herself to look away from whatever she found so fascinating. Because other than a slight hitch in his gait which raised the question *How?* there was nothing remarkable about the man. Just a country guy in jeans and plaid shirt worn open over a T-shirt, sunbaked features shadowed by the brim of a Purina ball cap.

Nothing noteworthy at all. But her eyes would keep moseying back over there, wouldn't they?

Her stomach rumbled, reminding her she hadn't had breakfast.

"I kind of figured that," she said to the kid, thinking maybe she should smile or something. "What's your name?"

"Travis. How come you got so many earrings?"

Carly's hand lifted to one ear, touching the dangling strand of beads hanging from her lobe. A pair of studs kept it company, while farther up a small gold loop hugged the rim. "'Cause I like 'em," she said. "And this way, I don't have to narrow it down to a single choice every morning."

Travis seemed to consider this for a minute, then said, "My sister, Libby, has holes in her ears, too. But only one set. Does it hurt?"

"No," Carly said as the dog—a mottled gray and black thing with enormous ears and a toothy grin—exploded out of the weeds in front of them, dancing around the boy for several seconds before realizing he'd been remiss in not acknowledging the other human standing there. The beast plopped his butt down in the dirt, his wagging tail stirring up a dust cloud as he *woofed* hello.

"His name's Radar," the boy said. "He likes everybody. Daddy says he's nothing but a big ol' pain in the butt."

The dog *woofed* again, and Carly laughed, which the dog took as an invitation to jump up and plant his paws on her thighs.

"Radar! Down!" "Daddy" said, striding over to grab the dog's collar, even as Carly said, "No, no—it's okay, really," and then she looked up into his face and damned if she didn't forget to breathe for a second or two. Because there was a substance behind those brandy-colored eyes that she hadn't seen in an extraordinarily long time. If ever. Something that went beyond the surface friendliness, or even the shrewd intelligence that masked—barely—a simmering sensuality that made her slightly dizzy.

It was honesty, she thought with a start. The completely ingenuous openness of a man with no hidden agenda, with nothing to hide.

Or to lose.

"Shouldn't be more'n ten, fifteen minutes before Darryl gets here with the wrecker. Hey," he said when she swayed slightly. "You sure you're okay?"

"What? Oh, yes, I'm fine. Just, um, hungry. I skipped breakfast," she hastily added, thinking, *Oh, brother.*

The crumples now rearranged themselves into a grin, one which created not a few wrinkles around his eyes and mouth and made her realize this was not a man in his first—or second—blush of youth. Either.

"Well," she said. "Thanks for stopping. But there's no sense in your hanging around any longer, since you said the tow truck would be here pretty soon…."

"And only one of you can fit in Darryl's cab for the ride into town, so I guess that means the other one gets to ride with me." Despite the man's grin, Carly got the weirdest feeling he wasn't all that happy about this turn of events.

Travis tugged on Sam's shirttail. "Did you see all her earrings, Daddy?"

"Yeah," he said, staring hard at the side of her face. "I saw 'em." Then his gaze swept down and she realized that wasn't all he'd seen. Or, she guessed, approved of. Well, that was his problem, wasn't it?

Travis and Radar wandered over to watch her father assess the damage to the camper's interior. Brave souls, the pair of them.

"You really swerved to avoid hitting a squirrel?" Sam asked.

She looked back at Sam. "I really did. Although my guess is he probably darts out in front of cars on a regular basis, just for the hell of it. Squirrel 'chicken,' or something."

"Dangerous game."

"Guess he figures what's life without a little danger to make it interesting? *Crap,*" she said on a wince as her knee tried its level best to give out on her.

Sam's hand instantly cupped her elbow, followed by a heart-piercingly gentle, "What is it?"

"My knee. Or what's left of it. I need to sit."

"Can you get up into the truck?"

She nodded, and Sam put an arm around her waist and helped her over to his truck, then boosted her up into the passenger seat. It smelled very…male, although she couldn't have possibly said what she meant by that.

"I'm not playing the damsel in distress, I swear," she said, lifting the hem of her pants to massage the muscles around her Ace-bandaged knee.

"Didn't figure you were." Standing by the door, he nodded at her knee. "What happened?"

"Repetitive stress injury, basically. I'm a dancer. *Was* a dancer," she added with a rueful glare at the offending joint.

"In your case, I'm guessing that's not a euphemism for stripper."

Despite pain bad enough to make her eyes cross, she laughed. "No, I don't exactly have the equipment for that line of work."

His grin managed to be both slightly devilish and very dear. And he was giving off this amazing, basic masculine scent of clean clothes and sun and that indefinable something that makes a woman's mouth water, and she thought, *Oh, God, just shoot me now.*

"I was a ballerina," she said, refusing to believe her dry mouth was due to anything other than a craving for orange juice. "In Cincinnati."

"No fooling?" Sam leaned one wrist on the truck's roof. "I always wondered how you gals danced on your toes like that."

"Painfully." His low rumble of amusement made her mouth even dryer. "What about you?" she said, nodding toward his right leg.

He grimaced. "Had a run-in with a bad tempered cow, Thanksgiving Day, a couple years ago. They tell me it healed perfectly, but corny as it sounds, I can definitely tell when it's going to rain. So…what brings you to these parts?" he said over her chuckle.

She pulled her pants leg back down over her knee, then nodded over to her father, who was showing something or other to Travis. Seemed a shame, really, to waste such great grandpa material on a daughter who had no interest in being somebody's mother.

"Road trip," she said.

"Now, why do I get the feeling there's a story behind this?"

She smiled, then shifted in her seat, trying to find a comfortable position for her knee. "My mother died a couple years ago," she said softly over the ache of loss that still hadn't quite dissipated. "Dad insisted he was okay—and here's the part where I blow any chance I had of making a good first impression—and I chose to believe him because it made my life easier. Except then when I suddenly didn't *have* a life, I took a good look at my father and realized I didn't like what I was seeing. So I suggested we hop in the camper and drive until we got bored."

"Is it working?"

"My dad, you mean?" She squinted over at the man. "Hard to tell. He's a master at putting up a front. I suppose twenty years in the Army will do that to a man. Oh! Is that the tow truck?"

Sam glanced over. "Sure is. So what do you say I take you into town, and your father can ride with Darryl in the wrecker?"

"Sounds good to me," she said, even though it didn't sound good at all. What it sounded, was dangerous.

Unaware of her rampant ambivalence, Sam shut her door before starting to walk away, only to twist back around and say, "Just so you know…as far as impressions go, you did okay."

"Oh," she said as blood rushed gleefully to her skin's surface. "Is this a good thing?"

He stared at her harder than a stranger had any right to, then shook his head. "No, ma'am, it most definitely is not," he said, then strode off toward the beeping wrecker, leaving Carly feeling as tilted as her father's truck.

Chapter 2

"My, my, my…wouldja lookee there?"

Having just attended a protracted birth that ended up getting transferred to the hospital in Claremore anyway, Ivy Gardner wasn't sure how much of anything she could see. Or cared to, frankly. At the moment she was beginning to think she was getting too damn old for this foolishness, never mind how much she loved her work. She could also do without Luralene Hastings's poking her before she'd had a chance to finish her first cup of coffee. But since the redheaded proprietress of the Hair We Are would only bug the hell out of Ivy until she responded, she peered blearily across the diner at the unfamiliar couple sitting in the far booth, both frowning at the twenty-five-year-old laminated menus that nobody local ever used.

Except then her vision cleared for a second or two and her brain managed a *Huh* of interest. Might've been more than that if she hadn't been sleep deprived. Then again, maybe not—she was long past the age where her heart fluttered at the sight of a good-looking male. Which this definitely was, she wouldn't deny it, with those good-size shoulders and thick, snowy hair. Ivy shifted uncomfortably in her seat, feeling very doughy, just at the moment.

"Wonder who they are?" Luralene said, poking Ivy again.

"Does it matter?"

Exasperated green eyes—which clashed with the turquoise eye shadow—met Ivy's. "You know, you have turned into a regular stick-in-the-mud. I remember when you used to be *fun.*"

"And I remember when you used to be subtle." Except then she took another sip of coffee and shook her head. "Strike that. You were never subtle."

"Damn straight. Oh, oh—don't look now—" this in a stage whisper you could hear in Tulsa "—but he's lookin' at you!"

And of course, Ivy lifted her eyes and yep, ran right into a pair of baby blues that set things to fizzing that hadn't fizzed in a long, long time. And even as she wondered if maybe the man needed glasses, a suggestion of curiosity wormed past the fizzing, dragging a tiny speck of feeling flattered along with it. Then the man returned his attention to the younger woman with him, it all went *poof,* and Luralene was asking Ivy how her mayoral campaign was going and Ivy found herself entertaining the idea of stuffing one of Ruby's blueberry muffins into the redhead's mouth.

She still wasn't quite sure how she'd gotten hoodwinked into running for mayor, although she seemed to recall the Logan brothers, the youngest of whom was her son-in-law, had a lot to do with it. But when eighty-something Cy Hotchkins decided not to run for reelection—it would've been his sixth term, but term limits were not a big issue in a town of a thousand where most people were just happy somebody was willing to do the job—who should throw her forty-year-old pillbox into the ring but Arliss Potts, the Methodist preacher's wife known more for her culinary eccentricities than her leadership qualities. And before Ivy knew it, her daughter Dawn, the town's only attorney, had gotten a petition going and amassed enough signatures to get Ivy on the ballot, and suddenly she was a political candidate. She, an aging hippie who'd had the nerve to raise her illegitimate daughter in a town not known for its liberal leanings. At least, not three decades ago.

But then, the reasoning went, a woman who believed in the town enough to stick around despite all that early censure was the perfect person to head its admittedly skeletal government. And besides, the reasoning went further, since more than half the people who'd looked down at her all those years ago were dead, and she'd delivered a fair number of all the younger voters, her chances of victory weren't too bad, considering.

Whatever. If nothing else, if she was elected, city council meetings would be spared an endless parade of deviled eggs made with ginger and horseradish and Cheez Whiz canapés topped with anchovy stars. But since she figured her winning was unlikely—Arliss was a good person at heart, even if she couldn't cook worth spit, and this was a picayune Bible-belt town, after all—she was basically only going along with the whole idea in order to make her deluded but well-meaning friends and family happy.

"Campaign's goin' fine," she finally lied, but Luralene had already moved on, her beady little eyes scanning the diner like radar. You could practically hear the *bleep…bleep…bleep* from underneath her bomb-shelter hairdo. Jenna Logan came in with her niece Blair, who was smiling like a goon at everybody until finally Ruby said, "Well, look who got her braces off!" and the out-of-towners—father and daughter, she was guessing—glanced over and smiled, which is when Ivy got a load of all the earrings marching up the outer rim of the gal's ears, the number of rings on her long, thin fingers. She seemed a little old to be dressed that way, to tell the truth, but then, Ivy supposed she had no room to talk with her long, gray braid and embroidered East Indian tunic. Not to mention the Birkenstocks.

Hey. Being a cliché took a lot of effort. Just ask Luralene.

The man's cell phone rang. He dug it out of his shirt pocket, said, "Uh-huh" and "I see" a few times, then clapped it shut (it was one of those fancy flip-up numbers) and frowned at the gal, mumbling something that made her mouth twist all up. She leaned over to get her purse off the floor while the man paid the bill and praised Ruby's cooking, which earned him the black woman's brightest smile. The two of them passed by Luralene and Ivy's booth on their way out, the man surprising the living daylights out of Ivy by meeting her gaze directly, then nodding.

Luralene poked her. "Didja see that?"

But Ivy barely heard her for all the blood rushing in her ears.

Sam had promised the Stewarts he'd check in with them after he'd run his errands to see how things were going, so that's what he was going to do. Because he was a man of his word, for one thing, and because it didn't seem right, abandoning them if they were going to be stranded—which he suspected they were—for another. However, to say he wasn't altogether comfortable with the prospect of seeing Carly Stewart again was one of the bigger understatements of the year. Why, he couldn't say, exactly. Other than the obvious, which was that something about her was tickling awake things he'd just as soon stay asleep, thank you. He always had hated being tickled. However, by the time he got back to Ruby's, they'd already left.

"And not lookin' particularly happy about things, would be my take on it," Ruby said, ringing up the breakfast burrito he and Travis were going to share. Setting foot in Ruby's without ordering something violated a basic law of nature. Then the white-haired woman frowned. "How'd you know about them, anyway?"

"We were right behind them when their truck landed in a ditch. Axle's shot, looked like." He pocketed his change. "I didn't have the heart to tell 'em it's probably unlikely Darryl's got a replacement lying around, which means they might be here for a while."

Ruby gave him a speculative look, the kind that preceded a comment he doubted he wanted to hear, so he was more than grateful when Blair Logan suddenly appeared at his side, grinning up at him.

"Well, hey, Blair," Sam said with a grin of his own for Libby's best friend. Her calm, rational, normal best friend who, in jeans and a long-sleeved top that skimmed her slender figure rather than strangling it, wasn't showing signs of going over to the dark side. At least not yet. "You got your braces off, huh?"

"This morning, yeah," she said, handing the check and a twenty to Ruby, then scooping Travis up into her arms to give him a hug, her cinnamon-colored hair glimmering in the streak of sunlight angling through a nearby window. "So," she said, setting his son on his feet again, "you know those people who were in here earlier?"

"Not really, no. I only stopped to help them out on the road."

"Oh. The woman looked kinda cool. For someone that old, I mean."

Then again, the dark side took many forms, he thought as Ruby handed the teenager her change.

Once back in the truck, now loaded down with enough fencing supplies to circle the state, Sam drove the three blocks to Darryl Andrews's garage, turning a blind eye to Travis's sharing his half of the burrito with the dog in the back seat. Sure enough, Carly and her father were standing out in front, backpacks and duffels strewn at their feet, looking like they weren't quite sure what to do next.

A vague feeling of impending doom came over Sam, coinciding nicely with the sharp ping of sexual awareness as he took in a scrap of her springy hair toying with her long neck. And he thought of Libby and the hormone riots she was no doubt inciting these days and how Blair thought Carly was "cool" and how Libby would no doubt see in this woman a kindred spirit, and Sam marveled at his brain's ability to produce so many thoughts simultaneously, not a single one of them reassuring in the slightest.

Except maybe for the briefly entertained idea of getting the hell out of there.

However. He pulled up beside them, and Carly leaned in the passenger-side window like she'd been expecting him and said,

"Darryl said it'd take a week to get the axle, so it looks like we're stuck," and now he noticed just how full her bottom lip was and he thought *This is nuts.* He also noticed she wore that resigned expression of someone who was actually ticked but knew giving vent to those feelings would serve no useful purpose. "So I guess we need someplace to stay for a few days. Is there a motel around here?"

See, this is the part he was dreading. Because he'd known before she'd even opened her mouth what the options were, and what the outcome was likely to be, both of which tied nicely in with that impending doom thing. "There's the Double Arrow out by me," he said as if reading a script, "but it's closed for the next couple of weeks while the owners finish up remodeling it."

"No place in town, then?" her father put in from over her shoulder. "A rooming house or something?"

Here's the funny thing: Any number of people could have been behind Carly and her father this morning when their truck went off the road. And any number of people would have made the offer he was about to make. But it hadn't been any number of people, it had been him. He could practically hear Jeannie saying, "Nothing happens without a purpose," although her voice wasn't nearly as clear as it used to be.

Still, Sam shook his head, a gesture which apparently rattled loose the words he knew he was going to say all along. "No, the Double Arrow's it. But if you don't mind family living, you could bunk with us. Libby, my girl, has an extra bed in her room. And there's a fold-out couch in the living room."

"Oh, now," Lane said, as Carly—Sam noticed out of the corner of his eye—simply stared at him as if not quite sure what to think, "we don't want to put you out—"

"It's no bother," Sam said, because logistically, it wasn't, really. "And besides, there doesn't seem to be a whole lot of choice, does there?"

Father and daughter regarded each other for several seconds; then Lane said, "We insist on paying you for putting up with us, though," and Sam laughed.

"You're talking about a ninety-year-old farmhouse, six kids and one bathroom. Somehow, it wouldn't seem right to take your money."

"Then I guess we'll have to take it out in trade," the older man said. "If you need some work done around the place, stuff like that."

Sam sensed an eagerness behind Lane's offer which surprised him. "Thought you folks were on vacation?"

"Believe me," Lane said, "if it was a vacation I wanted, traipsing around the countryside with this pain in the backside—" he jerked his head toward Carly "—would not be my first choice."

"Hey," she said, gently smacking him. But since nobody seemed to be taking anybody else too seriously, Sam figured he didn't need to, either. So they tossed all their gear into the back seat next to the kid and the dog, and Carly and her father climbed up onto the truck's bench seat and they took off. Within seconds, the truck was filled with conversation. And the faint scent of coconut, which Sam would swear he'd never in his life found arousing before now.

Six kids?

Carly stared straight ahead as they bumped and squeaked over the road, trying not to stare at how the veins stood out on top of Sam's hand cradling the gearshift. Who the hell has six kids these days? Thank God they weren't alone, was all she had to say, although she wasn't in much of a mood to thank God or anybody else for the situation as a whole. Her last relationship had ended just long enough ago to leave her dangling over that emotional hellhole between still stinging (she'd never been much good at being the dumpee) and really, really missing sex. Not that she hadn't dangled over this particular emotional hellhole a few—okay, more than a few—times before, so it wasn't as if she didn't know she'd survive. It was what she tended to do *to* survive that could be the problem.

She caught a whiff of Sam's aftershave and shut her eyes, drumming, *Wrong, wrong, wrong* into her head.

There. That should do it.

The men, having no idea of the horde of nefarious demons intent on colonizing her brain, had fallen into an easy conversation about sports or whatever, she wasn't paying much attention, while her thoughts orbited around a single idea (and those demons), which was that this little sidebar to their trip went way beyond her original proposal to "go wherever the mood struck."

Not that she was all that upset about the axle business. These things happen. And it wasn't as if they were on any kind of set schedule or anything. Nor did she have a problem with whatever the accommodations turned out to be. God knows—although her father did not—she'd spent more than a few nights in some pretty seedy places over the years. Her ability to crash almost anywhere had not, she didn't imagine, fallen into disuse simply because she'd been living more or less like an actual grown-up for some time. As long as she had a can opener and toilet paper (which she did), she was good.

However...turning back to the hellhole business for a minute: It was not exactly reassuring to discover that, at thirty-seven, her hormones were apparently every bit as out of control now as they had been at twenty. Or—her mouth pulled tight—fifteen. Now, Carly had long since accepted the fact that she clearly lacked whatever instincts steered other women to their life mates. And that, at this point, it was downright disingenuous to chalk up her inability to form a meaningful attachment to simply needing to mature a little more. So finding herself attracted to some farmer with a batch of kids—in all likelihood, a *married* farmer with a batch of kids, since that was one thing she did *not* do—was very depressing.

Wait. If Sam was married...

Carly cleared her throat and said, "Um...shouldn't you have cleared our coming with your wife first?"

She saw the muscles in his hand tense as he shifted gears to climb a hill.

"Jeannie's been gone for coming up on three years now," he

said softly, then twisted to give her what he probably thought was a reassuring smile. "Nobody to clear this with but me."

Her first thought—a slightly panicked realization that the marriage thing had been her ace in the hole—collided with the most bizarre sensation of…wait, the word was there, some-where…*caring,* that was it. Not that she never felt sympathy for anyone, because of course she did, it wasn't as if she was cold-hearted. No, it was the intensity of the moment that knocked her off her pins, the overwhelming rush of compassion for this per-fect stranger who was opening his home to them. The obvious love in Sam's voice, the residual grief—something she under-stood all too well herself—somehow made her feel very, very humble. And shallow.

"I'm so sorry," she finally said, even as her father put in about how hard it must be for Sam, raising all those kids on his own.

Indeed.

Sam wordlessly acknowledged their sympathy, then said, "That's the farm up ahead. It's just a small operation, but we call it home."

But Carly barely registered the small grove of fruit trees, the corn-stalk-stubbled fields, the modest two-story farmhouse, white with blue shutters, proudly standing underneath a huge old oak tree, its leaves rust-tinged. Because she was too busy processing the newsflash that even though there was no Mrs. Sam in the picture, the six kids should work quite nicely as a libido suppressant. Because no way was she messing around with a man with six kids.

No. Damn. Way.

Sitting by herself on a patch of hot, prickly grass outside the school cafeteria, Libby glowered at her bologna sandwich, then took a bite, seeing as she was hungry and it wasn't like it was gonna change, anyway. The "cool" girls—mostly juniors and seniors—sat in a cozy bunch under the massive cottonwood, their laughter drifting over on the breeze. Lunch—a trial on the best of days—really sucked when Blair wasn't there. And Sean was no help, since he liked to spend every spare moment working on whatever car was up on the blocks in Auto. So it was just Libby and her bologna sandwich. Oh, and chips and an apple. Big whoop.

Actually, in some ways it wasn't nearly as bad as she thought it would be. Most of her classes were okay, although she could do without Mr. Solomon, her English teacher, trying so hard to act like he was everybody's best friend. The homework was no big deal, and she'd already gotten a ninety-three on her first biology quiz, so she felt pretty good about that, but lunchtime—the girls giggled again—was the pits. Why most of the kids she'd gone all through school with had suddenly decided it wasn't cool to hang out with their old friends anymore, she had no idea. Not that any of 'em had anything to be stuck-up about—for the most part, everybody here was a farmer's or rancher's kid, just like her. When she'd bitched to Dad, he'd told her to sit tight, reminding her how hard her first weeks had been in middle school and how well that had turned out.

Like Dad had a clue how she felt. He used to be pretty cool, too, until he'd gone on this overprotective tear. Like showing two inches of skin or wearing makeup was going to turn her into a slut, for crying out loud. She was in high school, for heaven's sake! Why didn't he get that?

Libby glanced down at her breasts—36C and still growing—and sighed, thinking maybe he got more than she wanted to admit. Then she noticed Blair striding across the grass from the parking lot, her red hair looking like it was on fire in the sunlight, and felt a little better.

"Where were you?" Libby asked, knowing she sounded short. But Blair only plopped down beside her on the grass, not taking offense.

"I told you, I had to go get my braces off this morning."

"Oh, yeah, huh. I forgot. So let me see."

Blair bared her teeth, like a dog.

"It looks weird," Libby said. "I guess because I've only ever seen you with braces."

Blair and her aunt Jenna—who'd brought Blair to Oklahoma from Washington, D.C., in search of Blair's father, Hank Logan, only to fall in love with him and get married, which Libby thought truly one of the most romantic things she'd ever heard—had only been living in Haven for a little over a year. Blair and Libby had become best friends practically within minutes of meeting each other. Libby had sometimes thought maybe their instant friendship had something to do with Jenna being so much like Jeannie, Libby's mom's name, but this was not a theory she'd voiced aloud to anybody for fear of being thought silly.

"It *feels* weird," Blair said, running her tongue over her naked teeth. "But I got used to having 'em, so I guess I'll get used to not having 'em."

"So, you ate before you came?"

"Yeah, Jenna took me to Ruby's. Oh!" She sat up, her blue eyes all excited. "I almost forgot—there were these new people there, an old man and his daughter, she was so cool, like obviously not from around here—" Libby had found Blair's previous big-city experience to be pretty reliable when it came to pegging somebody as cool or not "—and I think your father took them out to your place."

Libby looked hard at Blair, because this information was not sinking in.

"What are you talking about? Why would Daddy be taking two strangers out to the farm? And how the heck do you know this?"

Blair snitched one of Libby's potato chips—it wasn't fair, since Blair could eat as many chips and candy bars as she wanted and never gain any weight, while all Libby had to do was think about the stuff and her jeans got tight—and said, "I saw your dad at Ruby's, too, and he said something about being behind them when their truck went off the road and landed in a ditch outside town—"

"Ohmigosh! Was anybody hurt?"

"No, I don't think so. But I got the feeling their truck was going to be out of commission for a while. Anyway, then Jenna and I stopped by Darryl's to get gas, and we saw them get into your father's truck with their backpacks and stuff and take off."

"Honestly, Blair, you'd make a rotten detective, you know that? Just because he was givin' 'em a ride doesn't mean Dad was takin' 'em home—"

Blair plucked another chip from the bag. "And where else was he gonna take 'em? You know the Double Arrow's closed until Dad and Joe get it finished."

Well, she had a point. But still. One thing did not necessarily lead to another….

"Hey, babe!"

Libby nearly choked on her Diet Coke, but she recovered in time to give Sean a bright smile as he dropped onto the grass beside her. She could feel at least ten sets of dagger glares coming from underneath the cottonwood tree.

"Hey, Blair," Sean said, "how's it goin'?"

"Fine," her friend said, and Libby swallowed a sigh—along with the Diet Coke—because Blair and Sean didn't really like each other all that much. Libby wasn't really sure why, although she had a feeling it had something to do with both of them wanting her—Libby—all to themselves. Well, they were just both going to have to learn to deal with it, weren't they?

Libby smiled into Sean's amazing coffee eyes and tried not to sigh. She knew he wanted to kiss her, but the school had a zero-tolerance policy about shows of affection, so that was out. It was so weird—Sean was easily one of the cutest boys in school, he could have had any girl he wanted, so Libby had been totally shocked when he'd started hanging around her. And she really couldn't believe it when he'd offered her a ride home a week ago and had leaned in and given her this really sweet kiss right before she got out. They'd kissed some more—okay, a lot more—since then, and to tell the truth, what she felt when they were kissing kinda scared her. Like when she was little and she'd spin around and around until she got dizzy and would fall over. But she figured it was like being new in school—eventually, she'd start feeling more normal about it.

"Thought you were working on Dawn Logan's old GTO?" People could bring in cars for the advanced auto students to work on. They'd been working on that GTO since the first day of school, with no end in sight, from what Sean said.

Sean grinned, a crooked thing that made Libby feel a little like she might throw up. "I was. Except then I remembered if I spent the whole hour in there, I wouldn't get to see my girl for another three-and-a-half hours."

Blair made a strange sound in her throat. Libby tossed her a "Don't say it" look before smiling back at Sean. Nobody'd ever called her *my girl* before and she was determined to squeeze every drop of pleasure out of the moment as she could.

The bell rang, bringing a chorus of groans, understandable since it was hot as hell inside. But before Libby could haul herself to her feet, Sean was standing with his hand out. Libby flushed, both with pleasure at being treated like a lady, and with embarrassment that he might not be able to heave her to her feet as easily as he thought. She resolved this dilemma by getting on one knee so he wouldn't do all the work, flushing all over again when, once she was standing, he placed a kiss on the inside of her hand, making her tingle all over.

Behind Sean, Blair rolled her eyes. Libby decided it was only because she was jealous. However, she was gracious enough not to hold it against her.

Showered and changed into her favorite voile blouse over a tank top and a pair of bold, floral capris too tacky to resist, Carly sat stiffly on Sam's porch swing, staring mindlessly out toward a clump of fruit trees—apple, mostly, she thought, but there were a few pears, as well, their leaves blushing scarlet—while nursing a cup of coffee long since gone cold. Sam had insisted she and her father were welcome to anything in the house, but she'd already started a list of what they used so she could replace it before they left. Since both she and her dad were big coffee drinkers, a can of Maxwell House went to the head of the class.

She'd hoped the shower and coffee would clear her muddled head. Wrong. If ever a situation brimmed over with "I know, buts…" this was it. Despite how well the situation had resolved itself, despite the shower and the coffee and a surreally perfect day with a sky so clear she felt buoyed by it, despite the rush of fond childhood memories brought on by the soothing, honest scents of hay and earth and animal, the ominous feeling that she was about to be tested in some way kinda shot all the good stuff to hell.

All the males, as well as a small pack of dogs, had been gone for a good two hours—something about repairing a fence, she gathered. Her father's enthusiastic offer of help had thrown Sam, Carly could tell, but he'd relented once Dad convinced him he'd helped fix plenty of fences as a kid growing up on his parents' dairy farm in Iowa. So off they'd gone, Sam's apparent lack of concern about leaving a stranger alone in his house unnerving her even further, tossing her own cynicism back at her like a hot potato. And like that hot potato, she wasn't quite sure what to do with such no-strings-attached generosity. Except she knew if she held on to it for more than a second, she'd get burned.

Carly downed another sip of coffee, only to grimace at its bitterness. The swing's chain jingled, startled, as she got up and tossed the dregs out into the yard. Then she stretched her arms over her head, hauling in a lungful of air before slowly swaying from side to side, then bending down to easily lay her palms on the floorboards in front of her feet, taking care not to hyperextend her bum knee. Almost more than giving up performing, the thought of losing her flexibility and control over her body gave her the willies.

Speaking of willies…she actually shuddered when she walked back into the house, it was so impossibly neat. Fancy, no—the blue and beige early-American sofa had a decidedly weary aura about it—but everything was stacked or shelved or hung up or otherwise relegated to its appointed place. Not a single cobweb dangled from the ceiling or clung to a lampshade, not a speck of grunge huddled in the corners of the bathroom, and the clawfoot tub had been as white as Miss America's smile. Creepy. While Carly wasn't prone to letting dishes pile up in the sink, her housekeeping philosophy generally ran along the lines of when she got grossed out, she cleaned.

And yet, how to explain the occasional wall painted bright blue or tangerine or lemon-yellow, the animals snoozing or lurking everywhere she looked, the exuberantly free-form artwork smothering one entire wall of the airy, teal-green hallway leading from the living room to the kitchen? Or the row of boots lined up with almost military precision in the mudroom, except for one tiny red pair, defiantly lying on its sides…the mad collection of family photos in mismatched frames, on walls, on shelves, on end tables?

Sam's wife was in at least half of them, a round, pretty woman who'd been clearly in love with her husband, her children, her life. Carly's chest tightened for the obvious hole her death must have left in this family. As generous as Sam was with his smiles, none of them even came close to the ones in these pictures.

She carried her empty mug back into the kitchen, where one of a dozen notes tacked here and there instructed whoever—in this case, her—to either wash it out or put it in the dishwasher. Smiling, she rinsed it out and set it in on the drainboard, then decided to see what she could throw together for lunch, since she imagined the guys would be back soon. Not that Carly was inclined to either domesticity or helpfulness, but it seemed silly to make lunch for herself and not go ahead and make it for everyone else at the same time.

A block-printed note on the refrigerator sternly reminded her to think about what she wanted *before* opening it, but since she didn't know what was inside, she supposed she could be forgiven for browsing, just this once. She found many of the same staples she remembered from summers at her grandparents': bologna and American cheese and lettuce and big, ripe, juicy tomatoes still fresh from the late summer garden, Miracle Whip and generic mustard, with loaves of IronKids and whole wheat bread in the large basket on the counter. The milk would be fresh, she knew—she'd heard the lowing of a cow or two while she'd been sitting on the porch—and nothing skim about it. And if you wanted water, there was the tap. Well water, she imagined, ice-cold.

A humongous ginger tomcat snaking around her ankles, she started slicing tomatoes on a wooden board she found by the sink, frowning at the wipe-erase board the size of a medium-size continent hanging on the only counter-free wall, divided into columns with chores listed under each name. Even little Travis was up there, with Feed Chickens and Collect Eggs as part of his duties. Although she did notice that there was always an older child listed with the same chores, so maybe the little guy was only in training. Still, this was a method that brooked no argument. And frankly seemed at odds with what she could have sworn was a laid-back demeanor on Sam's part. But there it was, irrefutable evidence that Sam Frazier apparently ran his home like a military institution.

Or an orphanage, she thought with a pang.

She heard the growl of a pickup outside; the cat tore over to the back door. A minute later, amidst sounds of laughter and a hiss from the cat as Radar burst inside, Travis trooped into the house, followed by her father, then Sam, both men wearing the unmistakable glow of satisfaction for a job well done. Or at least *done*. Her father, especially…when was the last time she'd heard him laugh like that, seen a smile that big on his face?

"I made some lunch," she announced, waving at the table. "Sandwiches, if that's okay. Bologna or cheese, or both, if you're feeling adventurous."

Her father said, "I think I need a quick shower first. If that's okay?" he directed at Sam, who said, "Sure, go right ahead," and then Dad vanished, leaving Sam staring at the table as though she'd set up a tray full of live snakes.

Wordlessly he plucked off his ball cap and slapped it up onto the six-foot-long pegboard mounted near the door, the move revealing a ragged, dark splotch plastering his shirt to a

chest more substantial than one might expect given his overall
leanness. Several strands of hair that could have been either sil-
ver or blond fell across his forehead; he swiped at them, his gaze
bouncing off hers before sweeping over the innocent sandwiches mounded on a plate in the center of the table. Travis's
grubby hand shot out to claim half a sandwich, but Sam grabbed
him with a "Not before you wash your hands, pup." Then, one
arm around his youngest's chest, he met her eyes again and said,
softly, "You didn't have to do that."

"No problem," she said with a bright, idiotic grin, trying desperately to lighten the inexplicably weighted atmosphere.
"Wasn't as if I had anything else to do. What would you like to
drink?"

Again with the weird look. Full of lots of angst and undertones
and all sorts of stuff Carly really didn't want to deal with. "I'm
all sweaty," he said, his eyes still locked with hers. Uh, boy.
Thank God her father was still out of the room, was all she had
to say.

"Hey. You want to talk sweaty? Try fifty dancers in an unair-
conditioned studio in July. At the end of a two-hour rehearsal.
You don't even rate."

That, at least, got a small smile, like a crack in the ice on a
warm day, and at least some of the undertones slunk away.

Some. Not all. Certainly not the ones that made her glad her
father wasn't around. And that *she* wouldn't be around for more
than a few days.

Sam carted Travis over to the sink, holding him up to wash
his hands, then dousing a paper towel with the running water to
mop the kid's face for good measure before freeing the protesting child so he could clean himself up. Leaving Carly to ponder
why—how?—after all the beautiful bodies she'd seen in motion
over the years, she couldn't seem to unhook her eyeballs from
this one. All he was doing was washing his hands, for crying out
loud.

Then she heard a dry chuckle and realized he was watching
her, watching him, and she felt a whoosh of desire so strong she

nearly lost her balance, followed by the calm, clear words, *You are so not going there.*

Well, hot damn—maybe, just maybe, she was finally growing up.

Chapter 3

It'd been a long time since a woman had made him lunch.

It'd been even longer since sex had tapped at the door to his thought and said, *Psst…remember me?* Okay, so maybe it had come a'knocking once or twice in the past three years, but for damn sure Sam hadn't had the time, interest or energy to open the door. In any case, the problem with both of these events was that Sam didn't need, or want, either one in his life.

On an intellectual level, at least. Which was the only level he was going to pay any mind, since listening to the alternative—which would be something not involving a whole lot of brain cells—was too darn scary to contemplate. Because right at this very moment, if he indeed removed his brain from the equation, he didn't mind at all having somebody make him lunch. And he really didn't mind that pleasant ache in his groin, if for no other reason than to be reminded that, hallelujah, brother, he wasn't dead yet. But he very much minded *not* minding, because…well, because what was the point?

Although the way the gal was looking at him…

He heard the pipes shudder, then groan, as Lane turned on the shower. Meaning it would probably be a while before they had a buffer. One big enough to count, anyway, he thought with a glance at his youngest, wrestling on the floor with Radar and growling louder than the dog. So much for the clean hands.

"So—" The word popped out of Carly's mouth like a blow dart, like maybe she'd been having similar thoughts. Sam realized he could see straight through that flimsy shirt she was wearing, and even though she had another shirt on underneath, the peekaboo effect was wreaking havoc on his common sense. "What's with all the notes all over the place?"

Not what he expected her to say. But after a quick scan of the room, he could see why she'd asked. "Huh. Guess there are a few, aren't there?"

"Twelve," she said. "Not counting that." She nodded toward the wipe-erase board.

Sam held one of the kitchen chairs steady so Travis wouldn't knock it over as he climbed up into his seat. Kid was still too short to really sit at the table comfortably without a booster seat, but Sam had a better shot at getting him to eat worms than use the "baby chair."

"Got tired of repeating myself, basically. And this way, nobody can claim they didn't know what they were supposed to do."

Carly took a seat at the table, her plate filled mostly with lettuce, it looked like. "And this doesn't strike you as just a tad…autocratic?"

"Only way to go when you've got six kids. Unless you got a better idea?"

"Move?"

"Don't think the thought hasn't crossed my mind a time or two." He handed Travis half a cheese sandwich. The kid gave him a wide smile, and Sam thought, with a little pang, *This is the last baby-toothed grin I'll see.* "For what it's worth," he said, turning back to Carly, "your dad was impressed as all get-out."

"He would be." With a loud groan, Radar collapsed on the floor in front of the sink, clearly untroubled by his status as wuss dog of the family. "Although," Carly was saying, "Dad never resorted to notes or lists. He tended to rely more on the bellow and glare method." Then her mouth quirked up. "With good reason."

Yeah, Lane had shared a few stories about his daughter. Stories he doubted Carly would appreciate being bandied about, Sam mused with a smile as Henry, an ancient, chewed-up-looking tomcat whose few waking hours these days were mostly devoted to tormenting the dogs, paused in his travels to sniff Radar's butt. The startled dog leaped to his feet, only to immediately cower against the cabinet door, ears tucked against his skull, eyes wide with terror. Satisfied, Henry flicked his tail and stalked off. Travis giggled; Carly gave the little boy a smile softer than Sam would have thought possible, given the sharpness of her features.

"Yeah," he said, unable to take his eyes off that smile, "Lane definitely gave me the impression that you were a bit of a handful."

She smirked. "Are you kidding? I made his life a living…" She glanced at Travis, then back at Sam, her eyes glittering, defiant, like her makeup, which, while anything but subtle, ventured no where near tacky. This was simply a woman who had no qualms about making herself look good. "Let's just say I took the concept of challenging authority to a whole new level. Which begs the question…" She swept one arm out, indicating the notes. "Does this work?"

"Mostly. Once everybody realized I meant business."

"And how old's your daughter?"

A cold, clammy chill tramped up his back. "Almost fifteen."

All she did was smile. And change the subject, her smug expression clearly indicating her belief that she'd won that round. "So. You get that fence fixed?"

"You're still doing it, aren't you?" Sam said.

A bite of salad halfway to her mouth, her eyes shot to his. "Doing what?"

"Challenging authority."

She shrugged, the gesture setting the dangliest of the earrings to shimmering. Her hair, a rebellious tangle of not-quite curls swarming around her neck and shoulders, strained against the single bright blue clip jammed impatiently at one temple. "Can't say as I've ever been real big on following the rules, no. So. The fence?"

Sam found it curious that, for someone so intent on being a badass, she sure didn't seem interested in discussing it. But no matter, especially as it was none of his concern, anyway. "All done," he said, loading up his own plate with several sandwich halves before turning back to the refrigerator. Carly'd already poured Travis a glass of milk, but Sam wanted iced tea. Preferably dumped over his head. "Thanks to your father. Can't remember the last time I saw anybody get such a kick out of replacing fence posts."

"Yep, that's Dad." Sam noticed how cautiously she was eyeing the four-year-old, giving him the feeling she didn't spend a lot of time around little kids. Then she picked up a napkin and wiped a dribble of milk off Trav's chin, which earned her a shy smile. She smiled back, sort of, then forked in a bite of lettuce and said, "So I guess that means the two of you didn't spend the whole time discussing my errant ways."

"Not the whole time, no. Just on the ride there. And back. And whenever we got close enough to hear each other."

She reached out to move Trav's cup of milk back from the edge of the table. "I wouldn't've thought there was that much to discuss."

"And here I was thinking it sounded like he'd barely scratched the surface."

That got another moment's stare before she said, "*Anyway*...I think Dad's missed working with his hands." Sam checked out hers—long fingers, smothered in all those rings, but no nail polish. "Mom was convinced he'd bought an old house on purpose so there'd always be something to fix. And believe me, there was. The kitchen alone took the better part of a year." She smiled. "I swear, all the clerks at Home Depot knew him by name."

"Sounds like a man after my own heart," Sam said, and she rolled her eyes, making him chuckle. But her smile dimmed as she stabbed at a hunk of lettuce.

Travis asked for another sandwich half. Carly beat Sam to it.

"Doing nothing makes him crazy. After he retired from the Army, he started his own security business. Except when Mom got sick, he sold it so he could spend as much time as possible with her. Then after she died, he got rid of the house right away and moved into an apartment. I understand why he did what he did, but he's been at loose ends ever since."

Sam waited out the twinge of sadness, faded more than he would have ever believed possible three years ago, but not entirely gone. For a moment, he almost envied the other man, being able to cherish what he had, to say goodbye. Losing Jeannie so suddenly had been like being shoved off a cliff into an ice-cold waterhole—there was no time to get your breath before you had all you could handle just to keep from drowning. But as hard as Jeannie's unexpected death had been on him and the kids, at least *she* hadn't suffered. Watching somebody you loved dwindle away…he could only imagine how hard that must have been. "Too many memories in the house?" he finally said, as his own echoed softly from every nook and cranny of the one they were sitting in.

"That's what I figured, but he never really said."

"I'm done," Trav piped up. "C'n I be 'scused?"

Sam said, "Sure," and the kid slid down from his seat, his feet hitting the floor with a thump before pounding out the back door, Radar—having recovered from the cat's brutal attack—hot on his heels. The screen door whined shut, leaving him and Carly alone. Together. With the water still humming through the pipes and Sam well aware that voicing Lane's probable motivation for selling his house could possibly let Carly more into his own head than he might like, especially since a few of those memories now whistled through his brain like wind through a canyon. With some difficulty, Sam swallowed the bite in his mouth and said, "Your dad must be bored out of his mind. In an apartment, I mean."

She gave him one of those looks that women do when they're trying to translate what you just said into their own language, then nodded.

"You have no idea," she was saying, taking another bite of lettuce, her posture bringing to mind the deceptive strength of a sapling.

"So you decided what he needed was a road trip to jump-start him again."

"Both of us, actually. Although when I brought it up, Dad definitely pounced on the idea."

"How long've you been on the road?"

"About a month."

"Since you lost your job?"

"That happened about three months ago, actually. Which is when the sports doctor told me I could have surgery, with no guarantee I'd ever dance again anyway, or quit dancing altogether and the problem might clear up on its own."

"Some choice."

"Yeah. That's what I thought."

Her bravado wasn't doing a particularly hot job of masking her disappointment. "And how long until you go back home?"

"We hadn't decided that. One of the perks of being in limbo," she said with a grand wave of her fork. "I've got a half offer from an old dance school friend who's married with munchkins and the minivan and the whole nine yards in a Chicago suburb, she wants to open a dance school and wondered if I'd be interested in teaching."

"Are you?"

That bite of lettuce finally found its way into her mouth. After several seconds of chewing, she shrugged. "It's an option."

The pipes groaned again, this time from the water being turned off. "But…not one you're very excited about."

"Hey. I'm thirty-seven. Even without my knee sabotaging me, I only had maybe five good years left, anyway. Eight if I didn't mind pity applause," she said with a short, dry laugh. "Still. Somehow, even though most dancers turn to teaching after they retire, I somehow never saw myself doing the Dolly Dinkle Dance School routine. Teaching a class full of everybody's precious darlings in pink leotards and tutus... I can't see it, frankly. I'm not really into kids."

Sam thought of her wiping Travis's chin and smiled to himself. "Yeah. I can tell."

"It's not that I don't like them," she added quickly. "Exactly. I just never quite know what to say to them. How to relate to them. I mean, my biological clock's merrily ticking away and I'm like, *'Fine, whatever.'* Shoot, it's all I can do to take care of *myself.*"

Chuckling, Sam polished off his last sandwich, then chased it with the rest of his iced tea. When he finished, he leaned back in his chair. "You always this up-front with people?"

She shrugged. "Pretty much. Does it bother you?"

"It's a mite unnerving, but no. Not particularly. Actually it's kinda nice to be around someone who has no trouble saying whatever's on her mind."

"Most men wouldn't agree with you."

"That's their problem," he said mildly. "So tell me about your dancing."

Brows lifted. "This isn't a date. You're not going to win any points by pretending to really be interested in what I do."

"Humor me. It's not every day I have an honest to God ballerina sitting in my kitchen. And I'd add 'eating my food' but that would be stretching it."

Her eyes followed his to her plate. "Ah," she said, with an understanding smirk, before her shoulders bounced again. "I'm not anorexic, if that's what you're thinking. I ate like a pig at breakfast, that's all."

"What? A piece of toast and a grapefruit half?"

"Hah. Three pieces of *French* toast, sausage and two scrambled eggs."

"I'm impressed."

"So was what's-her-name. The woman who runs the place?"

"That would be Ruby."

"Ruby, right. She wanted to know where I'd put it. Any-way…you sure you want to hear this? Okay, okay," she said when he let out an annoyed sigh. "Not sure how much there is to say, really. I've been dancing literally since I could walk, even though I didn't start formal training until I was ten and Dad retired, so we weren't moving every five minutes. I went to dance camp as a teenager, then on to North Carolina School of the Arts for high school. After I graduated, I danced with a major New York company for a couple of years, which for anybody else would have been a total dream job. Except I realized that staying there would have meant basically dancing in the chorus of Swan Lake for the rest of my career. So I decided I'd have more opportunity in a smaller regional company, even if it meant a cut in pay. Never expected to end up back in Cincinnati, but there you are."

On the surface, her words seemed straightforward enough. And yet, something about the way she wouldn't look at him, the fingers of her left hand constantly worrying the edge of the plastic placement the whole time she was talking, led Sam to wonder if that part of her life had really been as straightforward as she was making out.

He took another bite of his sandwich before saying, "You ever regret your decision? To leave the bigger company?"

"No," she said immediately. "See, dancing isn't something I do, it's who I am. Not that I expect anyone else to understand that. I mean, how much sense does it make to be so passionate about something that pays squat, that leaves you in virtually constant pain, and offers zip job security?"

"Sounds an awful lot like farming."

She grinned. "Hadn't thought of it that way. But hey—at least farming feeds people."

"Who's to say what you do doesn't feed people, too?" he said, and a rich, startled laugh burst from her throat. "What? You think a country boy can't appreciate the arts?"

Her laughter died as another blush crept across her cheeks. "Well, no, but—"

"Hey, the tradition of farmers letting loose with music and dancing goes way back. Why is it you suppose that whole wall out there's covered in the kids' artwork? And why else would I put myself through the torture of listening to a twelve-year-old murder the violin for a half hour every day? Or scrape together a few extra bucks so one or the other of 'em can take a special art class or music class after school? Maybe it's not 'art' in the way a lot of folks define it, but whatever it is, it's not something tacked on—it's just the way people are wired." He allowed himself a second or two to stare into those wide eyes, then said, "Not what you expected, is it?"

She blinked. "No. Not by a long shot." Lowering her eyes, she poked at her salad for a couple beats, then looked at him again. "So. Do you dance, Sam Frazier?"

"I've been known to do a mean two-step in my day."

Again, that wonderful, rich sound of her laughter filled the room, like something that had been let free after being confined for far too long. Then their eyes locked and need kicked him in the gut, swift and hard, and man, was he ever glad to see Lane.

"Well," Sam said, rising, "I reckon I've goofed off long enough. Still got a ton of work to do before the kids get home from school. Thanks for lunch," he said with a nod, grabbing his hat off the rack and screwing it back onto his head. "And if either of you need to go into town or want to go sightsee or something, feel free to take the Econoline. Keys are on the rack over there."

A week, he thought, striding out to the barn. Surely he was strong enough to last a week.

Only then a little voice in his head said, *Don't bet on it,* and he thought, *Oh, hell.*

She could make it through one lousy week, right?

A single week. Seven piddly days. Maybe less, if the axle came in earlier…

"You sure your knee's okay?"

Which made at least the sixth time her father had asked her this since they'd set out on their walk around the property. His idea. One her knee actually hadn't been in total agreement with, but she knew she'd be okay as long as she took it easy. Staying in that house, however, was another matter entirely.

"This isn't exactly like running the marathon, Dad. I'm fine."

A loud, obnoxious cackle sounded inside her head.

"And I know you," Dad said. "Used to drive your mother and me nuts, the way you wouldn't admit defeat if your life depended on it."

Well, maybe not out loud. Because she was definitely feeling, if not defeated, certainly poleaxed.

By a quiet, soft-spoken farmer with six kids. And how messed up was that?

She simply wouldn't think about it, that's all.

Carly laughed, the sound maybe a little shriller than it should be. Her father gave her a funny look. "You know me well. But really, it's okay. Actually," she said, realizing with moderate panic that attempting to not think about Sam was like trying to get gum out of her hair, "I'm kind of surprised you suggested this. I would have thought you'd be all worn out from this morning."

Eyes like deep ice cut to hers; chagrin toyed with his mouth. "Because I've got one foot in the grave, you mean."

"No, of course not—"

"I'm only sixty-three, Lee. Not ready for the home yet."

She smiled. True, the morning's outing seemed to have done her father a world of good, provoking a pang of guilt that she hadn't been pushier about getting him out and doing long before this….

Did you see the way Sam kept looking at you?

Shut up, she said to…whoever. The spook squatting in her brain, she supposed. Except the spook cut right back in with some annoying observation about how Sam was like some innocuous-looking Mexican dish—wasn't until you'd taken several bites before you realized your hair was on fire.

Of course, this is not a problem if you like spicy food.

"Lee? Are you okay?"

"Yes, Dad," she said with a bright smile, because whatever this craziness was, talking it over with her father wasn't gonna happen. Actually, up until this little trip, it had been years since she and Dad had talked about much at all. Not because they didn't love each other, but because they did. At some point several years ago, after what Carly assumed was a mutual revelation that they came from different planets, and that they'd both grown weary of every conversation degenerating into an argument within five minutes, she'd simply stopped bringing up touchy subjects. Which mostly involved her vocation (he tolerated it, but had clearly hoped it was a phase and that eventually she'd come to her senses and pursue a "real" career), her lifestyle (enough said), and her love life (about which, for everybody's sake, her father knew far less than he thought).

Fortunately her mother had been more inclined to take Carly's side—the natural outcome, Carly supposed, of Dena Spyropoulos Stewart's having been brought up in a strict Greek-American family with a father who exerted an iron-fisted control over his wife and children. And since Lane was totally besotted with his wife, he usually lost the battles with his hardheaded daughter. Without her mother to run interference, however, Carly frankly hadn't been as inclined to seek out her dad's company. Realizing you simply weren't the child your father always thought he'd have had tended to have that effect on a person. In fact, part of her problem with Sam—aside from the farmer with the six kids business, which was a deal-breaker in any case—was how much he reminded her of Dad. All those notes and lists brought back way too many memories, most of which involved her father expecting her to do things one way and Carly's determination to do exactly the opposite.

So it had been easier, especially after Mom's death, to simply stay out of each other's way rather than enduring visits that neither of them really enjoyed very much. Not something she was proud of, but there it was.

And only the threat of either, if not both, of them disintegrating into pajama-clad blobs spending their days watching game shows and infomercials had spurred her—in a moment of pure insanity—into suggesting they take this trip. Especially considering the odds of their killing each other within the first forty-eight hours. What they'd discovered instead was that, somewhere along the line, they'd both mellowed. Not that they now shared a brain or anything, but at least enough to enjoy each other's company.

Especially during those long, lovely periods that people referred to as "companionable silence."

The countryside in this part of Oklahoma tended to be hilly, nestled up against the Ozarks the way it was, and Sam's farm was no exception. The spread wasn't particularly large, her father said, fifty acres or so—but Sam was determined to wring every drop out of the land he could. Dad explained that the larger fields were devoted to wheat, alfalfa, and corn, with a large vegetable garden that yielded not only plenty of produce to feed the family, but enough left over to sell at a local farmer's market as well. Then there were the fruit trees—three kinds of apple, not to mention pear and cherry—the chickens, the cows, the two pairs of hogs that produced several litters a year…and plenty of pork in the freezer, he added.

Carly shuddered, which got a chuckle. "That is what farming's all about, you know."

"Yes, I do. It's just all a little too hands-on for me."

"You loved it as a kid."

"Gram and Gramps had a dairy farm. They milked the cows, they didn't eat them."

"No, they ate somebody else's. And where do you think those fried chicken suppers came from? KFC?"

"Dash my idyllic childhood memories, why dontcha?"

Her father laughed, a good sound. The sound of someone on the mend, she decided.

They'd come to a fallow field smothered in late season grasses and wildflowers. A lone oak alongside another farmer's post-and-rail fence, its side scarred from a long-ago lightning strike, beckoned them to rest a while. Carly's knee was more than ready to take the tree up on its offer. They lowered themselves onto a patch of cool dirt, both taking long drinks from their water bottles. At a comfortable distance, a pair of cows munched, their ears flicking, tails swishing. One of them disinterestedly looked in their direction.

"Your mother would have loved it here," Dad said. "The mountains, the trees…she used to say there was nothing finer than the smell of country air."

"If you like earthy."

"You're too young to be so cynical," her father said mildly, twisting the cap back on his water, and she thought, *Young, hell. I feel as old as these hills.*

And very nearly as worn down.

But truth be told, some of her best childhood memories had come from summers spent on her grandparents' farm. Except that was then and this was now, and that little girl had up and taken off some time ago.

Leaving in her place a cynical, lame woman destined to become a dried-up old prune of a dance teacher with dyed black hair and too much eye makeup who still wore gauzy, filmy things in an attempt to fool herself that she was still young and lovely.

There was a heartening thought.

"I'm glad you suggested this," Dad said.

"The walk was your idea, remember?"

"Not the walk. The trip."

Drawing up her legs to lean her forearms on her knees, Carly angled her head at her father. "Even though I drove the truck into a ditch?"

"Especially because you drove the truck into a ditch."

"You know, you might be more ready for that home than you think."

Dad laughed. "What I mean is, this gives us an excuse to stay put for a few days. Absorb some of what we're seeing. Get to know the people who live here."

Oh, yeah, a definite selling point. Carly turned around to stare at the cows. They stared back. Sort of. "I suppose," she said, mainly because she didn't want to argue.

"Guess we're both at a sort of crossroads, aren't we?"

Since that sounded a heck of a lot better than *dead end,* she said, "Yeah. Guess so."

Her father took another swallow of his water. "You got any idea yet what you're going to do when we go back?"

A logical question from a man who'd—logically—expect his thirtysomething daughter to, you know, have a *plan?* Since she no longer had a job? Never mind that it now struck her, like the proverbial bolt of lightning, that she'd apparently suggested this trip in order to avoid thinking about The Future. And now here The Future was, planted in front of her like a used car sales-man, refusing to go away until she at least sounded as though she'd made a decision.

But she'd gotten real good at faking out her dad over the years. Goading him was one thing. Worrying him was something else, she thought as a surprisingly cool breeze sent a shiver over her skin. Dad had no idea how much about her life she'd cho-sen *not* to let him find out. A situation she had no intention of changing.

"I thought I'd see about teaching at the company school." Ac-tually she hadn't, not yet, but it sounded good. "And you know Emily offered me a job."

"That's in Chicago, right?"

"Right outside. Lake Charles."

"Gets damn cold up there."

"Oh, and like Cincinnati's so tropical?"

"I'm just saying."

Saying what was the question. But, as she was so good at doing, she turned the tables on him. "What about you? Planning on going out for canasta champion at the Senior Citizen cen-ter?"

Lane blew out a half laugh, then shifted to lean against the tree trunk. It seemed strange, seeing her father so relaxed. Not bad, just strange. "Actually bumping along on all these back roads the past month must've jostled something loose in my brain, because I'm thinking of starting up some sort of consulting business. Something I could do from home, mostly, by computer."

Well, hell—this was the first positive thing to come out of her dad's mouth since Mom's death. "Seriously?"

"Yep."

"That's a terrific idea, Dad."

"Seriously?"

"Seriously."

His gaze sidled to hers. "You could help me, you know."

"Oh, right. Doing what, for God's sake?"

"Haven't figured that part out. But I'm sure we could think of something."

"Dad. What on earth do I know about business?"

"You're a smart cookie. You'd catch on."

"Man, you weren't kidding when you said you knocked something loose."

"I've always thought you were smart, Lee. It was just your common sense I had issues with."

"A subject I gather you brought up to Sam," she said before she even knew the words were in nodding distance of her brain.

Dad skimmed a palm over his short hair, looking everywhere but at her. "Your name might've come up once or twice."

"By whom?"

"I don't remember, actually. What difference does it make?"

"None, I suppose. Except I'm not sure I appreciate being described as a 'handful' to a total stranger."

"As if the man wouldn't have figured that out on his own after five minutes in your company. Besides, don't tell me you've haven't always prided yourself on being a pain in the can."

This was true. Except she was beginning to wonder how, exactly, this had benefited her in the long run.

She got to her feet, prompting a "You ready so soon?" from her father.

"My butt's going to sleep sitting on the hard ground. And I'm getting cold."

Her father rose, as well, slipping off his lightweight overshirt and handing it to her. "Thanks," she muttered, poking her arms through the sleeves. The shirt fluttered around her, cocooning her in his scent, and she felt, just for a moment, like the little girl who used to love cuddling with her daddy before she turned into the big bad pain in the can.

Back when she still let people all the way in.

They started back toward Sam's house, both lost in their thoughts. It had been a long time since she'd wanted to let anybody in, she realized. She wasn't sure she knew how, anymore. Or even if it was worth it. But there had to be something more than this chronic emptiness, an emptiness that seemed to yawn wider with every affair, every pointless relationship. Yeah, she'd lived life her own way. And still would, hardheadedness being definitely a chronic disease. But perhaps it was her definition of things that needed tweaking.

Maybe.

Through a stand of pines, Carly spotted a pair of buildings, apparently belonging to another farm. Although she had the feeling nobody lived there, the barn—an old-fashioned number in soft grays—appeared fairly sturdy. The house was something else again. To Carly's dismay, she realized she felt a lot like that house—old, abandoned and half-eaten up with decay. Terrific.

They returned by way of the front road, right as the big yellow school bus pulled up, its hydraulic brakes letting out a groan like an old woman taking off her girdle. The doors slapped open, belching out four buzz-cutted boys of assorted sizes, all in jeans and T-shirts and sneakers, still-new backpacks slung by a single strap across a skinny shoulder or dangling from one hand as they hurled good-natured insults back at their buddies still on the bus. The doors squealed closed; the bus let out a fart of exhaust and continued on, as the boys turned up the road leading to the farm, totally oblivious to being followed. Not surprising, since they were far too busy swinging their backpacks in a wide arc as they spun around, or bumping each other off balance, or yelling, "You take that back!" and "Nuh-uh!" and "What do you care, he's stupid, anyway," their soprano voices still high and clear and—God help them all—shrill as nails on a blackboard.

Then, like a turbocharged beetle from a fifties sci-fi flick, a metallic green Mitsubishi Eclipse roared past, kicking up a cloud of peach-colored dust and provoking the older boys' taunts of "Libby's got a boyfriend, Libby's got a boyfriend!" Carly caught a glimpse of long dark hair, sucked out of the window along with some remark or other, which turned the taunt into "Oooh, I'm gonna tell!"

They were close enough to the house by now to have alerted the dogs, who streaked down the road to greet the dusty, noisy little group with blurred tails and sharp barks, one or two dashing back and forth from house to boys to house to boys, as if not trusting the boys to find their own way home. The seen-better-days Eclipse screeched to a stop in the yard; a teenage girl got out, her gaze longingly following the car as it did a three-point turn and zoomed back up the road, past Carly and Lane again. The boy inside spared them a brief, curious glance, just long enough to understand the reason behind the girl's pining look.

Then Sam came out onto the porch, and Carly was defenseless against her stomach's little *whoomp* at seeing him again, this unassuming, unremarkable farmer who moved with the unconscious ease of a person who has far more pressing things to think about than his own body. Or the crazy woman gawking at him, Carly thought with a sigh as a sharp whistle knifed through the air, bringing all shenanigans to an immediate halt. She couldn't hear what he said, but five heads swiveled in her and Dad's direction. When she and her father got closer, the boys all said, "Hello," with various degrees of interest and enthusiasm as Sam introduced each one in turn. As if she'd remember all their names.

"And this is Elizabeth, my only girl. But everybody calls her Libby." He put an arm around the pretty girl's shoulders and gave her a squeeze. "I told Carly she could bunk with you for a couple of days, since you've got an extra bed and all. Didn't think you'd mind."

With a smile, Carly turned to Libby…and nearly lost her breath.

Never mind that she and Libby Frazier looked nothing alike, not in body type or coloring or stature. And yet, a single glimpse into those warm brown eyes, and Carly felt as though she'd been slammed back more than twenty years…

…to meet her fifteen-year-old self.

Somehow, Carly doubted it would be a joyous reunion.

Chapter 4

As if they weren't crowded enough already, jeez.

Libby stormed around the house and up the back steps, dumping her backpack with a thud on the royal-blue carpet remnant she'd picked out when they moved her in back here. She'd thought the color had been so cool in the store, but now she knew it attracted every piece of dirt and lint in the county, which was a real pain because who the heck had time to vacuum every five minutes?

She caught sight of what she guessed was Carly's stuff—an oversize backpack and a bright red duffel bag—and irritation sucked the breath out of her. Where'd Dad get off telling some stranger she could stay in Libby's room? And for a *week?* Okay, yeah, so maybe Carly did look kind of cool—certainly not like most of the women around here, that's for sure—but that was beside the point. It was like everything else these days—Dad simply didn't *get* it. Get *her.*

Not that she got herself much these days, either. Sometimes she felt as if somebody else had taken over her body, because she kept getting pissed off about stuff that never used to bother

her before. Like there was a constant storm going on inside her head, only occasionally interrupted by blue skies and sunshine.

Libby yanked off her "good" jeans and top and struggled into an old pair of jeans and a sweatshirt, her bedroom doorknob bouncing off the wall as she tromped back out through the mudroom to haul on her boots. It hadn't rained for a couple of days, but Jasmine, one of the sows, had recently figured out how to push down the float to her water tank to flood the pen, much to the delight of her penmates. Sure enough, when Libby got there, the sow—blissfully stretched out in a mud puddle—grinned up at her.

"Nobody can accuse you of being a priss, that's for sure." The sow grunted contentedly and flopped back into the ooze, and Libby's bad mood backed off a little.

Until she saw Dad headed her way.

She stepped into the feeder pigs' pen—there were nearly sixty of them, about half of which would be ready for market in a few weeks—and flipped open the top to the automatic feeder to knock down the finely ground grain packed against the sides and in the corners, as a sea of young pigs swarmed around her calves, nosing open the metal lids to the trough to eat.

"Thought you just did that yesterday?" Dad asked softly over the *bang, bang, bang* of the feeder lids dropping. He hardly ever yelled, at least not at Libby or her brothers. He didn't have to.

"Did I? I don't remember." She shut the lid again; her father chuckled.

"You remembered that, though."

Her cheeks warmed. "Honestly, Dad, it was only the one time. And two years ago at that."

"Some things," he said, grinning, "a father doesn't forget. Like the disgust on your face when you had to clean out all the moldy feed after it rained and rotted it all."

"Not an experience I want to repeat, believe me."

"I imagine not."

Libby dusted off her hands on her jeans, then came back out of the pen, leaving her snorting, snuffling charges behind, eating their butts off. Or on, in this case. She folded her arms and met her father's calm, but firm, gaze.

"What?"

"You know what. You didn't exactly give our guests a warm welcome."

She blew out a sigh, contemplating the cows in the pasture beyond. For a moment, she wished she was one of them. "It's not like I was rude or anything."

"Exactly."

She looked back at her father, noting with a start how much older he suddenly seemed. In the sunlight, the lines around his mouth and eyes were more noticeable, as was the gray in his hair. No matter that for their sake, Daddy had kept his grief over Mama's passing mostly to himself, Libby still knew how hard it had been on him, dealing with the farm and everything all by himself. How hard it must have been to smile and laugh for Libby and her brothers when there were times when he couldn't have felt much like it. So she felt bad, she really did, about all this weirdness churning inside her, making her feel like somebody else. And if she knew how to make it go away, she would.

But she didn't.

"It just…irritated me, is all, to come home and find out some stranger was stayin' in my room with me. Without my even having a say in it."

"I know. And I understand. But it was just one of those unforeseen things, you know? And, hey, Carly'll be somebody for you to talk to. You know, another woman."

Libby's eyes widened a little that Dad had implied that she was a woman, too, but that didn't change the situation. "I have other 'women' to talk to. Like Blair. And April. Who I'd planned on having spend the night on Friday. Now I suppose I can't."

Dad leaned one hand on top of the pen, his other hand fitted halfway into his jeans' pocket. "And I would've thought if you hadn't learned anything else by now, it was how to roll with the punches. Be flexible. I'm sure we can figure something out."

Libby nodded, because it was true, what Dad was saying, and she knew she was just being hardheaded, but it wasn't her, it was this itchy feeling inside her making her feel like this, act like this.

"You coming back inside?" he asked.

"Not yet. Thought maybe I'd check to see what needs to be picked from the garden. The tomatoes are still growing like gangbusters."

"I'm seeing a lot of spaghetti sauce in my future."

That pulled a smile from Libby. Mostly they had an arrangement with some of the ladies in town to do their canning and freezing for them in exchange for eggs and meat and some of what they'd put by. But spaghetti sauce, from one of Mama's recipes, was Libby's specialty.

"Yeah. I guess so."

Daddy gave her one of those long, assessing looks that made her nervous, gave her a wink, then walked away. Libby watched him, then crossed to the garden shed for a bushel basket, hoping like hell her nerves would settle down some once she set foot inside the garden.

But she wasn't counting on it.

Carly was waiting for Sam out by the back door, her arms crossed over some lacey little sweater that seemed kinda pointless, if you asked him. Funny the way she managed, even when she was completely covered, to still allude to what was underneath. Not that there was much underneath to allude to, but Sam had long since realized that sexiness had little, if anything, to do with a person's body. From inside the house he heard the comforting roar of his sons, working out the kinks from being stuck inside a classroom for six hours.

"You left your dad alone with them?" he asked, and a slight smile touched her lips.

"Are you kidding? You're talking about a man who coached Little League, soccer, football. He can't get enough of kids. Especially boys."

"And let me guess." Sam hooked one foot on the porch's bottom step. "You're an only child."

"Yep. And then I had to go and be a ballerina at that."

"And he didn't approve?"

"It was more that he didn't *understand*. Who I was, what made me tick…" Under the holey sweater, her shoulders bumped. "That sort of thing." Her eyes shifted toward the barn, then back to him. "Did you just talk to Libby?"

"Uh-huh."

Worry—and understanding, Sam thought—crumpled her features. "You know, I don't have to stay with her, if it really makes her uncomfortable. I've got my sleeping bag, I don't have a problem with crashing in the living room with Dad. Or even the barn, for that matter—"

"Like I'd let a guest sleep in my barn."

"I've slept in a lot worse places."

Sam thought maybe he heard a touch of regret mixed in there with the defiance, but he hadn't had enough practice to be sure. "By choice?"

After a moment she said quietly, "Most of the time."

"Well, it's *my* choice where you're sleeping now," he said, even as he thought whatever this woman had done in her past, it was none of his business. "And sure as hell it's not in my barn."

"But if Libby feels I'm encroaching on her space…"

"You're not. And Libby will just have to deal with it."

To his surprise, she laughed. "Because you say so?"

"Because she's normally the most laid-back kid I've ever known. And the friendliest. Why she's suddenly acting like this, I have no idea."

Pure pity sparkled in her eyes. "She's acting like this because she's fourteen and her hormones have jammed her brain cells and somebody she's never met is about to violate her private space. Right now, she's probably out there wondering if her dad's totally lost his marbles. I mean, I sure am, so I imagine she must be."

It took a second. Sam lowered his foot and crossed his arms over his chest. "And what's that supposed to mean?"

"Not many people would offer their home to two complete strangers. For all you know, we could be on the lam from the law. Or out to steal you blind."

"You're not serious."

His certainty—that Carly and her father were neither—seemed to catch her off guard, her expression making Sam speculate on how long it had been since she'd felt able to really trust another human being. He supposed she figured that made her tough. Emotionally impenetrable. Sam—despite more than a nodding acquaintance with emotional defenses—didn't see it that way. An inability to trust might make you safe—in some ways—but as far as Sam could tell, it didn't make you strong.

So he smiled and said, "Well, seems to me that deliberately breaking your axle so you'd get stuck in one place for a week isn't the kind of thing someone on the run would do. And as you've probably noticed by now, there's not a whole lot to steal, so no worries there. Although if you decided to take an extra cat or dog when you leave, I wouldn't have a problem with that." That got a little laugh, enough to make Sam feel it was okay to add, "So why don't you relax and not worry about anything more pressing than if the hot water heater can handle an extra two showers every day?"

"Deal," she said, but something in those damn eyes of hers told him she was lying through her teeth.

"Don't let me disturb you," Carly said to Libby as she quickly crossed the dark blue carpet to get to her duffel bag, lying expectantly on the floor by the extra twin bed. The girl sat at her computer, her dark hair shimmering down a back which stiffened at Carly's entrance. "I'm just getting a few things so I can change in the bathroom, so I won't bother you when I come to bed."

"Fine, whatever." Libby resumed typing. In a chat room, Carly noticed when she glanced over. She hauled the bag up onto the bed, unzipping it to get to a sleep tee and her toothbrush, Libby's annoyance humming between them like a pissed off bumblebee.

"Dinner was great, by the way," she said, moving to the door, the shirt and brush clutched in her hand.

Libby's hair shuddered from her shrug. "Just chicken and corn, no big deal."

"Been a long time since I had fresh corn, though. Not since I was a kid." She hesitated, then said, "I take it you knew the main course, um, personally?"

She could easily have gotten a God-what-a-dork eye roll for that one, but to Carly's surprise, the girl only said, "Can't say as how we were on a first name basis, no." She tapped out a response, then added, "I learned a long time ago not to get attached to anything that would eventually become dinner."

"That makes sense." A beat or two passed, then Carly said, "Look, I'm really sorry about this. I told your Dad I'd be happy to camp out in the living room. Or even the barn…"

"Don't worry about it, it's okay."

"You sure?"

Finally the girl twisted around. "No. But it's not like I've got much of a choice. Dad seems to have this sixth sense or something about running into people who need help. And he's never been real good at saying 'no.'"

Carly took heart that the girl didn't sound angry as much as resigned. But she said, "Except to you, right?"

After a long moment, she said, "Only like every five minutes."

"Sounds familiar."

"Your dad?"

"You got it."

"Yeah, he doesn't look like somebody who'd let you get away with much."

Carly decided not to go down that road. So she said, "Anyway, if it makes you feel better…I promise to be a good little roommate. I don't play loud music or have wild parties and no one's ever told me I snore."

Libby did something with her mouth that might have passed for a smile. "Well, I do. Not the loud parties, but I definitely play loud music. And my friends say I snore. I always have to sleep in another room when we have sleepovers."

"Huh. Maybe I'll sleep out in the barn after all," Carly said, and Libby actually laughed, followed immediately by her mouth turning down at the corners.

"I'm sorry for acting like a snot earlier. It's just…"

"You don't have to explain. I totally understand."

"Wish I did," the girl muttered, then got up from her chair, only to sink onto the edge of her bed, flopping back to rest on her arms. "It's a real pain in the butt, being the only girl."

"I can imagine." Cautiously Carly reentered the room, lowering herself to the hardback chair Libby had just abandoned. After all, it wasn't as if she had any pressing engagements. And since she was sharing the girl's room, it probably wouldn't hurt if Libby didn't think of her as the enemy.

"And what really sucks is that I can't even talk about how I feel to any of my friends, because they don't get it, either. Especially my friend Blair, who's been acting all weird ever since I started hanging out with Sean."

"Sean…that's the boy who brought you home?"

"Yeah."

"A real hottie."

Libby grinned, pleased. "Totally, huh?" Then she sat up, crossing her legs under her, assuming the my-life-totally-sucks pose common to every teenage girl through history. "Sometimes I think maybe she's, I dunno, jealous, maybe? But then I think it's more like…she doesn't approve, or something…" She seemed to catch herself; Carly could practically see her reach out and grab the words back.

"Hey," Carly said softly, "I'm just passing through. I have no stake in any of this, so if you're worried I might say something to your father—"

"No, that's not it. Well, maybe a little. But it's more…" The girl heaved an exasperated sigh. "Sean treats me like…like I'm really special, you know? And for heaven's sake, I'm not even fifteen yet! It's not like I'm plannin' on running away or anything! But if Daddy had his way, he probably wouldn't want me to have a boyfriend until I was thirty!"

"That sounds about right." At the girl's whose-side-are-you-on? look, she smiled. "All fathers are like that. All the good ones, anyway. And somehow, their daughters all manage to not only live through it, but to go on to have perfectly nice lives."

Libby shook her head, not looking at all convinced. "I really wish he'd trust Sean more. Or at least that he'd trust *me*. I'm not stupid, I've known how babies happen since I was four years old. So I'm not about to do anything to make one, not for a long time. And Sean knows how I feel and he said he'd never ask me to do anything I didn't want to do."

Carly bit her tongue. Because she'd known a whole bunch of Seans in her day, and heard a whole bunch of sorry-assed promises that meant exactly the opposite. But it wasn't her place to either counsel this girl or shatter her illusions. Especially since, by Libby's age, Carly had a very different outlook on life and sex and boys, one she was pretty sure would give Sam Frazier a coronary. So she said, "Have you said any of this to your father?"

"What's the point? It's not like he's going to believe me."

Carly had the feeling it wasn't his *daughter* Sam would have a hard time believing, but again, she kept her mouth shut. "He might feel better, though, hearing what you're thinking. If you don't say anything…"

She let the girl come to her own conclusions. Which she did after a couple of seconds. "Yeah, maybe you're right. I just wonder, though…"

"What?"

"Whether maybe he's overreacting because he's the only parent, you know? I just can't help thinking if Mom were still around maybe she'd calm him down a little so he wouldn't get on my case so much."

Carly heard the longing in the girl's voice, one which echoed all too clearly inside Carly's head. And heart. As much as she'd been secretly grateful to see Mom released from the prison of her illness, and even though they'd grown apart more than Carly might have liked, she still hadn't quite accepted that she couldn't pick up the phone and call her mother, or drop in to see her, whenever the mood struck. She really missed her, even though she'd been in her midthirties when her mother died. She could only imagine how Libby must have felt, losing hers at eleven.

"If my own father was anything to go by," she said, "I doubt your mother—or any other woman—would make any difference. My mother certainly didn't. In fact, the more she tried to take my side, the worse Dad got. Trying to protect daughters is what dads do."

"Yeah, well, maybe she'd at least distract him every once in a while. If you know what I mean."

The blush caught Carly totally unawares, stealing across her cheeks and down her neck like a brushfire. So she got up, making some excuse about needing to use the bathroom, adding she probably wouldn't be back until after Libby went to sleep since she could rarely get to sleep herself before midnight.

"Carly?" Libby said before Carly could get out the door. She turned. "I guess it won't be too bad, having you stay here. I mean, talking to you is kinda like talking to a shrink, huh? I can pretty much say whatever I'm thinking, but you won't say anything to anybody else, right?"

Oh, dear God. All she'd wanted was to smooth over the resentment so she wouldn't feel ice daggers in her back every time she walked into the room. Becoming a teenage girl's confidante, however, was something else entirely.

"Sure," she said with a weak smile, hightailing it out of the room, realizing with a sickening thud that she'd never been much good at saying "no," either.

The squawk of a floorboard was Carly's first clue that she wasn't alone on the back porch. She flinched, turning her head in the direction of the noise, willing her eyes to adjust after the bright lights of the kitchen.

"Didn't mean to scare you," came Sam's low, soft voice out of the darkness.

"You didn't. Exactly." She rubbed her arms through her sweater, against the chill of the evening, against the warmth of Sam's chuckle. "Thought farmers all went to bed by nine."

The floor groaned again; she could now almost make him out, sitting in a rocking chair with one foot parked up on the porch railing.

"I've never needed more than five or six hours sleep, for some reason. Long as I'm in bed by eleven, I'm up by five, no problem."

"Hell, I'm not sure I'm even *breathing* at that hour."

Another low laugh drifted across the porch. Then: "Where's your dad?"

"Watching TV."

"Ah."

"I take it you don't?"

Her eyes had adjusted to the dim light enough to see him shake his head. "Don't have much use for it, to tell you the truth. If I'm looking for entertainment, I like to read."

"Oh, yeah?" Another rocker sat expectantly a few feet from Sam's. Close enough for conversation, far enough away to still be in the safety zone. "Like what?" she said, lowering herself into the chair.

"Pretty much anything I can get my hands on. History, biographies, mysteries. The classics, sometimes. Hemingway, Dickens."

"Tell me you're one of the two people on the planet who's actually read *War and Peace?*"

"It's next on my list, as a matter of fact."

"You are one sick puppy," she said, and he laughed. Then she said, "Gotta admit, it's nice out here. Listening to the quiet." Well, *quiet* if you didn't count the late crickets and the constant *bang! bang! bang!* of the pig feeder.

"Yep," Sam said. "That's why I come out here almost every night, even in the dead of winter. Gives me a chance to collect my thoughts, think on everything I've got to be grateful for."

A definite fall breeze whisked across the porch, making her shiver. She tucked her arms around her middle and said, "This can't be an easy life, though. It certainly wasn't for my grandparents, even though I know they loved it, too."

"Guess that makes me a man who likes challenges," Sam said, and Carly smiled. "So…your grandparents were farmers?"

"My dad's folks, in Iowa. They had a dairy farm. I used to spend summers there as a kid."

"And you hated every minute."

"Actually, no. I had a blast. Just couldn't see doing it twenty-four/seven for the rest of my life."

"I can understand that. Farming's definitely not for everybody. It's either in your blood or it isn't." He leaned back in his chair, looking out into the darkness. "This land's been in our family for four generations. But my daddy didn't want to split it between my brother Josh and me, so he bought the farmstead next door before he passed, when Josh and I were still in our early twenties. Unfortunately he had no idea my brother wasn't the least bit interested in being a farmer."

"So what happened?"

"With my brother, you mean? He took off for Seattle and eventually became an architect. His place has been up for sale ever since. Well, actually, he had one taker, about five years ago, an artist from back East who'd gotten halfway through redoing the barn—apparently he wanted to live in it and tear down the old farmhouse—when he ran out of money."

"Oh…that must be the place Dad and I saw when we were out." She scanned the dark horizon, trying to get her bearings, then pointed east. "Over…there?"

"Yep. That's it. I've been working about half the acreage until we find a buyer. House needs a lot of work, though. Place is structurally sound, just badly neglected. You warm enough over there?"

Her head jerked around; she hadn't even realized she'd shivered again, let alone that he'd noticed. "What? Oh…yeah, I'm fine."

"It gets chilly at night this time of year," Sam said, shifting in his chair to work out of his jacket. "Here, put this around your shoulders."

"No, I'm okay, really…"

He got up and walked over to her, his footsteps sure against the floorboards, the jacket dangling from one hand. "Lean forward," he gently commanded. After a second or two, she did, a tingle racing down her spine when the stiff material draped over her back and shoulders. "That better?" he said above her head.

"Yes." She pulled the jacket more closed; it was impregnated with his body heat, his scent. "Thank you," she said, even as she steeled herself against the onslaught to her senses.

Sam walked back to his chair and dropped into it. "You're welcome. I figured, considering you don't have enough insulation on your bones to keep a flea warm, you had to be cold."

Now huddled under the jacket—okay, so it did feel pretty good—she glanced over. "Look who's talking."

She saw a flash of teeth in the darkness. "Oh, my engine's always idlin' on high. I hardly ever feel the cold. Never seem to put on any weight, either."

"You do realize I may have to kill you for that?"

His laugh warmed her far more than the jacket, and she thought *Not good.* She also thought, because things were getting far too cozy, *Get up, fool, and go back inside. Now.* Except then Sam said, "Guess you survived your first supper with my brood okay," and it would have seemed rude to cut him off.

"If you don't count the slight ringing in my left ear."

"Yeah, I guess it does get a little loud when they all get together. But I figure they'll all scatter soon enough. Until then, I can deal with a little noise."

A *little* noise? She'd been to quieter rock concerts. Then she heard herself say, "Did you and your wife actually plan on having six kids?"

"Can't say as we *planned* on that many, no." Amusement tinged his words. "Can't say as we planned on *not* having that many, either."

"Would you have had more?"

"No, I think it's safe to say we were done." He gave a low chuckle. "You really do come right out and say whatever's in your head, don't you?"

She thought of her conversation with Libby. "No. Not always."

"You and Libby work out a few things?" he asked, as if he'd read her mind.

"Enough. We…talked for a while after dinner."

"I don't dare ask what about, do I?"

"No."

"I figured as much. But I tell you, she gets those girlfriends of hers over here and brother—you can hardly hear yourself think for all the yakking." He was quiet for a moment, then said, "I know she misses her mom. The two of them…well. It was really something to see them together."

"You still miss your wife, too, don't you?"

Sam took his time before answering. "One day, I realized I'd gotten through a whole hour without thinking about her. And at first I thought something was wrong with me, that somehow, it didn't seem right *not* to hurt, not when you loved somebody as much as I'd loved her. Then, when the hour stretched to two, then sometimes even half a day, it finally began to sink in that missing somebody implies a vacuum of some kind, a hole in your life where this person used to be. And I thought, hell—after all those years we'd had together…" He shook his head. "All these kids, each one of 'em reminding me of her in some way. Travis has her eyes, and Frankie's got this weird way of looking at everything like she did. And Libby gets this set to her mouth that's Jeannie all over. It was Jeannie's idea, painting the walls all those bright colors. The snowball bush out front, the lilac over there in front of the kitchen window, the row of cherry trees over there…all her doing."

With a gentle smile, he turned to Carly. "I suppose some people would find all those reminders painful. But I find 'em a comfort. After all, it's kinda hard to miss somebody who's everywhere I look."

Unable to move, hardly able to catch a breath, Carly sat, staring over the porch railing as the night absorbed Sam's words. She'd never been particularly religious, but she thought this was what people meant when they talked about "grace"—the ability to not only accept a situation, or even to make the best of it, but to be lifted above it. And without warning, regret swept through her, not that she hadn't experienced a loss like that, but she'd never loved, or been loved, that completely and deeply and thoroughly.

And she doubted she ever would, if for no other reason than she wouldn't know what to do with that kind of love if it smacked her in the face.

Her lungs suddenly expanded, like those of a drowning person breaking the water's surface; the cool, earth-sweet air rushed in, clearing her head, if not those deeper, darker places inside her that had been shut off from light and proper ventilation for far too long. She slowly rose from the chair, her legs stiff—she hadn't stretched at all in two days, and her muscles were giving her grief for it. Aware of Sam's eyes on her, she let the jacket slip from her shoulders, her back tensing as the night's chill instantly wicked away the borrowed warmth.

"Going inside?" he said, slowly taking the jacket from her.

"Yeah. Guess I'm more tired than I thought. Besides, I interrupted your head-clearing time, so I'll let you get back to it."

His gaze was steady. "You didn't interrupt anything, Carly. Believe me, if I'd wanted to be left alone, I'd've let you know."

Way in the distance, a train blew its whistle, the sound comforting and mournful at the same time, and she thought of how that train had a purpose, a direction. Like Sam. Like she used to, before she realized she'd only taken half her life into account, and now that half had been shot out from under her.

Dear God, she was in a maudlin mood tonight. She sucked in another breath and said, "Dad and I thought we might do some sightseeing, if you're sure you don't need the van?"

"I'm not planning on it, no. So you go right ahead."

Her throat tightened, at this stranger's kindness and generosity and how the-God-she-wasn't-entirely-sure-she-believed-in was clearly having a good laugh at her expense. Especially when she started to leave and Sam's hand caught hers, the rough honesty of his calluses almost a rebuke to her softness.

"You okay?" he asked.

"Sure. Just tired, like I said. Well…g'night."

He dropped her hand. "Night. Oh, and if you hear footsteps overhead? It's just me checking on the kids before I turn in."

She nodded once, then left.

Instead of getting up, doing his final check of the barn and pens, Sam stayed put as if glued to the rocking chair, listening to the silence and breathing in the remnants of Carly's perfume, lingering in the air, on his jacket.

It was a damn good thing she wasn't sticking around long, was all he had to say. Because what he'd said about not missing Jeannie was true, as far as it went. He *had* taken solace in all those reminders of her, reminders that had blunted, then reformed his grief into a kind of contentment he'd had no reason to doubt before this. His life was full, and full of meaning, and he had no right to ask for a second helping of something a lot of folks never even got to taste.

And yet something about this gal was shaking him up but good. Something he couldn't figure out—not surprising, considering that with one regrettable exception his experience with women started and ended with Jeannie, whom he'd known better than he'd known himself. But whatever it was, Sam didn't want it. Didn't need it. Not when it had taken him the better part of these three years to finally trust that contentment, that peace, both of which he'd come to count on as surely as the Mason jars full of beets and applesauce and peaches lining the shelves in his cellar storeroom.

Except every so often, for all sorts of reasons beyond his or anyone else's control, those shelves went empty.

He forced himself out of the chair and slipped his jacket back on, then headed out to check on his livestock, feeling the cold in a way he couldn't ever remember.

Chapter 5

The sun razored through the cloudless sky, making it feel much hotter than the sixty-five or so it probably was. Lane took a swig from the bottle of cool water, swiping his shirtsleeve across his forehead—it had been more than forty years since he'd smelled the sweet, pungent tang of newly mowed alfalfa. Or felt the itch of it against his damp skin. When Carly had suggested this trip, the last thing he expected was to find himself driving a tractor, helping a farmer bale his last hay cutting of the season. Or that doing so would make more sense than anything had since Dena's death.

Except that it did didn't make any sense at all.

He could see the derelict farmhouse from here, could barely make out the faded For Sale sign; he forced his gaze away, telling himself *no*. Infatuation, was all this was, his senses bombarded by the sheer novelty of being away, doing something different. Doing something, period. They'd only been here for four days, for God's sake....

"Here," Sam said, dragging Lane away from the path that led to madness. He tossed him a ham sandwich from the cooler, then called over the kid who'd been working alongside them all morning, Billy something-or-other. Big guy, just shy of twenty, Lane thought, hardworking from what he could tell, but not inclined to conversation. Billy took a couple sandwiches and a jug of milk, nodding his thanks before striding away to sit by himself in the narrow patch of shadow hugging one of the large round bales. Lane lowered himself to the cool, bare ground underneath the lone oak still in full leaf at the end of the field, considering his host, wondering what exactly was going on underneath that ball cap of his. They weren't that far from the house, they could easily have gone back for lunch. But Sam had said, since he'd had to substitute teach the last two days, he was in a split to get the alfalfa baled before the weather turned and he risked losing the whole cutting, so he hadn't wanted to take the extra time.

Right.

Not that he'd ever let on, but Lane had overheard enough of Sam's and his daughter's conversation on the porch that first night to not only get a pretty good idea that something was bubbling between them, but that neither of them had the slightest idea what to do about it. Probably not a bad thing, all told, since from where he was sitting, they didn't seem to have much in common. A shame, in a way, since Sam struck Lane as somebody a woman—or anybody else, for that matter—could count on. Solid. Stable. Words he unfortunately couldn't use to describe his daughter, as much as he loved her.

Yes, she was a grown woman. And no, it wasn't any of Lane's business how Carly chose to live her life. But watching her flit from relationship to relationship—and noticing her valiant attempts at shrugging off each breakup—Lane had begun to wonder if it was a desire for freedom, or simply habit, driving her choices these days.

Sam lowered his butt to the ground beside Lane, biting off half his sandwich at one clip, and Lane herded his thoughts in another direction. He nodded toward Billy. "So what's the story with the kid?"

"Why's he here, you mean? He's working off some community service hours by helping out the various farmers and ranchers in the area."

"Oh?" The kid was quiet and seemed polite enough, from what little contact Lane had had with him. Hard worker, too. "What happened?"

"About a year ago, Billy got the bright idea to hold up the Git-n-Go with a fake gun. Stupid kid prank, but one that definitely needed nipping in the bud. But the judge decided sending him to jail would serve no good purpose, so he came up with the community service idea instead."

Lane watched the young man for a second, then said, "You think the judge made the right decision?"

"Absolutely," Sam said around the bite in his mouth. "I've seen a big change come over him in the past several months. He still keeps to himself, but doesn't goof off, never gives me lip, and you can practically see his confidence swell when he's done a good job." Sam knocked back several swallows of water and said quietly, "Most everybody makes a few bad choices along the way. I sure as hell have. But it seems to me, especially with kids like Billy, the trick is to catch 'em and get 'em turned around before they start believing their own bad press. You know what I mean?"

"Yeah. I do."

Sam leaned back against the tree, one leg stretched out in front of him. "I think with Billy all it took was having somebody believe in him, somebody willing to look past all the crap to see the real kid caged up inside."

"And that would be you?"

"Not just me, no. The judge, for one. And all of us who said we'd give the kid a chance." He sort of laughed. "Hell, guess we figure there's so few of us as it is, we can't afford to let one of our own go down the tubes." Then he looked over at Lane, his eyes shining with a conviction that stems from something far deeper than blind faith, Lane thought. "It doesn't always work, I know that. Some folks seem bound and determined to shoot themselves in the foot, no matter what. But I think most people appreciate a hand to help pull them up out of the hole they've dug for themselves."

Lane let his gaze drift out over the mowed field dotted with bales. "You sound a lot like my wife. I don't know how I would have made it through Carly's teenage years without Dena. She was always the calm one. The trusting one."

"Yeah. I know what you mean." Sam exhaled loudly. "I've got six kids, Lane. And God knows I'm trying to do right by them, to set the best example I know how, but even the best kids sometimes pull some real dumb-assed stunts. So I'd like to think, if I wasn't around for whatever reason, and one of 'em screwed up, that there'd be somebody willing to give them another chance to get it right, that's all."

"You're worried about Libby, aren't you?"

Sam stilled, water bottle halfway to mouth. "What makes you say that?"

"Because I still worry about Carly, even though she hasn't been a teenager for almost twenty years. And I hate to tell you this, but your girl gets this look on her face that's like looking back in time."

"You know, I could have gone all day without knowing that."

Lane chuckled, his laughter fading as he realized Sam was holding something back. "And...?" he prompted.

"Don't take this the wrong way, but I had some reservations about putting the two of them together."

"Afraid my girl would corrupt yours, you mean?"

"I wouldn't say that, exactly..."

"Yes, you would. And it's okay. In your position, I probably would have thought the same thing." Sam grunted. Lane glanced over at Billy, who was lying down, his hands braced under his head, plugged into a portable CD player. "You didn't have to take us in, you know."

"No, I didn't. But I decided any gal who volunteers to take her father on an extended road trip can't be all bad."

Lane smiled. "You've got a point."

Sam sloshed the water around in his bottle, then said, "I could be dead wrong, but something tells me that underneath all that attitude, she's got a soft spot she doesn't let many people see."

Lane felt the helpless pang of any father whose child is so obviously hurting. "I think you're probably right," he said, once again thinking about Dena and how little he'd realized, until this minute, exactly how much of his strength he'd gleaned from his wife.

"You think you'll ever get married again?" he asked, the question surprising him as much as it apparently did Sam.

Sam took another swallow of water and said, "I think I'll have to give you a qualified 'no' on that."

"Why qualified?"

"Because I learned a long time ago that nothing's set in stone, that what seems perfectly logical one minute won't make a lick of sense the next. So all I can say for now is, it took me a long time to adjust to life without Jeannie, to get the kids adjusted to getting along without her, and frankly, I'm not sure how anybody else would fit in. Or even if anybody'd want to." He turned to Lane. "What about you?"

"I don't know. Carly's mother would be a hard act to follow, that's for sure. But I liked being married. Liked the constancy of it."

"Yeah," Sam said. "Me, too." He shifted again, keeping his eyes fixed ahead. "Nights are the hardest. And I don't mean the sex, necessarily. I mean having someone to talk to. To listen. To make me laugh. I miss that."

"I know what you mean."

A browned hand streaked a hand through hair not much darker than Lane's. "The other night, I gave Carly this whole song and dance about how it's hard to miss somebody who's still so much a part of your daily life. But anymore… Maybe I'm fooling myself. About not needing anybody else, I mean. I liked being married, too. Liked it a whole lot. I just don't know if I could pull it off with anybody else."

"Which isn't enough to stop you from being attracted to my daughter." Sam's eyes shot to his; Lane chuckled. "Yes, it's that obvious."

Sam's gaze held in his for several beats before, on a rush of breath, he looked away. "I haven't even been tempted to get emotionally involved with somebody else since Jeannie passed. Still not sure I want to, or that I'm ready, or whatever. But even if I thought Carly and I had anything in common, even if I was absolutely sure I was ready to move on, for sure I'm not about to let my feelings get all tangled up about a woman who's leaving in a few days."

"I can understand that." Lane paused, then said, "Three years is a long time."

"Not compared with more than twenty," Sam said, but without much conviction. But then he rallied with, "Besides, I don't know what your daughter's looking for, or even if she's looking for anything, but I'm pretty sure I'm not it."

"Then why are you going out of your way to avoid her?"

Sam laughed, a hollow sound. "Because in spite of everything I just said, there's a little devil in my head hell-bent on convincing me I don't know what in the blue blazes I'm talking about." He stood, tossing his empty water bottle back into the cooler, then signaled to Billy it was time to get back to work. "If we haul ass, we should be able to finish this by sundown—"

Lane got to his feet, as well. "You know, now that I think about it…"

"Billy and I can finish up, if it's too much for you."

"No, it's not that. It's…"

And what did he think he was going to say? *I think you're exactly what my daughter needs?* Oh, yeah, that'd go over really well. With both parties.

He laughed softly, tapping his head. "Too late. Whatever it was, it's gone now. One of the hazards of growing old."

"Shoot," Sam said with a grin, "I've been doing that ever since I can remember. So…you wanna rake or bale?"

And that was the end of that discussion.

For now, at least.

Carly had to admit the past few days had been among the more peculiar of her life. Not because of anything that had happened—heck, she was in the middle of nowhere, *nothing* had happened, other than that one of the sows had given birth to about a million piglets—but because of all the weird stuff going on in her brain.

She'd assumed she'd go crazy in the country: she didn't. She'd assumed she'd miss her life back in Cincinnati. She hadn't. At least, not all that much. She'd assumed, when it became obvious that Sam was avoiding her, she'd shrug, say, "Whatever," and stop thinking about him.

She couldn't.

Even despite the one reaction that hadn't surprised her in the least, that all these kids gave her the heebie-jeebies.

Nope, no dormant maternal instincts suddenly blossoming here. If anything, every time somebody clobbered or yelled at or wrestled with somebody else, she could feel her ovaries shrink in horror, clutching their little eggs and hanging up a little Sperm Not Welcome sign.

But back to Sam. Who was avoiding her. Whom she had to admit made her widdle jaded heart go *awwww* every time she saw him with one of the ovary-shrinking darlings. Because, well, there was a lot to be said for a man who could walk into the middle of a fracas, utter a single, deep-voiced, "Cut it out," and cut out, it was. There was a lot to be said for a man comfortable with hugging and kissing his sons, a man who'd tear the house apart—and commandeer everyone else to help him—in order to find Travis's favorite stuffed animal. An animal that Carly had yet to identify as having ever been part of the known animal kingdom.

There was a lot to be said for a man who could look a woman in the eye in such as way as to leave no doubt of his interest, but who also made it clear that nothing was going to come of it and yet, somehow, *not make the woman feel rejected in the process.* Truly, this was a gifted man.

Not that—between his work, her father, and all these kids— there'd been any way for anything *to* come of it, but still. A girl can dream.

And in less than three days—since Darryl Andrews had called and said the axle had come in, so he'd be finished up by Monday—that's all this would be. A dream.

"You ready?" Libby said from the kitchen door.

"Yep," Carly said, finishing her coffee. "Just let me go pee and we're off."

Okay, so maybe she'd sort of bonded with one of Sam's off-spring. After that first rocky night, she and Libby had settled into a fairly calm relationship, based mainly on Libby's grip-ing about life in general and Carly's sympathetic "Hmms" at appropriate places.

Another assumption blown to hell. That having a young girl dump on her would irritate the life out of her. Of course, know-ing that the dumping had a limited run might have something to do with her tolerance level.

Libby—and Carly's father, and Travis, and Radar, sheesh— were in the van already when Carly got outside. Sam was still doing his thing with the alfalfa, and apparently all the other boys were otherwise engaged, either helping their father or…what-ever boys did when they weren't at school or doing chores. So Carly and Dad, who needed to go into town anyway to stock up for the next leg of their trip, had volunteered to haul Libby, and whoever, along with them. Not that there was a whole lot of shopping one could do in Haven, but Libby said the Homeland would be fine for what she needed, that she had too much to do to take the time to go to the Wal-Mart over in Claremore.

Carly's father opted to sit in back with Travis and the mutt, leaving Carly to drive and Libby with the passenger seat, which she clearly didn't mind. Although her makeup was done more expertly than Carly's, the skin under her eyes still sagged from her being up all night with Bernadette, the sow who'd given birth. *Farrowed,* Carly reminded herself, even though she predicted scant opportunity to work the word into the conversation once she left here.

"How're the babies?"

That got a bright smile, even if the sow's labor had put the kibbosh on Libby's friend April spending the night. "Did you see them? Aren't they gorgeous?"

"I did. And they are." For pigs. "How many did she have again?"

"Seventeen." Carly's ovaries whimpered. "But she only has fourteen teats, so we're all taking turns feeding the extras."

That would account for the pig-filled box on the back porch. And to think, they'd all had bacon this morning. Bacon from something that had once maybe been a tiny piglet in a box on the back porch, being bottle fed every few hours. Definitely a strange way to live.

A few minutes later, she parked the van in the supermarket's lot and they all scrambled out, except for Radar who took his vehicle protection duties very seriously. All along the front of the store, letter-size photocopied posters of two women apparently running for mayor were stapled, taped and hung, the papers making a weird buzzing sound when the wind blew across them. Her father stopped in front of one for a second—maybe ten seconds, actually—before they all went inside, where he promptly plodded off to the magazines and books. Carly pulled out a cart and was contemplating how to haul the runny-nosed little boy beside her up into it without doing herself a mischief, when Libby took Travis's hand. "We'll meet you out front in like, twenty minutes?"

Knowing what Libby was planning on buying, Carly glanced at the four-year-old, then back at his big sister.

Libby laughed. "I know what you're thinking. But being the only female in a house full of guys, you get over feeling self-conscious about certain things *real* fast. At least, a lot faster'n they do! And he's been missing me since school started, haven't you, short stuff?"

The kid nodded, snot glistening on his upper lip.

Oh, brother.

Carly dug a tissue out of her shoulder bag and cleaned the kid up, then stood there as Libby and Travis disappeared into the Saturday morning crowd, the tissue pinched between her thumb and forefinger as though it were radioactive. A situation readily handled when she spied a trash can tucked under the counter behind one of the cashiers. The tissue duly dispatched, she steered the cart toward the magazines, but there was nobody there except a couple of young mothers with what looked like a dozen kids between them.

Carly scanned all the nearby aisles, frowning. Now where on earth could Dad have gotten to that fast?

Ivy nearly caused a cucumber avalanche when her daughter nudged her.

"Don't look now," Dawn said, "but you're being seriously cruised."

Ivy glared at Dawn, then smiled for Max, her six-month-old grandson toothlessly grinning at her from his baby seat in Dawn's cart, before oh-so-casually moseying over to the tomatoes, despite not needing any since everybody and their cousin had had a bumper crop this year and kept pawning them off on Ivy. Dawn followed her, hissing, "Not over here, over there," which made Ivy turn to do some more glaring, which is when she saw him.

Her head whipped back around. "That's the man I was telling you about," she whispered. "The one who kept staring at me in Ruby's the other morning."

Dawn handed Max a teething biscuit, angling herself to get an eyeful, then frowned at Ivy. "And you're not staring back why?"

"What would be the point?"

"If you have to ask—"

"Morning, ladies," said a deep baritone beside them.

They both jumped; three tomatoes rolled off onto the floor,

two of which became tomato puree at their feet. The third one, however, bounced, then took off toward the lettuce. Everybody took two steps over like they had nothing to do with the mess.

"Aren't you the lady running for mayor?"

"She sure is," Dawn said, and then he smiled, and Ivy knew, with that sinking feeling one gets at times like this, that it was gonna take a whole lot more than heaven to help her.

"Ivy…Gardner, right?"

A come-on in the produce section of the Homeland. Yeah, that sounded about par for the course. Dawn made like she was gonna nudge her again, but Ivy leaned out of range.

"Your picture doesn't do you justice," the man said, and Dawn started coughing, since Ivy had comfortably settled into her cronedom some years ago. Despite Luralene's nagging her about ditching her braid for a more stylish 'do—which, translated from Luralese, meant something involving teasing combs and copious amounts of AquaNet—Ivy had determined from the start of this so-called "campaign" that if the town really wanted her for mayor, then they'd just have to take her as she was— saggy, baggy, and crone-headed. Then Dawn started in about needing to get Max some Huggies, she was nearly out—Ivy'd given up on trying to get her to switch to cloth diapers, there was just no talking sense to the woman sometimes—and disappeared. Ivy wasn't sure if that was a good thing or not. Especially when the man smiled again and put out his hand and said, "Lane Stewart. My daughter Carly and I have been staying with Sam Frazier, maybe you know him?"

Ivy laughed, even though he was holding her hand in both of his, gently, like a bird he'd captured, and her heart was beating about as fast as that bird's, proving that there really was no fool like an old fool. However, she composed herself enough to get out, "Know him? I delivered all six of his babies."

"You're a doctor, then?"

"Midwife." He had yet to let go of her hand. Not that this was a problem. Except for Millie Pennyweather's standing there, gawking. Ivy was tempted to glower at the woman until she remembered she needed her vote. But then she remembered she also needed to take control of this bizarre situation, so she extricated her hand from Lane's, shoving it into the pocket of her sweater coat. "You enjoyin' your stay in Haven?"

"Very much." He paused, his eyes full of intent. "It's a shame we're leaving on Monday."

Ivy couldn't remember the last time a man had looked at her with anything even remotely resembling intent, let alone when one had gotten things to fluttering inside her. Except, since the man wasn't sticking around, anyway, she couldn't even count on him for a vote, much less anything to make the fluttering worthwhile.

"Well. It was nice to meet you, Lane," she said, pleasantly enough, she thought. But no sooner had she picked up a pair of cucumbers off the stack in front of her—which she didn't need, either, not to mention having no cart to put them in—than he said, "Would you do me the honor of having dinner with me tonight?"

Slowly she replaced the cucumbers, then turned to meet what sure as hell looked like a sincere gaze. "Thought you said you were leavin'?"

He smiled in the way of a man having something up his sleeve. "It's not written in stone," he said, and the fluttering increased twenty-fold. By this time, a small crowd had gathered around Millie Pennyweather like iron filings to a magnet, which meant, if Ivy accepted, within a hour half the town would know she'd just allowed a total stranger—his having stayed out at Sam's for the past few days notwithstanding—to pick her up. In broad daylight.

And then those blue eyes twinkled and she thought, *Eat your hearts out, you old bats.*

"In that case," she said with a smile she hadn't had occasion to use for more than twenty years, "I'd be delighted to have dinner with you, Lane Stewart."

She heard a collective gasp, followed by—from clear over by the deli counter—what sure sounded like her daughter's whoop of approval.

All of which was completely obliterated when Lane gave her a wink that warmed her clear down to her worn-out Birkenstocks.

Chapter 6

All Carly could think was, *I do not believe this.*

They were standing downstairs in the empty farmhouse next to Sam's. Her father was grinning like Jack Nicholson in *The Shining*. She, however, was not. "Dad. You can't be serious."

Oh, boy—she hadn't seen *that* look in a long time. "I hate that apartment, Lee. I miss having a house to work on, and I've got nothing left in Cinci anymore. So give me one good reason why I shouldn't do this?"

She could hear Sam's footsteps creaking on the floorboards upstairs. "You'll be glad to know," he called down, "that all the windows are sound up here." Sam was clearly tickled pink about the prospect of having her father as his neighbor. Not that she blamed him, but still.

"Because…because this is a whim! You haven't thought this through—"

"Actually, I've been thinking about this practically nonstop ever since we saw this place. It's not as spur-of-the-moment as you might think." Stuffing his hands into his khaki pockets, Dad walked over to the window looking out over fields she knew he'd never work. "Even though I know it must seem out of character."

"There's an understatement."

He turned, smiling. "Some things can't be explained, honey. Like how a man knows when he's come home. And frankly, it doesn't have to make sense to anybody but me."

"Does this by any chance have something to do with the woman in the store?"

His expression got all hazy. "Maybe."

"That *is* nuts, Dad! You talked to her for, what, five minutes? What do you know about her?"

He shrugged, unconcerned. "Nothing." Then his mouth curved. "Yet."

"But she's nothing like Mom!"

"And maybe I'm not looking for a copy of my favorite movie. Maybe I'd like to see something where I don't already know the words."

Whoa. Not that his words made him sound any less crazy— if anything, they only reinforced her conviction—but whoa, all the same.

Dad wandered out onto what passed for a porch, but Carly dragged herself over to the stairs—each wooden tread more bowed than the next—and sank onto the third step from the bottom, understanding neither her father's calm nor why her brain felt as though it was being ripped apart by some brutal centrifugal force. She rammed her hands through her loose hair: Why did she feel so…left out? After all, it wasn't as if she and Dad hung out all the time, or that either of them *needed* the other. And wasn't this what she wanted, for him to move past his grief, to see him jump-start his life?

Except jump-starting his life in rural Oklahoma hadn't exactly been what she'd imagined.

"Hey," she heard behind her, a split second before she caught Sam's scent, felt his warmth through her cotton sweater. "Where'd Lane get to?"

"Outside," she said, with a quick swipe at her cheeks, a vague gesture toward the front door. The stair treads not being wide enough for two butts, Sam lowered himself to the step above hers, the outside of one long leg grazing her shoulder. She was so distraught, she almost didn't notice.

"You don't want him to do this, do you?"

"Wouldn't be my first choice, no."

"Got any idea why?"

She twisted around, her breath hitching at the gentle strength in those warm green eyes. A strength that did a pretty good job at masking the loneliness she knew lurked right on the other side. "This isn't like him, you know? He's never been impulsive in his life." Turning back, she said, "I'm the one who goes off half-cocked. Dad was always the one telling *me* to think things through…." Her throat constricted; no one was more surprised than she to hear herself say, "I'm supposed to be the one escaping him. Not the other way around."

She started at the steady, warm pressure of Sam's fingers massaging the juncture between her shoulder and neck. Her head was determined not to respond, but her body clearly had other ideas. "And then," she plowed on, "he apparently has a…crush or something on this woman he met at the store."

"You mean Ivy?"

That was worth screwing herself back around for. "You already know?"

"Honey, high-speed Internet has nothing on the Haven grapevine. In any case, Libby couldn't get the words out fast enough when y'all got back from the grocery store. Said it was the first time she'd ever seen Ivy look flustered."

Carly frowned. "She didn't look flustered to me."

"Which only goes to show how serious this is." He stopped massaging; a twinge of regret passed through her. "Whether or not your dad and Ivy would ever work together, I have no idea. But you won't find a better human being, or a bigger heart. She speaks her mind, that's for sure, and heaven help your dad if he screws her over." Carly made a face, and his chuckle did things to her insides that scared her half to death. "I'm just saying. But I've known Ivy Gardner for more than thirty years, and if anybody deserves happiness, it's that woman."

"So does Dad, but…" She turned back around. "Oh, Sam…what on earth is my sixty-three-year-old father going to do with a *farm?*"

"Well, it'll take him a good ten years just to fix up the house," he said behind her, his smile evident in his voice. Carly huffed out a sigh, which he apparently found amusing. But then he said, "Actually, he and I have already discussed it, and he's going to lease a good portion of the land back to me. I've been working it anyway to keep it in shape, paying my brother part of the profits. Lane's not planning on being a farmer, if that's what's worrying you. I expect he just wants to live out in the country. Have you seen the barn?"

"No, I haven't seen the barn. I don't want to see the barn. I want…"

"What?" he said softly, his breath teasing her hair. Or it might have been a breeze whisking down the stairs from an open window. "What do you want, Carly?"

"My life back, dammit!" she said, and the tears started up all over again. She clamped a hand across her mouth, although in a lame attempt to staunch the tears or the thought that brought them on, she had no idea.

"Change is damn scary, that's for sure," Sam said. "Especially when there's no time to prepare for it."

Refusing to look at him, she nodded.

He released a breath, then said, "I think what most shook me up after Jeannie's passing, even more than the obvious fact that she wasn't here anymore, was that nothing—nothing—was the same. I hadn't realized how much I'd taken my life for granted, how much I'd somehow expected everything to keep on the way it had been. I knew there'd be changes, sure—the kids would grow up and eventually go on to have lives and families of their own—but it was still part of the plan, you know? Jeannie dying wasn't part of the plan." After a moment, he said, "Your knee givin' out on you wasn't part of your plan. Neither was your daddy deciding his idea of 'moving on' wasn't the same as yours."

She dug a wadded up tissue out of her pocket, blew her nose, and scowled. "Do you always have an answer for everything?"

He chuckled, the warm sound filling the emptiness of the room, even as it maybe plugged up a tiny hole in her heart as well. "Hardly. Hell, half the time, I don't feel like I've got an answer for anything."

She dared to look at him, a reluctant smile tugging at her mouth. "Like when you're talking to Libby?"

"Exactly." Then his own smile softened, even as his eyes linked with hers in a way she couldn't ever remember happening before, as if he somehow understood her in a way she didn't even understand herself. "But I've had a lot of time to think about that particular subject, so I thought it wouldn't hurt to share." Underneath his plaid shirt, the kind of shoulders a woman could get used to leaning on rose, then fell. "Take from it what you will. It's free, after all."

A laugh burst from her own throat, a surprised sound, like a car backfiring. Then she said, "All my life, I've been fighting my father for the right to live my life as I saw fit, without his interference. Or commentary. I guess…the tables are turned, aren't they?"

"In other words, you have to let him go."

"Yeah. Oh, God…how I must have scared the crap out of him."

"So what are you going to do?"

Twisting one of her rings around her index finger, she pushed out a sigh. "I suppose, if he really wants this…"

"I really do," Dad said from the doorway.

Oh, hell…how could she deny him his shot at whatever peace he could find? "Then I guess the least I can do is help you move out here."

With a grin, Dad opened his arms. Carly pushed herself off the stairs and walked into them, thinking how ironic it was that she should finally feel close to her father, right when he was about to remove himself from her life. While she might find it in her heart to eventually accept his harebrained idea, if this was where he wanted to live, he was on his own. Because no way in hell would she ever call Haven, Oklahoma, *home.*

"What makes you so sure she's gonna end up staying here?"

Firmly planted in one of the porch rockers, Sam narrowed his eyes at the dark-haired man ensconced on the ancient glider a few feet away. Joe Salazar's eight-year-old half brother, Seth, and Sam's Wade had spent the afternoon together after school, but when Joe'd come to pick Seth up, the boys had insisted they were "in the middle of somethin'." Hence the ten minute break on Sam's porch. Hard to believe that Joe, who'd only come to Haven to oversee the remodel of the Double Arrow, had been a complete stranger not four months ago. But the town had sucked the brothers to its bosom, as the town was wont to do, and now it was as if they'd always been here.

As witnessed by how easily, and completely, Joe had grafted himself onto the grapevine. True, most of the male population viewed gossiping as women's work, but every once in a while a subject came up that transcended gender. And Carly Stewart was apparently one of those topics. Ruby's husband Jordy down at the diner even had a pool going, about whether she'd stay or not. Last Sam heard, the pot was up to a hundred bucks.

Not that he was a part of it or anything. Sam was not a gambling man, his long-standing game of craps with Mother Nature notwithstanding.

So now he took a swallow of his iced tea, watching his other boys—and half the dogs—chase a soccer ball around the yard, and said, "I'm not *sure.* I've just got a hunch, is all." He balanced his glass on the arm of the rocker, half expecting to hear a little *hissss* as the condensation trickled over his heated fingers. After a couple of fall-like days, the temperature had bounced right back up again, like the weather couldn't make up its mind what it wanted to be. Just like Sam couldn't decide what, exactly, he felt about Carly. "She cares too much about her father to just leave him, for one thing. No matter what she says. And for another…" He let another swallow of tea slide down his parched throat. "I get the feeling that gal's lookin' for something."

"Like what?"

He remembered her wretched expression last Sunday afternoon in her father's "new" living room, an image that hadn't diminished any in the five days since she and Lane had left. "A life. A new one, I mean."

"And you think she can find it here?"

"You did, didn't you?"

The other man chuckled. "Walked right into that one, didn't I?"

"Yes, you did. And speaking of which…you and Taylor pick a date yet?"

That got another grin, obviously for the pretty red-haired kindergarten teacher, a relative newcomer to Haven herself, who'd stolen Joe's heart. And healed his little brother's, broken to bits after the little boy's parents' sudden deaths this past spring.

"Around Christmas, maybe. Since we're not interested in waiting too long."

Not that they had, from what he'd gathered, Sam thought in amusement as he kicked back the rest of his tea, then set his glass on the floor beside the rocker. Like wisps of fog, memories of the weeks leading up to his and Jeannie's wedding floated through his brain, all that seemingly endless agony of anticipation, made even hotter in no small measure by their youth, he imagined. Except then he glanced over and caught the funny smile on Joe's face and thought, then again, maybe being older doesn't lessen the thrill at all.

"You think it's true," Joe said, "about Lane moving here because of Ivy?"

Then Sam thought of the look on Lane Stewart's face the morning after his date with Ivy Gardner and thought, nope, the thrill doesn't diminish one iota. A fact that might come in handy, some day down the road.

"I think it's safe to say she's a large part of it, yep."

"Think he's got has a chance?"

"Have no idea." Much to everyone's chagrin, the couple had gone clear to Tulsa for their date, so nobody had a firsthand account of the event. And Ivy wasn't talking, not even to Dawn. Who, as the town attorney, had drawn up the papers for the property sale. And Sam, acting as proxy for his brother, could tell it was clearly irking her that the first man to take Ivy out in more than twenty years was being as closemouthed as her mother.

"How about you?" Joe asked.

"What about me?"

"Well, since you brought up the subject of Carly's sticking around, or not…" He let the sentence trail off.

Sam let it stay trailed for some time, then said, "Stating my opinion about whether or not she'll stay is not the same as expressing a personal interest."

"Of course not."

"You know, you could at least *try* to keep a straight face."

Joe laughed. "I'm only saying for somebody without a *personal* interest, you seem to be staring at the woman a lot."

"That's only because it was driving me nuts, trying to figure her out."

"I see. Like she was one of those mind-bender puzzle things."

"Exactly." Sam folded his hands behind his head, savoring the rare moment of relaxation. Except there was nothing at all relaxing about this conversation. "I'll admit I find her intriguing. But that's all." At his friend's smirk, he said, "Oh, come on…what on earth would I do with somebody like that?"

"It'd come back to you, I'm sure."

Sam grunted, then said, "Joe, half the time the woman looked at my kids like they'd escaped from the zoo." A loud, rude noise sounded from across the yard, sparking peals of laughter. "Not that I blame her," he said, as whoever was responsible for the sound effect gave an encore. "Shoot, there were times when I'd no sooner walk in the door that Jeannie'd go sailing out of it, declaring if she didn't get away from them immediately, she couldn't be held accountable for her actions. And she was their mama. She'd *wanted* them. And she loved them, even in those moments when I think she'd've taken a buck-fifty for the lot and never batted an eye. And then there's Libby in the throes of teen-age angst…."

The screen door slammed behind them as Seth and Wade came barreling outside and down into the yard. Joe propelled himself to his feet, digging out his car keys from his pocket, then turned amused, dark eyes to Sam. "So what you're saying is—" he slipped on his sunglasses "—there's no room in your life for this woman, right?"

Suspicion pulled up a chair and settled right in beside him. "Where are you goin' with this?"

"Just wondering if you realize that—what, two weeks ago?—you would've said there's wasn't room in your life for *any* woman?"

"C'mon, Joe—let's *go!*" Seth called out. "I'm hungry!"

"Yes, *sir,*" Joe muttered good-naturedly before, with a wave to Sam, he made his loose-limbed way down the porch steps and over to his Blazer, neatly removing himself from the scene before Sam had a chance to come up with a fitting response to Joe's "observation." And no sooner had Joe and Seth driven off than everybody ganged up on Sam, demanding food. Everybody except Libby, who was holed up in her room with homework. Or so she said. So it wasn't until Sam took himself down to the cellar to find something to feed all his baby birds that he finally had a chance to mull over Joe's words.

Words that, unfortunately, couldn't have been more dead-on.

Still, he thought as he rummaged around in the smaller of the two SUV-size freezers, grateful for the billowing cold soothing his heated face, whether or not Sam had crossed the big, scary line between "never" and "maybe" in regard to his love life had nothing to do with whether or not Carly was the woman he'd crossed that line for. Even if—and here's the part he hadn't gone into with Joe, nor was he likely to, with Joe or anybody else—Sam's kids weren't an issue.

Because right now he was guessing she was one discombobulated lady. One discombobulated lady who needed the space to figure out what came next without sex and romance and all that stuff clouding the issue. Even if Sam had been a hundred percent sure he was ready to reconsider his stance on there not being room for another woman in his life (or his house), which he wasn't, even if he'd been even reasonably sure Carly was the woman he was ready *for,* which he definitely wasn't, even if she'd reacted to his kids like Snow White to the seven dwarfs, the timing just plain stank.

It was a shame, though, Sam thought as he slammed the freezer door and trudged back up the cellar steps, hamburger patties in tow. Because he had a pretty good idea—from things her father had let slip, mostly—that it had been a long time, if ever, since a guy had treated that gal the way she deserved to be treated. Since somebody had taken the time to see past the prickly armor she hugged to herself to see the dynamite, caring lady hidden away underneath.

And under other circumstances—if the timing hadn't been lousy, if he'd had a few less kids, if the thought of losing his hard-won ability to go it alone didn't scare him spitless—he might have welcomed the challenge of trying to pry off some of that armor. Since it was, and he did, so he couldn't, he really didn't care one way or the other whether or not Carly Stewart decided to stay in Haven.

He just wouldn't be surprised if she did, that's all.

Libby cradled the cordless phone between her shoulder and her ear, frowning at herself in the mirror on the back of her bedroom door as Blair went on about how much English sucked, why'd they have to read *Moby Dick,* anyway?

"Yeah, huh?" she said distractedly, partly because she'd already read *Moby Dick* on her own like two years ago—it wasn't too bad, once you got past the draggy beginning—and partly because she was trying to decide if the stretchy top she'd bought off Merrilyn Jasper for five bucks showed too much cleavage or not. Merrilyn had said the bright yellow turned her skin practically the same color as her Uncle Willie's right before the cirrhosis took him under, but it looked fine on Libby. More than fine—she tugged the neckline down a little more—it made her look *older.* Lord, Daddy would have a freaking *cow* if he saw her in this.

"So, you coming over to do homework or what?" Blair said.

"Can't tonight. Got too many chores. Besides, Sean said he might call."

"Oh," Blair said, and Libby could tell she was holding back saying what she was really thinking. Libby didn't encourage her, however, because whatever it was, Libby doubted it wasn't anything she was much interested in hearing. Sometimes Libby wished things could go back to how they used to be between her and Blair, but their age difference made them view things from totally different perspectives, she supposed. After all, Libby already thought of herself as fifteen, but Blair had only been fourteen for a few months.

Except then Libby had a pang of conscience and said, "Maybe we can hang out Friday night or something."

"Oh, you mean you don't have a date with *Sean?*"

Libby ignored the other girl's sarcasm and said, "You know Daddy won't let me date until I'm sixteen. Which only makes me like the biggest freak in the entire state."

"We can be freaks together, then," Blair said on a sigh. "'Course, it's a moot point at the moment, since I don't have a Sean. Or anybody else."

"You jealous?"

"Of you and Sean? Please."

"Could you sound any more disgusted?"

"I'm sorry, it's just…"

"Blair? You've already made it plain you don't like him. So could we just drop it?"

"Fine, whatever. So…you wanna come spend the night over here on Friday? Jenna said she'd drive us over to Claremore to catch an early movie, if we want."

Outside, one of her brothers started howling for no discernible reason. At least it would be quieter over at Blair's, jeez. "Okay, sure. Sounds good."

Blair then started in about some girl at school, but Libby was only half paying attention because her mind had drifted to thinking about Carly, and how well she and Carly had gotten along, even though Carly was *old*. Like Carly would totally approve of this top, she thought, turning sideways and sucking in her breath. Unlike everybody else in town, however, she doubted seriously if Carly would stick around, once she got her father settled. Why should she? Why *would* she?

Although the thought had crossed Libby's mind a time or two that having a stepmom like Carly might not be the worst thing in the world. Somebody who'd just listen without nagging or judging her. Somebody cool. Oh, Mama had been cool, too, in her own way, and there were still times when Libby would wake up in the middle of the night missing her so much she thought her chest would cave in. But that happened less and less as time went by.

Daddy had told her that would happen. That it would stop hurting, eventually. Now Libby wondered, as she dug her new glittery pink lipstick out of the Homeland bag and applied it generously to her way-too-skinny lips, if Daddy had stopped hurting over Mama yet. If she was just imagining the looks that passed between Carly and her father. Not that she particularly wanted to think about her father getting it on with anybody, but these were hard times. Whatever it took to mellow him out was okay by her—

"Butthead!"

"Dork-face!"

"That's enough, guys," she heard Daddy say.

God, she was never having kids, she thought, pouting at herself in the mirror as Blair started in about the latest Orlando Bloom flick. Well, maybe she'd have one kid, when she was around thirty or so, but if it wasn't a girl she was giving it to somebody else to raise.

This lipstick totally *rocked*.

The call-waiting signal beeped; she glanced at the caller ID and her heart bucked inside her chest. "Blair, sorry, gotta take this call—I'll see you tomorrow, 'kay?" She hit Flash before Blair's "Okay, bye" had even faded in her ear.

"Hey, babe," Sean said when she answered. Oh, man, Daddy'd have *two* cows if he heard Sean call her "babe."

"Hey," she said, trying to sound sophisticated and worldly, like boys called her "babe" on a regular basis. Like boys called, period, on a regular basis. "This is a surprise," she said, in what she hoped was a cool purr. She'd read somewhere that a girl should never act like she was sitting by the phone or anything, waiting for a guy to call, because it ceded them far too much control in the relationship.

"Huh," Sean said, sounding a little confused. "I thought I said I'd call tonight?"

Oh, crap. She'd forgotten. "Um, guess I didn't hear you? Sorry. But I'm really glad you did," she added, since she didn't want him to think she was one of those nose-in-the-air-girls who got off on stringing boys along.

"Anyway," Sean said. "I was wondering…you wanna go to a movie over in Claremore Friday night?"

Libby's breath caught in her throat. He was actually asking her out? Ohmigod, ohmigod, ohmi…

"Sure, I guess that'd be okay," she said, because Sean was the hottest boy in school and there was no *way* she was going to let this opportunity slip through her fingers, even if she wasn't allowed to date until she was sixteen. Which was a dumb, stupid, totally arbitrary rule anyway. Why should she suffer just because her father still had one foot in the eighties?

"So, like, should I pick you up there or what?"

"No! I mean…I'll have to get back to you on that—"

"Lib?" her father said, knocking on her door.

"Hold on a sec, okay?" she said, then held the phone to her chest, her mind racing. If Jenna did drive her and Blair over to Claremore, maybe Sean could meet her there. But how on earth was she going to convince Blair not to tell…? "Yeah?" she called out to her father.

The door opened just enough for Daddy to stick his head in the room. "Oh, sorry, I didn't realize you were on the phone. But when you get off, could you help me with the little ones' baths? I have no idea what they got into but…"

"Yeah, sure, I'll be out in a minute."

Then she caught his frown. Damn—she'd forgotten she was still wearing the low-cut top.

Not to mention the lipstick.

"Ignore this," she said. "It's going right back. I mean it's *way* too low and stuff."

Her father cleared his throat. "It certainly is that. But as long as you're returning it…"

"Oh, yeah, definitely. I mean, God, I look like a total slut in this."

She thought maybe Daddy blushed, but all he did was make a let's-wind-it-up motion toward the phone, then popped back out.

"Sorry," she said to Sean. "My dad."

"Oh. I get the feeling I'm not exactly his favorite person, you know?"

"Don't take it personally. He's just being protective and stuff."

"I don't blame him. I'd be protective of you, too, if you were my daughter." Libby's heart gave a little blip—God, she'd *so* lucked out! "So…is he cool with me takin' you out? 'Cause I definitely do not want to piss off your daddy."

"Uh, sure. I mean, yeah, it's fine." Her insides got all quivery, half from excitement, half from stark terror—she'd never told a lie in her life. At least not one this big. "But I've gotta get off, go help give my little brothers baths. So we'll talk tomorrow, okay? About Friday?"

"Sure, I guess."

"I…I can't wait."

"Yeah. Me, too."

"Okay," she said on a rush of breath. "'Night—"

"Hang on a sec…" Sean's voice got all soft. "Close your eyes."

"What?"

"Just do it, babe. Close your eyes. You got 'em closed?"

She had no idea what was going on, but she shut her eyes and said, "Uh-huh."

"Now imagine me kissing you, my lips real hot on yours, and I'm holding you tight against me…."

Libby's eyes popped open, her heart pounding so hard she could hear it.

"Can you feel it? Can you feel me kissing you, babe?"

"Uh…yeah. It's, um, nice?"

His low laugh set her skin to prickling all over, but not unpleasantly. Not unpleasantly at all, in fact. "Okay, then. I'll see you tomorrow. 'Night."

Libby replaced the phone on the stand and thought, *Ohmigod,* about five dozen times.

Things were not exactly going to plan.

Of course, Carly silently groused as she and Dad stopped at Haven's only stop light, the moving van impatiently growling behind them, if she'd had a plan to begin with, she might not be in this situation.

"Did you ever see a prettier day?" her father asked, grinning like an idiot, as the light changed and they took off again, every inch, foot, mile bringing her closer to her doom. Carly slumped down in the passenger seat of the truck—her Saturn leashed to the truck's rear bumper like an obedient puppy—ramming her face down inside her oversize turtleneck, her eyes stubbornly shut against the onslaught of all those damn yellow and red and orange leaves vibrating against a brilliant blue sky.

Against the nasty wee voice whispering *Home…home… home.* To which her response was *Like hell…like hell…like hell…*

"Yeah. Gorgeous," she said.

"And smell that air!"

"Dad? You are seriously going to make me sick."

He laughed, jolly as Old Saint Nick. Well, hell, why shouldn't he? His life was falling into place quite nicely, thank you, while hers had made an express, first-class trip to hell in a handbasket. All Dad had talked about the entire two weeks they'd spent packing up his place—how he'd managed to accumulate so much junk in a one-bedroom apartment was beyond her—were his plans for the stupid, bloody farm. And his new Internet-based business. And Ivy.

Oh, God, yes. Ivy. "Smitten" didn't even begin to cover it.

"Ivy told me to call her as soon as we got into town."

As she was saying.

Of course, no word yet on whether Ivy returned her father's smittenness, Dad's version of their date being obviously one-sided. Mostly, they'd argued about politics, from what Carly could glean. Long enough to close the restaurant, apparently. But although Dad had clearly found the evening invigorating, who knew how Ivy felt? While there'd been more than a few phone calls while they'd been back in Cinci, what she didn't know was who'd initiated them.

Carly opened her eyes and peered over the turtleneck at her way too mellow, humming father, and her heart cracked. Even though the man could be a major pain, he still deserved to be happy. But if he'd moved here for all the wrong reasons, if this thing with Ivy was one-sided…

By all accounts, her father's experience with women began and ended with Mom. Which meant he hadn't dated in more than forty years. Her guess was his immunity to heartbreak had long since worn off.

Unlike hers, of course.

A thought which bounced off her head as they pulled up in front of her father's new house and her heart did this bizarre *boing* at the sight of Sam standing there. Surrounded by a million little boys and nearly as many dogs.

Well, hell.

They parked, they got out, the men did the whole shoulder-clapping, good-to-see-you thing, kids swarmed, dogs barked, and Carly was nearly overcome with an oh-gee-isn't-this-just-*swell* urge to barf.

Or run. Something.

Then Libby was giving her a hug and whispering in her ear, "I have *so* got to talk to you," and then she kind of got swept up in the tidal wave of dogs and people moving toward the house, as the moving van rumbled up behind them, *beep-beep-beeping* as it positioned its butt as close to the porch as possible.

A perfect October breeze toyed with Carly's hair as she took in the house, and all these chattering, excited people, her father's expression of pure bliss and Libby's of what she could have sworn was relief; then, finally, her gaze came to rest in Sam's. He smiled, and for the life of her, she couldn't turn away from his eyes, or the questions lurking in them.

Any more than she could turn her thoughts away from wayward musings about how solid and confident and uncomplicated he seemed, traits she'd always thought of as boring. Before now. Which only went to prove that packaging really is everything.

Then he was in front of her, his hands stuffed in his pockets, his eyes still on hers, the understanding in them nearly taking her breath as everyone else drifted off to help the movers or whatever, she really wasn't paying much attention.

"You seem awfully agitated for somebody who's just here to help her father get settled in."

Her mouth twitched, but not into anything even remotely like a smile. "Good call," she said, then added, meeting Sam's gaze dead-on, "since I guess this is my zip code for the foreseeable future."

"You're *staying?*" Libby shrieked behind her, then spun her around for another hug. "That is so freaking *cool!*"

Carly hugged the excited teenager back, as if by doing so, some of the girl's enthusiasm would rub off.

Chapter 7

"So basically, all my options dried up."

Sam's insides clenched at Carly's words, spoken in the way of someone who's resigned herself to the inevitable before she's come anywhere near making peace with it.

He could tell she'd tried her best to keep a lid on her composure after she and her father had first arrived, but her jerky movements and short, obligatory replies to everyone's questions clearly indicated how overwhelmed she felt. So Sam had hauled her off to the half-remodeled barn so she could vent an emotion or two in relative peace. Now she stood in a shaft of light knifing through the glittering dust motes from a window the previous owners had installed in what had once been a hayloft, three rectangular pools of sunshine from as many windows spilling across the pine floor. What had at one time smelled of animal flesh and hay and manure was now perfumed with a bouquet of dust, unfinished wood, the residual tang of polyurethane.

Carly's back was more or less turned to him, her hands stuffed into her jeans' back pockets, the toes of her pointy, fancy boots headed as usual in two different directions. Even at rest, energy pulsed from her body like a racehorse itching to be given its head.

His own arms laced across his chest, Sam leaned on one of the barn's support beams, far enough away to keep their molecules from intermingling. To prevent either one of them from feeling threatened.

"What happened to the teaching jobs?"

She turned then, her mouth pulled tight. "No openings. Anywhere, apparently. And my friend Emily's pregnant again, so she decided to put off starting her own school for another year at least." She walked across the evenly laid planks, the skinny heels of her boots making soft, sexy tapping sounds. Crouching, she ran a hand over the gleaming surface. "Nice floor."

"It is that. Like I said, the previous owners had planned on living here and tearing down the old house…"

"Oh, God, Sam…what am I going to *do?*"

Her anguish bounced off the high walls like panicked birds searching for a way out. She was still squatting, her hands gripping her knees as she stared at the floor, shaking her head. Then she laughed, an empty sound, mirthless, and pushed herself to her feet. "Sorry. That was a rhetorical question. Besides, I need to be here right now anyway, right? Because of Dad, I mean."

"Seems to me your father's more than capable of taking care of himself."

"I'm not talking about the day-to-day stuff. I'm talking about…"

"Ivy?"

"Yeah."

"I imagine he can take care of that all by himself, too. And wouldn't he be pissed to find out his daughter thinks he can't?"

A rueful smile tugged at her lips. "True. But you didn't see him right after Mom died. And for many, many months after that. He was absolutely wrecked. And this…thing with Ivy… At this point, it's based on *air.*" Her gaze touched his, then skittered away before she said softly, "I'm afraid for him."

"That he might get his heart broken?"

Air rushed from her lungs. "Dad and I might drive each other crazy, but we're all each other has. I can't prevent his getting hurt, if this doesn't work out. But at least I can stick around for a while… I mean, if it takes off, great. I'll be thrilled. But if it doesn't…he might need me to help pick up the pieces." Another wry smile. "Then again, he might tell me to go to hell."

"Or at least back to Cincinnati."

"To do what?" she said flatly, then let out another one of those hollow laughs. "See, this is why parents tell their kids who want to make a career in the arts that they need to have something to fall back on. A 'real' vocation of some kind. Except dancing was all I ever wanted to do." She paused. "All I could do, really."

"What makes you say that?"

After a second's hesitation, she said, "Because I'm dyslexic. Well, mildly, anyway. Enough to make school a challenge, though. And almost any job that entails processing written information or entering numbers in the right sequence." Her mouth twisted. "Dancing was my lucky 'out.' Or so I'd thought."

"Well…our part-time housekeeper quit a few months back. I suppose I could use a replacement."

Alarmed, pale blue eyes shot to his. "You're kidding, right?"

"Yes. I am." She let out a huge sigh of relief, and he chuckled. Then he said, "So let's break your problem down into pieces. First off, you hard up for money?"

"Sam, this isn't your problem—"

"I'm well aware of that. I also know sometimes it helps to talk these things out with somebody else. Unless you think I'm gettin' too nosy…?"

"No, it's not that." Her earrings sparkled when she shifted to face away from him. "Exactly."

"Then what is it? Exactly?"

She apparently decided it was easier to answer the original question than deal with that one. "Okay, fine, I'm not exactly rolling in it. But I've got enough to scrape by for a while. And

Dad said he'd hire me to help with his new business. Not that I have a clue what I'm going to do to help him."

"So you're not in danger of imminent starvation."

"No."

"And you've obviously got someplace to live."

"This is true."

"And you could probably keep searching for teaching positions, right? Or is there some age cutoff?"

Her laughter ricocheted off the rafters. "Considering that some of the teachers I've had over the years could've given Methuselah a run for his money, I think it's safe to say there's no age limit."

"So what's the problem?"

She gave him an odd look, then clicked across the floor and back outside to the dirt-packed barnyard. Sam followed, but not too quickly. From the house, they heard thumps and bumps and lots of voices. Some fussing, but mostly laughter. His kids' laughter, primarily, mingled with Lane's, a moving guy or two. Then he caught sight of Sean's Eclipse out front and thought, *Hmm,* even as Carly, who was hugging herself against the cool breeze, said, "The problem is, this is all way too…normal for me. And I don't know what to do with 'normal.'"

Sam tore his attention away from the Eclipse and the *hmming* and not wanting to think about where his daughter was and/or what she was doing to say, "You don't feel like you fit in here?"

"Not much, no. Although that's a reflection on me far more than on anybody else, believe me."

"I doubt you're anywhere near as different as you think. So maybe you should stop being so hard on yourself."

She turned to him, a funny smile playing across her mouth. "Being self-aware isn't the same as being hard on myself."

"Isn't it—?"

"Miss Carly?"

They both turned to see Frankie, standing there with a bunch of scarlet oak leaves clutched in his hand. "I brung you these," the six-year-old said proudly.

"Brought," Sam automatically corrected, then whispered to Carly, his mouth barely brushing her hair. "He doesn't hear well out of his left ear, so make sure you direct anything you say to his right."

She nodded, then knelt to take the leaves from the little boy. "Thank you, sweetie! They're beautiful!"

Frankie beamed, showing off the gap where his front teeth used to be. Then the boy threw his arms around Carly's neck and gave her one of his no-holds-barred, I'm-gonna-love-ya-til-you-cry-mercy hugs, nearly knocking her off balance. Sam quickly moved to rescue her, only to stop dead in his tracks when she hugged the little boy back, nearly as fiercely as he had her. Then the mushy stuff was over and Frankie took off back to Lane's house, his little flashing sneakers raising tiny puffs of dust as he ran.

"Sorry about that. He's always been the touchy-feely one of the group."

Carly turned to him, her eyes glittering like icicles in the sunshine. "Actually, I think I really needed that."

Well, hell, if it's a hug you need…

Only then she said, "So who's he take after? With the touchy-feely stuff, I mean? Your wife?"

He knew better, he really did. And nothing had changed since he'd had his heart-to-heart with the hamburger patties. Nothing except he'd forgotten just how much proximity counted for, well, a lot, really.

A hell of a lot.

"No, ma'am," he said softly, brushing a strand of hair out of her eyes, thinking about how the harder it was to dig a gemstone out of the rock, the more precious it was. "He gets that from me."

She froze, just for a second, her eyes locked in his. Eyes in which he saw, in that instant before she took off, disbelief tangling with hope.

And over it all, sheer, undiluted terror.

Head down, hands fisted, Carly veered away from the house and toward the woods forming a natural windbreak along the farms' northern boundaries. A few minutes alone, was all she needed. A few minutes to catalogue her thoughts, deal with her reaction to Sam's...whatever that had been back there. Her pulse raced; the distant highway sounds, the wind whispering through drying leaves and intrepid evergreens, were all muffled by the roar of panic in her ears. Bolting wasn't her usual style. Especially from a man. Yeah, she'd spurned a few along the way, but she'd never in her life actually *run away*. That she should flee from someone as gentle and...and *safe* as Sam Frazier made no sense whatsoever.

Except it was Sam's very safeness that made him such a threat, wasn't it?

She hadn't missed the hesitancy, before he touched her hair. Hadn't expected the flood of need that simple touch had ignited, a need that went way past wanting to placate a few thousand jittery hormones...

The voices, soft and urgent, cut through her panicked musings. She stilled, cloaked in the deep hush of the woods, listening, before a flash of red caught her attention. She could barely see the couple, but she knew Libby'd been wearing a red sweatshirt, dimly remembered seeing Sean's car parked in front of her dad's house. And Sam's silent, but no less readable, reaction to the car.

From what she could see, and hear, all they were doing was making out. And standing up at that. And the trees in this part of the forest were a little puny for anything too serious. Still, she knew better than to ever underestimate the ingenuity of a horny teenage boy. Let alone his persuasive abilities on a young girl in the heady throes of sexual self-discovery.

Damn.

To say she was torn didn't even begin to cover it. As if it were yesterday, Carly remembered all too sharply her desperate craving for privacy as a teenager; she also remembered, even more sharply, *why* she'd craved that privacy, the hormone flood that had nearly drowned her good sense.

Nearly? Who was she kidding? At Libby's age, younger,

even, the path to adulthood had seemed excruciatingly long. Shortcuts begged to be found. And find them, Carly had. Just as she imagined Libby would do, given encouragement. Which, judging from the scene in front of her, she was definitely being given.

And if anybody'd told her twenty years ago that she'd feel impelled to break up the very thing she'd fought like the devil for the freedom to do at that age, she'd've never believed it. However, at the very moment she decided to make enough noise to let the teenagers know they weren't alone, Sam barged past her from behind, all fury and fit-to-be-tied paternal protectiveness.

"Sam!" Carly hissed. "Don't—"

But he either didn't hear her, or chose not to. *"Libby!"*

A thousand shrieking birds shot from the trees; the couple sprang apart as if somebody'd thrown a firecracker between them.

"Daddy!" Carly could barely make out the girl's sweeping her long hair out of her face as Sam continued his relentless approach. "I…I…"

"We weren't doing anything, sir," she heard Sean say, contrition soft-edging macho cockiness. "I promise—"

"Get back to the house, Libby."

"Daddy! Jeez…"

"Now. We'll talk later."

"This is *so* unfair!" the girl cried, then spun around and tramped back through the forest, too upset to notice Carly standing a few feet away. Carly ached for her, even as she realized she had no idea what she'd say. How she'd explain things she didn't even understand fully herself.

But Sam had Sean in his sights by now, his arms crossed over his chest.

"It's not what you think, Mr. Frazier," the boy said, his obvious nervousness eroding his machismo a little more. "I really care about Libby—"

"I don't doubt you do," Sam said in a voice so low, so calm, shivers streaked down Carly's back. "In your own way. But Libby's not yet fifteen. And I remember all too well what it was like to be seventeen. And how easy it is to slip from 'not doing anything' to 'we didn't mean to.' Judging from what I just witnessed, I think maybe the two of you need to cool things off for a few weeks."

"But we've got a date for the Harvest dance next weekend!"

"I somehow doubt that, since Libby knows she can't date until she's sixteen."

"But…" The boy scratched his head, clearly confused. "She said you said it was okay…I mean, we've gone out the past two weekends—"

Uh-oh, Carly thought as Sam's *"What?"* cannonballed through the forest, rousting even more birds from their roosts. "You took her out? *Alone?*"

"Y-yes, sir."

"And she told you I gave her *permission?*"

"More or less. Sir."

By this time, Carly figured the poor kid had probably wet his pants, a situation guaranteed to cool his ardor. For a while, at least.

She moved closer—what the hell, she was this far in, anyway—in time to see Sam let out a long breath. "Go home, Sean," he said quietly. "And don't bother coming to pick Libby up for school tomorrow. She can ride the bus."

The kid nodded, his shoes crunching in the leaves as, head bowed, he started off. Except then he turned and said, "Does this mean she can't go to the dance with me?"

Carly expected a bellowed *"Yes!"* Instead, after a moment's obvious wrestling, Sam said, "We'll talk about it later," and the boy traipsed off.

Then he faced Carly, his face like stone. "Before you ask…yes, I followed you. Because I was worried I'd done something to upset you."

After a split second to absorb his words, she hooked her hands in her back pockets and said, "That wasn't necessary."

"Maybe not to you."

Above her head, wings rustled as a bird or ten reclaimed abandoned perches. "You didn't…" She glanced away, then back. "I'm fine. Really."

"Good." His stare burned right through her. "But tell me something—if I hadn't come along, how long would you have waited to break up the lovebirds?"

She should have seen it coming, but she was still blindsided by the "if I'd upset you" comment. So it took her a second to recover before she got out, "I was about to, as it happens. Only I'd planned on a taking a more subtle approach. Like making noise or something so they'd realize they weren't alone."

"And what good would that have done?"

"It wouldn't have embarrassed them, for one thing! And you do realize that any obstacle you throw in their path is only going to fuel their determination to be together?"

"Spoken from experience?" he said softly, sending that chill up her spine again.

"Yes, actually," she said, meeting his gaze. Which, annoyingly enough, she couldn't read. But it was clearly time for a few offensive maneuvers.

"Look, Sam…I don't know what that was about back in the barn. If it was even anything, I'm not making assumptions, believe me. But I think you need to realize that…" She stopped, trying to order her words. "There's no point in our starting anything, because I can't be the one thing you most need, which is a mother to your kids. No, hear me out," she said when he started to protest, "because I'm not saying what you think I am. Not exactly, anyway." She hauled in a breath. "This is about more than my inexperience with kids, although that's no small thing. Your sons scare me, I won't deny it. But even if that weren't the case, even if I got all warm and tingly inside at the thought of being around the little darlings—" his mouth twitched into a half smile "—I don't exactly have the right resume for the job. I can't counsel your daughter, or anyone else, on how to stay on the straight and narrow, because I've never been there."

"Carly, everybody's done a few things they later regret—"

"Not a few things, Sam. Lots of things. A whole boatload of things I'm sure you do not want to know about. And for sure you wouldn't want any of your children to know about. Trust me on this," she finished, briefly touching his arm before walking away.

And this time, he didn't try to follow.

One of these days, Lane thought as he ran the USB cable from his printer to his computer, his daughter was going to figure out he wasn't a total idiot. Not that he was holding his breath, but he was a great believer in miracles. But dammit, it was obvious something was bugging her, since she'd hardly said two words since Sam and his gang had left a couple hours ago. Which might lead him to think her foul mood had something to do with Sam.

"Okay," she said, hands on hips, standing at the doorway to what would be his office. "I've lived here—" she glanced at her watch "—for exactly six hours and fourteen minutes and I'm bored out of my mind."

Then again, maybe Sam wasn't totally responsible.

"Spoken like a true city girl."

"And your point is?"

Lane chuckled softly. "Kitchen unpacked?"

"Yep."

"What about your clothes?"

"Dad."

"Fine. What about *my* clothes?"

"That bored, I'm not." Then she came in and slid bonelessly into the armchair that used to be in his bedroom in the old house. Lane took this as a good sign. That she was sulking in his company instead of in her own room. He sat down at his desk and booted up his computer, peering down at the screen through the reading glasses he absolutely detested.

"You want to talk about it?"

He could feel her eyes dart to the side of his face, sense the shrug that followed. "No, I don't want to talk. I want…something to *do*. Besides unpacking your clothes. Or sitting outside and watching the stars twinkle."

"Nobody told you to tag along back here," he said mildly. At her grunt in reply, he added, "Can't be easy, moving back in with your father at your age."

"Try *demoralizing*."

"Well," he said, squinting—these damn glasses weren't worth the $12.95 he'd paid for them, "Sam sure seemed glad enough to see you."

Ah. Apparently that was worth one of his daughter's famous Frozen Silences.

He decided to change the subject. Since the other would inevitably work its way to the surface sooner or later, anyway. "So. You know anything about why Libby went storming past the house and back over to her own a while ago? Or Sean's car peeling out of here like bigfoot was after him?"

"Unfortunately, yes. Sam caught them making out in the woods."

"Oh, dear." He peered over his glasses at her. "I take it he wasn't amused?"

"No more than you would have been in the same situation."

"You were there?"

"Not exactly. I mean, I saw them, too, but it was all between Sam and the kids." She swung her legs down and pushed herself out of the chair to squat down by a box of books he hadn't unpacked yet. "You want these in any particular order?"

"No. Now you want to tell me what's really bothering you?"

"It's not Sam," she said, too quickly.

"Of course not."

A blush the color of Bing cherries took possession of her cheeks. She clunked several volumes of the old Britannica they'd bought for Carly when she was ten up onto one of the shelves—she'd given him grief for carting it out here, but he still used it from time to time for research. "Okay, it's nothing I can't handle. That better?"

"Got any ideas why you think you should 'handle' it to begin with?"

"Yeah. Six of 'em. All sharing his last name."

"He's a good man."

Instead of answering, she leaned back on her haunches, spearing him with her gaze. "Since we're playing the butt-in game…you hear from Ivy yet?"

"As a matter of fact, I spoke with her this afternoon, while you were off with Sam. We're meeting up in a little while at her house."

"Her idea or yours?"

"What difference does it make?"

Another four or five books slammed up onto the shelf. Then she faced him, swiping a hand across her forehead, leaving a streak of dirt in its wake. "I don't want you to get hurt, Dad."

"What makes you think that's going to happen?"

"You've fallen awfully fast, don't you think?"

"Says the woman who's been in love how many times?"

She bent over to pick up more books, her hair sweeping across her face. Not until the next batch was in place did she say, "Would you think any worse of me than you already do to find out that I've never really been 'in love' at all?"

Her admission sliced right through him. Not because he was shocked—he'd realized some time ago that his daughter's romances were about as substantial as soap bubbles—but because of the sadness weighting her words.

"Honey, believe me…I have never thought badly of you."

She shoved the next few books onto the shelf with a breathless, "Yeah, right."

"Lee?" After a long moment, she finally turned to him, her hands slipped into her back pockets, a defiant "I'm fine" pose she'd affected before she'd finished elementary school. "Maybe it's hard for me to hear that you've confused sex with love—"

"Oh, jeez, Dad…"

"Hey, you brought it up, not me. But you're missing the point. It's your having reached the ripe old age of thirty-seven without making any real connection with another human being that's giving me pause, not the other. For *your* sake, not mine. Seeing you unfulfilled and unhappy is far more likely to keep me awake at night than anything else you might have done." When she averted her eyes, he added, "I'm aware of more than you probably realize. And yes, I worried about you. Still do. Because I've had the feeling for a long time there's something deeper behind some of your choices I just don't understand. That you're…I don't know…" Lane hesitated, struggling for the right words, *any* words that might make sense of something that didn't. Finally he settled on, "It's almost as if you're a prisoner to something inside you I'm not sure you understand yourself." He waited, then said, "No comment?"

"I…" Her brow knotted. "No."

Lane leaned forward, his hands loosely gripping the arms of his chair. "Just for the record? You're not nearly the badass you'd like the world to think you are."

A startled laugh burst from her throat, cracking the tension. Somewhat, anyway. Lane stood and crossed the still-bare, uneven floor to his little girl, cupping her bony shoulder. "But the thing is, I *have* been in love. Deeply. And I know the difference between love and infatuation. Yes, I'm infatuated with Ivy Gardner. And no, I couldn't tell you why. Sometimes, there's just no rational explanation for these things. But I can 'handle it,' too. If it doesn't work out, I promise you I won't fall apart."

"But after Mom…"

"We were married for nearly forty years, honey," he said softly, gently squeezing her shoulder. "I've been out with Ivy exactly once. Big difference."

"So…this isn't just some desperate attempt to stave off loneliness?'

Lane dropped his hand from her shoulder and thought about that for a second or two. "It's no secret I've been lonely since your mother died. But desperate?" He shook his head. "I don't think so. Even though I've never really bought into the idea that *staying* lonely somehow honored the person who'd gone on. I know some people prefer their own company, but I happen to get pretty tired of talking to myself all the time." She smiled. "I've also never thought much of sitting around and waiting to see what comes my way. You've gotta grab opportunities, girl. Or make them, if it comes down to that. Be an active participant in your own destiny, if you will."

One side of her mouth hiked up. "How very New Agey of you."

"Oh, wait. One of the first things I'm going to do is change the location of the front door—the feng shui is terrible in this house."

"Oh, God," she said, laughing.

"You think I'm kidding?" he said, then left the room before she could find her voice.

Ivy's first thought when she opened her door to Lane Stewart ran along the lines of, nope, her mind hadn't embellished on her memory of his good looks one bit over the past two weeks. Followed immediately by one of those vague *This is not good* kind of thoughts that usually happens right before the plane begins its plummet to earth. She wasn't sure what it said about her that she let the man in anyway.

Let alone that she allowed him to pull her into his arms and kiss her.

Her mind hadn't embellished on that memory, either.

"It's been a long two weeks," he whispered into her hair, loose tonight, hanging nearly to her waist over her favorite sweater. She thought she might have agreed with him, except her brain was too busy processing the glorious sensation of being held and wanted—very obviously wanted, she thought with a smug smile—by this man to be sure of much.

"Smells good," he whispered, nuzzling her neck.

"I made coffee—"

"Not talking about the coffee."

"Oh. Must be the skin cream Dawn gave to me for Mother's Day, then."

The nuzzling got more serious. "Tell Dawn I said 'thank you.'"

"Like hell," she said, and they both laughed.

That they would end up in bed, as they had on their first "date," wasn't even a question. At their ages, there seemed little point in playing coy. Or in kidding herself that years without a man's touch hadn't made her…not desperate, exactly, that sounded too, well, *desperate*. But anxious would do nicely. Or that there had been lot of leftover grief, blended with a soul-sucking loneliness that had blistered her own soul, in Lane's frantic, but thorough, lovemaking. In other words, it was all about convenience and timing, as far as she could tell. Maybe not what she'd envisioned for herself, once upon a time, but a helluva lot more than she'd had in a very *long* time.

"There's pie, besides the coffee," she said, taking him by the hand and leading him to the kitchen of her little bungalow a block or so off Main Street. "Apple."

"Homemade?"

"Yep. But not by me." He sat at her table, exuding the skin-tingling, potent masculinity of a man who no longer feels any need to prove himself; she cut a big slab of pie and set it on a handpainted plate she'd picked up at some garage sale probably twenty, twenty-five years ago now.

"You know, I haven't had homemade apple pie since Dena passed. She was one helluva cook, let me tell you."

Ivy looked away. It really felt like fall tonight, the wind rattling her loose windowpanes as if seeking refuge in her house. Time to weatherproof for the winter, she guessed. "A local gal makes 'em for Ruby's," she said. "Although she's so busy, between her new baby and more orders than she can handle, that she's got two other women working for her now." Lord, she was making small talk like some nervous young girl. And here the man had already seen her naked, for heaven's sake! She set the pie down in front of him, then went to fix him a cup of coffee—she already knew he took it black with one spoonful of sugar.

Lane picked up his fork and sighed in obvious anticipation.

Of the pie, for now, she thought. "How's the campaign coming?"

"Far as I can tell," Ivy said, pouring out two mugs of coffee, "it could go one of two ways. Either I win or Arliss does. So Carly decided to come back with you, after all?"

"She did…oh, God, that's good," Lane said of the pie, and Ivy puffed up as though she *had* made it herself. "But not just to get me moved in."

Halfway to the table with the coffee, she halted in her tracks. "She's stayin'?"

"For now."

"She okay with that?"

"Not really," he said with that weariness common to all parents with grown children who still haven't found themselves.

Ivy set the coffee on the table, then tugged out her full, long skirt to sit down at right angles to Lane. "She okay with *this?*" she said, pointing back and forth between them, never mind that *she* wasn't sure she was okay with it, yet.

"Not really," Lane said again, but this time with a soft chuckle. "She's afraid for me. That you'll throw me over and I'll die of a broken heart."

"Well, you never know. I just might at that."

For a moment, heated, amused blue eyes lanced hers; then he resumed putting away the pie. "I told her I'd take my chances." He glanced up, then back down at his plate. "She thinks it's too soon. After Dena's passing."

"Maybe it is," Ivy said softly, but he didn't appear to have heard her.

"You know what she told me tonight?" he said, his fork suspended in midair. "That she's never been in love. Not even once."

The pain in his words echoed inside her, as she remembered her own daughter's terror of falling in love, a terror finally healed through Cal Logan's infinite patience not all that long ago. Whatever had kept Carly Stewart from finding whatever it was she needed, Ivy had no idea, since she didn't know the woman. But she understood all too well Lane's feeling of helplessness about the situation. An understanding which prompted her to reach over and intertwine their fingers. Lane lifted her knuckles to his lips, then said, "It's hard not to wish her mother were here to help translate some of this for me."

Ivy removed her hand, reminding herself that this was only about coffee and apple pie and sex. And if a third person happened to show up in bed with them later, she'd just as soon not be overtly reminded of that fact.

Chapter 8

Three days after they'd moved in, Carly was still sweeping up piles of crusty, weightless bug bits from behind appliances and scrubbing mildew from the grout between the yellowed bathroom tiles. Fine time to discover her father's meticulousness had apparently rubbed off on her when she wasn't looking.

Not that she was complaining. Exactly. If nothing else, each scrubbed out cabinet and scoured sink and newly sparkling window nudged awake a sense of belonging she hadn't experienced since she couldn't remember when. Nothing like reducing her hands to the same state as her pointe-shoe-ravaged feet, she thought, frowning at her chapped, callused hands, all the nails broken but one, to bond you to a place. But besides that, she thought as she wrestled the Eisenhower-era fridge back into place, her frenzied cleaning was keeping her too busy to worry about anything.

Like her dad, who obviously wasn't going over to Ivy's every night to watch TV. Please—either that was an afterglow or the woman's house had a serious radon problem. Or about her and

Dad's conversation about her not ever having really been in love before, and all that stuff about there being something inside her keeping her from…

From what? Panting, on high alert against any unsuspecting, lurking filth as she stripped off the zipper-fronted sweatshirt she'd thrown on this morning over a tank top and yoga pants, Carly let her gaze dart around the room. Her eyes burned—from the dust, no doubt—as she tried, for the thousandth time, to finish that damn sentence. At least, finish it without *Sam* trying to wedge itself in there somewhere.

He'd stayed out of her way, thank God. Of course, she imagined he had a few more pressing things to tend to than playing cootchie-coo with her. One or another of the boys had wandered over on occasion—Frankie, the first-grader, had an obvious crush on her, which she had to admit was kind of a hoot—and she'd found herself standing out back, barely able to make out Sam messing around with the tractor or something in the distance, the sun glinting off his pale hair when he'd yank off his ball cap and dash it to the ground in frustration. The way he moved, lean muscles effortlessly obeying his brain's signals…

She could imagine his grin, almost hear his laughter with his boys as they tended to the livestock each morning and evening.

But other than that, she thought as she hauled her skinny booty up onto the stepladder to attack the grease-caked soffit, she hardly ever thought of him.

And certainly not in conjunction with whatever it was her father had been talking about.

Definitely not.

She'd no sooner begun her assault on the sludge of the ages when the doorbell rang. Out in the middle of freaking nowhere and the doorbell rings. At ten o'clock in the morning. Her father and Sam had gone off to Claremore to inflict serious damage on the local Home Depot, all the kids should be in school, and, as far as she knew, pigs hadn't yet developed the ability to push doorbell buttons, Libby's testaments to their remarkable intelligence notwithstanding.

Grumbling, she climbed down and trekked out to the living room, letting out a small "Oh!" of surprise when she swung open the door to see the girl herself standing there, shivering slightly in her bulky, boxy sweater and bell-bottomed jeans, her grin a little unsure. "Hey."

"Why aren't you in school?" Carly said, cringing at the accusatory sound of her own voice, as the chilly air raised goose bumps over her damp skin.

"Cramps," Libby said, inviting herself inside, her head swinging in a wide arc as she took in the room. "Wow. You'd never know this was the same place. Cool furniture."

"Too much furniture, is more like it," Carly said as her gaze followed the girl's. "The funky stuff is mine, the nice stuff my father's. Left over from the house I grew up in."

"All you need now is a cat."

"I think not. Libby…why are you here? And pardon me, but you don't seem all that crampy to me."

"I took like four Midols, so I don't feel too bad. Other than feeling a little loopy." She flopped down onto the overstuffed gold brocade sofa that had been Carly's mother's pride and joy, shrouded in plastic all through her high school days, much to her profound mortification. Then Carly caught sight of the girl's big amber eyes and thought, *Uh-oh.* "I've been tryin' to figure out a way to talk to you without Daddy finding out ever since Sunday—"

"Libby, please—I really don't want to be dragged into the middle of this."

Her dark brows crashed together. "I'm not trying to put you in the middle, I just need somebody to talk to. Somebody at least *reasonably* objective." On a dramatic sigh, she crashed back into the cushions, then winced, rubbing her belly.

"Tummy or back?"

"What?"

"The cramps."

"Oh. A little of both." She sat forward, as if trying to get comfortable. "So much for the Midol."

"You want some hot herbal tea? Sometimes that helps."

"Yeah, okay." She followed Carly into the kitchen. "You get cramps?"

"Not anymore," Carly said over the sound of water thrumming into her mother's old silver-colored kettle. "But I used to when I was your age. Until I went on the Pill."

Damn.

"Oh, wow—you went on the Pill when you were a teenager?"

"The doctor said—" Carly commended herself on her sangfroid "—it would help lessen the flow so my period wouldn't interfere with my dancing."

"You still on it?"

She clunked the filled kettle up onto the burner and turned on the flame. "Yeah."

"Doesn't it, like, really mess with your system and stuff?"

"Not if you're careful." A chill skated up Carly's nearly bare back; she plucked the sweatshirt off the pine kitchen table where she'd discarded it earlier and slipped it on again.

Libby took a leisurely tour of the kitchen, poking inside cabinets and drawers, one foot clearly still in childhood, even as her body was rushing toward adulthood at an alarming rate. "Daddy caught me and Sean kissing and stuff the other day and nearly came unhinged."

After several seconds, Carly said, "I know." When the girl whipped around, she added, "Actually I was there. I saw you before your dad did."

"God! Did half the world see us or what?"

Carly smiled. "No. Just your father and me."

"And you didn't say anything?"

"I didn't figure it was any of my business."

The kettle shrieked; Carly poured the boiling water over chamomile tea bags in a pair of mugs, nearly dropping the teakettle when Libby asked, "How old were you when you lost your virginity?"

Steaming water sloshed all over the newly disinfected

counter. Which was still butt-ugly, but at least it was clean. And now it was sterilized, to boot. Carly grabbed a sponge to wipe up the water, her eyes meeting the teenager's. "And I'm not sure that's any of *your* business."

Libby smirked, then carried one of the mugs back out into the living room. After a moment, Carly followed, folding herself up onto a brown velvet chair-and-a-half she'd found in some thrift shop. Her boyfriend of the moment had hauled it home for her in his truck; that she couldn't remember his name was a little disconcerting.

"I'm not ignorant about how stuff works," Libby said. "In case you were wondering." She took a sip of her tea, then made a face, although whether due to the tea or the subject matter, Carly couldn't be sure. "Mama and I had 'the talk' when I was like ten or something. And I've been reading romance novels for years. Not that I believe it really happens like that or anything. But I definitely get the general idea." Her eyes veered to Carly's. "Mama swore she and Daddy didn't do it until after they got married, but I'm not sure I believe them."

"Some people do wait, Libby."

"Yeah, well, if you could've seen the way they couldn't keep their hands off each other…there's a reason I've got five brothers."

Carly hid her smile behind the rim of her mug, then sobered enough to say, "I thought you told me you weren't going to do anything before you were ready?"

"That's the problem. I'm not sure I'm not."

"Oh, Libby…" Carly lowered her mug. "You're *fourteen*."

"Fifteen next week. And I really love Sean, no matter what Daddy says. I mean, when he kisses me and stuff—"

"Define 'and stuff.'"

"It's just an expression. He hasn't even touched me." Carly's brows lifted. "Not with his hands or anything. I mean, when he holds me really close, um…" Pink swept across her cheeks. "That doesn't really count, does it?"

"Trust me. It counts," Carly said, thinking, *I am so dead.* Then she said, "Are you sure this is what *you* want?"

The girl's brow puckered. "See, that's what I can't figure out. I mean, if I love him, and we're careful…but then…I don't know. I want to, but I don't want to, you know what I mean?"

A charred scrap of a memory drifted to the surface of Carly's thought. "Yeah. I do."

Except the sound of Sam's truck pulling up outside sent the teenager jumping up, the tea flying out of the mug. "Oh, God, I'm so sorry!" she said, backing away, her eyes wide. "But Daddy'll have my hide—!"

"Go," Carly said softly, getting up and shooing her with her hands. "I'll clean up the mess."

The girl hadn't been gone ten seconds before the front door opened and Travis—followed by Radar, natch—burst into the room, followed immediately by her father and Sam, grinning like a pair of cavemen after a successful hunt.

"You two leave anything for the next guys?" she asked, the brittle, blackened memory floating away as her insides warmed at the satisfied gleam in her father's eyes.

"Maybe one or two items," Sam said, cupping the four-year-old's head when he wrapped himself around his father's thigh. The little boy gave Carly a shy smile that might have melted the heart of a softer woman. "A pack of lightbulbs, I think, on Aisle 36…" His head suddenly lifted. "Is Libby here?"

Carly froze. Her father held out his hand to Travis, enticing him back outside with promises that he could help unload the truck. Kid, dog and dad swept back out of the room, leaving Carly alone with Sam's suspicion and her own ambivalence. "What makes you think that?"

"I can smell that junk she uses on her hair a mile away."

"Maybe I use the same junk?"

"No, you always smell like coconut." His attention caught on the mugs. "And I'm guessing you don't normally drink out of two cups at the same time."

Carly pushed out a sigh, then grabbed the mugs and carted

them into the kitchen. "See, this is why I hate getting stuck in the middle."

"You're not stuck in the middle," Sam said, following her. "You're on my side." She thunked the mugs onto the counter and glared at him. "Fine," he said. "I'll be sure to absolve you, how's that? Now you gonna tell me why she was over here or what?"

Carly leaned back against the counter, her arms crossed. Just what she needed today, a good old-fashioned rock-and-hard place scenario. Betray the kid, or keep important info from the father. Either way, she was screwed.

Okay, bad choice of words. And if Libby had been older, no amount of strong-arming would have made Carly give up the girl's confidences. But no matter how she sliced it, Sam had a right to know what he was dealing with. Especially as he'd have to be the one to handle it, not Carly.

"She's confused, Sam."

"Aren't we all?" he muttered. Then his gaze sharpened. "Confused about what?"

"The usual. Boys. Sex." She hesitated, then said, "She does know about birth control, doesn't she?"

He blanched slightly, but all he said was, "Of course she does. And has for some time. My father didn't hold with the notion that the way to keep his kids out of trouble was to keep them in the dark, and I'm the same way. I just didn't think…I mean, I hoped…" Worried eyes met hers. "Has she…?"

"No. But she's definitely thinking about it."

He breathed out a swear word, then said, "Just out of curiosity…what did you say?"

"Nothing. Since we'd just gotten to that part when you and Dad barged in."

"So what *would* you have said?"

"I have no idea." That merited several seconds of hard staring until she thought it prudent to bring up their earlier conversation. "Did you think I was kidding when I told you I wouldn't be any help with this?"

"No," he said after a moment. "But I did think maybe you were using it as an excuse to keep me at arm's length."

She grabbed a couple paper towels and trudged back out to the living room to wipe up the spilled tea. "Then I would have said 'keep away from me.' Or some such."

His footsteps echoed behind her. Then: "But you didn't, did you?"

"In any case," she said, turning around and pretending she hadn't heard him, "I did tell you I'm the worst possible person to give advice to your kids. Which I also told Libby."

"I take it she didn't listen, either."

"No. She didn't."

His gaze held hers like a vise. "She could really use a woman's point of view on this."

"Maybe so. But probably not one whose virginity was long gone by the time I was Libby's age."

Sam told himself he was just imagining the pain behind the defiance, the regret lancing the pride in those pale eyes. Needing a moment, not to absorb her confession as much as to give her time to recoup, he walked over to take a gander at some photos lining one of the bookcases. "I see," he said in an noncommittal a voice as he could manage.

"Sam," she said behind him, almost wearily, "I was the epitome of the wild child. Nobody could tell me nuthin'. Just ask my father. And trust me, he doesn't know the half of it. So how can I be an example for her? How can I possibly advise her to keep *her* legs crossed when I…" He heard her blow out a breath. "What kind of hypocrite would that make me?"

An alarm sounded inside Sam's head, that there was more to the story than she was telling. Or willing to tell, at any rate. Oh, he didn't doubt she was being truthful—just not *completely* truthful. Outside, Radar barked; he heard the thumps and bumps of the truck being unloaded, Lane's deep laugh mingling with Travis's breathy, innocent giggle. "So tell me something," he said mildly, picking up a silver-framed picture of Lane, Carly and a smiling, dark-haired woman he assumed was her mother. "You ever kill anybody?"

"What? No, of course not—"

He turned, swallowing a half smile at the shocked expression. "Inflict bodily harm?"

"Not counting myself?" She shook her head.

"Work for the Mob? Sell drugs to small children?"

"No. To both. Although…"

"What?"

"Since I'm being honest and all…you're skating close to the truth with the second one."

Again, the pain. Not shame, though. Not exactly. More like she didn't want anybody pitying her, would be his guess. He kept his expression unreadable. "Are you still using?" he asked quietly.

"No," she said on a huge breath. "Not for a very, very long time."

He approached her then, until he stood so close she had to lift her head. Not to intimidate her—fat chance of that happening, in any case—but almost as if he was trying to shelter her. "Frankly," he said, "I really don't give a damn about your past. Or at least, I'm not seeing it as the liability that you apparently do. No, hear me out," he said when she started to protest. "Yeah, I know it's my responsibility to help Libby see her way clear through all this. I'm also guessing nobody knows better than you how often teenage girls think their fathers know squat. Especially about sex and love and giving in to urges." His gaze lanced hers. "Or not. Seems to me her wanting to talk to you is a positive sign—"

"Well, yes, but—"

"—and it also seems to me that maybe you'd have a slightly broader view of the issue than somebody who waited until his wedding night to finally make love to his wife."

He saw the pulse jump in her throat, had to push aside the whispers to go ahead and soothe it with his thumb. If not his mouth. She shoved her hands into her sweatshirt pockets. "You don't expect me to believe you'd be *happy* about Libby having sex so young?"

His laugh scraped his throat like sandpaper. "Not hardly. And I have every intention of letting her know exactly how I feel about the situation every chance I get. Which by my reckoning should make her real pissed off at me for a good long time. But it might not be a bad thing for her to have someone she can come and bitch to about her idiot father every now and again."

Their eyes remained locked for several seconds, a weird contest of wills, until Carly walked over to the living room window. Past her, he could see outside, Travis chasing Radar around the dusty yard. "You're putting an awful lot of trust in someone you really don't know," she said.

"What can I say? I've always had good instincts."

She chuckled, then turned around. "For what it's worth, I won't encourage her to give in to her hormones."

Again, he sensed a wealth of unspoken reasons behind her words. "I didn't figure you would."

"But…I really think trying to keep them apart is only going to backfire." Her mouth twisted. "God knows, it never worked with me."

A conclusion he'd already reached about Sean and Libby some time ago, unfortunately. He hooked his thumbs in his front pockets and pushed out a breath. "Got any suggestions?"

"Well…she really wants to go to this dance with Sean. Maybe if they had another outlet for their…energy?"

It wasn't a half-bad idea, actually. "You're probably right. After all, she needs to see there's more than one way to enjoy a boy's company."

"So you'll let her go?"

Dang. He doubted Libby's expression would be as hopeful as Carly's was right now. And with that, he realized that, somehow, the woman had fallen under his daughter's spell. In spite of her best intentions, he imagined, as a half-formed idea with no basis whatsoever in common sense roared from the back of his brain and out of his mouth.

"On one condition," he said, even as he thought *You're not really going to say this, are you?*

"And what's that?"

"That she go with another couple. Double date."

"Actually that's not a bad idea. Depending on the other couple, of course. Who'd you have in mind?"

"Us," he said, and watched her mouth fall practically to her knees.

"It's that or nothing, Libby."

Half appalled, half incredulous, his daughter sat cross-legged on her bed, a pillow clutched to her chest. "That is *so* lame! What kind of baby is Sean going to think I am, double-dating with my *father?*"

Already rattled from that scene with Carly, Sam was in no mood for a teenager with her nose out of joint. "Considering you went behind my back to see him, I could have said you couldn't go at all. Frankly I think this is a pretty generous offer, myself."

That took the outrage down a notch or two. In fact, she ducked her head, her eyes fixed on the corner of her bedspread.

"And by the way, did you ever apologize to Blair for making her cover for you?" When she didn't answer, he said softly, "You know that wasn't fair, putting her in that position."

One shoulder shrugged. "She said she didn't mind."

"Friends don't take advantage of each other, Lib—"

"Jeez, Daddy—I got it! I'm sorry." Her eyes filled. "It was stupid and I won't do it again, I promise. Okay?"

"Okay."

"But…I don't understand," Libby said, still hugging that pillow. "How come you asked Carly? I thought you weren't even interested in her?"

"You know anybody else I could invite?"

"Well, no, but—"

"So there you are. And for your information, asking Carly to the dance doesn't necessarily translate into me being *interested* in her. Friends can go to these things, too, you know."

"But she's supposed to be *my* friend, not yours!"

"So go with her instead of Sean and all our problems will be solved."

For the second time, tears welled in her eyes, which is when he remembered—too late—that at certain times of the month, the female of the species has no sense of humor. "Why do you always have to make fun of everything I say, or do, or think?" she hurled across the room at him. "It's like you never take me seriously, ever!"

Ah, hell. Cows, he could handle. Locusts, he could handle. Drought, he could handle. Teenage girls...? Sam dared to sit on his daughter's bed, slinging an arm around her shoulder, longing for those halcyon days when she'd crawl up into his lap and regale him with her adoring, trustful gaze. Right now, hormones had just shot to the top of his S-list. And unfortunately, not only his daughter's.

"I'm sorry, honey. No, really," he said to her snort. "I was having a dumb male moment, okay? I didn't mean to hurt your feelings, I swear. But sometimes...I make jokes because it's easier than facing all this stuff I don't understand." He squeezed her shoulder. "Don't let this go to your head, but you scare the living daylights out of me."

That got a tiny laugh. "Really?"

"Really." He placed a kiss on top of her head. "Bear with me—I've never raised a teenage girl before. And it's kinda like trying to build a car from scratch. Without any instructions."

She giggled again, then reared back to frown into his eyes. "Carly's all wrong for you, you know."

"Yes, I do." The look on her face when he'd suggested they go to the dance together had been priceless. Probably about as priceless as on his. "But I thought we'd already established nothing's going to happen on that front."

"Dad. It's been a long time for you. Temptation happens."

It took everything he had in him not to laugh. But Libby looked so damn earnest, he didn't dare. Unfortunately she was also more right than she knew. There was a big difference, however, between wanting to help diffuse whatever darkness that gal sure seemed to be carrying around inside her, and wanting *her.*

A *big* difference.

"Well, I wouldn't worry about it too hard, if I were you. Especially since you and Sean are going to be right there to make sure things don't get out of hand. Sorry, sorry," he said in response to her rolled eyes. "I know you're serious, and I don't mean to make light of it. Although I thought you were so hot to see me get married again?"

"I am." Her brow furrowed. "I think." Then she let out a sigh. "And I really like Carly. But…" She pushed out a breath. "This isn't about what I'd like. It's about what's right for you. And Carly's so…"

"Different from Mama?"

"Yeah," she said on another released breath.

Sam stood, wondering how to put this so the girl wouldn't get the wrong idea. Wondering how to put it so *he* wouldn't get the wrong idea. "Honey, I think it's safe to say that, even if I did end up getting hitched again, it wouldn't be to a clone of your mother. I wouldn't want that, in any case."

"Why not?"

"Well, it's not possible, to begin with. Mama was definitely one-of-a-kind. But besides that…" He paused, trying to get his thoughts lined up before once again meeting his daughter's questioning gaze. "I'm not sure how to put this, but I don't feel like the same person I was before your mother died." Not that he'd known that was what he was going to say, but it was true. Jeannie's death had changed him in some intrinsic way he couldn't even define.

Libby's features seemed to relax. "Yeah. I know what you mean."

Under normal circumstances, this might have been a good note on which to end to the conversation. Except, for all the ground they'd just covered, Sam hadn't brought up the topic that had led to the double date idea to begin with. Feeling like scorpions were making nests in his belly, he rapped the palm of his hand against the door frame a couple of times before clasping it for support, then said softly, "By the way, I know why you went over to Carly's. What you talked to her about."

Her softened expression of moments before went instantly rigid; twin dots of crimson stained her cheeks. "She wasn't supposed to tell."

"She promise you she wouldn't?"

The dots got darker. "Not exactly, but…" A harsh breath rushed from her lips. "So much for being able to trust her."

"She felt real strongly that I needed to know what you were thinking, Lib. And it wasn't any more fair to expect her to keep something like that from me than it was for you to expect Blair to cover for you."

Libby grimaced. "Yeah, except Blair at least kept my secret."

"Which, one, didn't stay a secret anyway, because these things never do. And two, grown-ups usually have a different take on what it means to be a *real* friend."

She had nothing to say to that. But she crammed her hair behind one ear and said, "I wouldn't expect you to even *begin* to understand."

"About sex?" Her eyes shot to his. "Oh, I understand, all right. I understand a heckuva lot more than you know."

"Oh, yeah? Then I suppose Mom made up the part about you and she waiting until you were married?"

"Nope, we really did wait. But nobody said it was easy."

"So why didn't you just *do* it, already?" she blurted out, only to immediately bury her face in her hands. "I cannot *believe* I just said that to my father!"

"That's okay. I can't quite believe I'm having this conversation, either. Now do you want the answer to your question or not?"

She peered over her hands, then nodded.

"We held off because neither of us felt we were ready," he said simply. "I'm not talking about physically, I'm talking about mentally and emotionally. I'm not going to give you a lot of hogwash about saving yourself for marriage, but no way in hell am I going to say I think it's okay for somebody your age to have sex. Because things happen, Libby. Like diseases. And babies."

She scoffed, her embarrassment clearly taking a back seat to what she probably thought was sophistication. "I know all about condoms, Dad."

"Then I suppose you also know they don't always work. That they sometimes break? So are you prepared to deal with the consequences if that happens?" He paused, then added, "Is *Sean?*"

Apparently she had no answer to that.

"Any other questions?" Sam asked. She lowered her eyes, shaking her head. "Okay. Then the lecture's over. Except for one thing—I think you had the right idea, going to Carly."

Libby's head bounced back up. "Why? Because she ratted on me?"

"No, because she can give you a different perspective on some of these issues than I can. I think you *can* trust her, if nothing else to be straight with you." He hesitated, thinking of the disbelief in Carly's translucent eyes, the war going on in them between being touched by Sam's trust in her, and conviction that his trust was completely unfounded. His chest cramped: What on earth had happened to make her so completely blind to her own goodness?

And why did Sam feel compelled to be the one to strip the veil from her soul?

Pushing the disturbing thought off to one side where it wouldn't get him in any more trouble than he was apparently already in, he focused again on his daughter. "Because she's *not* Mama," he said quietly.

After a long moment, Libby nodded, her lips curved slightly in a smile of understanding.

Chapter 9

"**Y**ou know what this means, don't you?" Blair said to Libby as they both sat in the dirt, their backs braced against the outside wall of the barn, holding bottles for two of the not-quite-weaned piglets. Blair'd come over to bring Libby the work she'd missed in class and practically begged to feed the baby pigs. A chore she was completely down with, apparently, as long as she didn't think too hard about *why* she was feeding the pigs. "It means," the redhead went on before Libby could respond, "your dad is seriously crushing on Carly."

Libby adjusted her grasp on the bottle before the noisily nursing pig on the other end yanked it right out of her hands. "Tell me something I don't know."

Blair stopped making baby talk with her piglet long enough to say, "You're not okay with that? I mean, Carly's so cool."

"Yeah, but she's not exactly a kid person, is she?"

Blair got her how-could-anybody-not-like-kids? look on her face, an affliction, Libby privately thought, due in large part to her being an only child. Then she shrugged and said, "Well, any-way, at least you still get to go to the dance with Sean."

"Oh, yeah. With my dad chaperoning us the entire time. Can't wait." Except then the guilt she'd barely managed to keep at bay for weeks came and tapped her on the shoulder. "By the way…I'm really sorry about asking you to cover for me. Pretending we were at the movies together when I was really with Sean. I shouldn't've done that."

"S'okay," Blair said, but Libby could tell she was real relieved. Except then her mouth puckered up, like she had a secret she was dying to tell.

"Okay, spill, before you pop or something."

Blair shoved her hair behind her ear, not doing a real good job of acting nonchalant. "Kirk Hauser invited me."

Libby nearly dropped the piglet, bottle and all. "You're not serious."

"Of course I'm serious! What? You don't think somebody like Kirk would be interested in me?"

"No, no, I'm sorry, I didn't mean it like that! It's just…oh, my God—he is so freakin' gorgeous!"

"I know!" Blair said on a squeal to rival the pig's. "I couldn't believe it, either. Of course, I'm in the same boat as you, since he's only fifteen so he doesn't have his license yet. So Jenna and Dad are taking us."

Libby groaned in commiseration. Although, in a way—not that she'd let on, goodness knows—it was kind of fun, having so many grown-ups come to the dance, too. It used to be only for the high school kids until somebody suggested they make it a community thing. So now everybody in the county, practically, came. There was this local band who could play all sorts of stuff, both rock and country, and with all the women attending, there was always more food than you could shake a stick at. Which meant all the boys, even the ones who didn't have dates, showed up, too.

Although, Libby thought with a little tingle, that was not something she needed to concern herself with this year, since she had her own date, thank you.

The pigs were done with dinner, so the two girls got up, dusting off their bottoms. Libby had to admit that, for a city girl, Blair was pretty cool about helping out around the farm, that she never seemed to mind about the dirt, or that you couldn't spend any time at all with pigs without smelling like one afterward. Now that they were on their feet, her friend had to look down at Libby slightly, being a good four or five inches taller than her. "How's Sean feel about the double-dating business, anyway?"

Libby tossed the empty bottles into a plastic bucket to wash out later, deciding to give Blair the PG version of his comments. "He's says he guesses it's better than nothing. And that it's not like my dad's gonna be glued to our sides all night or anything."

The feeder checked, the girls let themselves out of the pen and started back toward the house. The sun was already low in the sky, a brisk wind laced with the scent of animal and earth—smells Libby wouldn't feel complete without, she realized—pushing them along as they walked.

"I'm sorry I was acting so weird about Sean," Blair now said, startling Libby.

"What are you talking about?"

"You know exactly what I'm talking about. And it was only because I *was* jealous that you had this really cute guy falling all over you and I didn't. I don't blame you for being pissed with me, I was acting like a brat about it."

"I wasn't—"

"I'm not stupid, Lib, okay? But I am sorry. Really, really sorry."

"S'okay," Libby said, linking her arm with her friend's, thinking there was a lot more to this growing up business than she'd ever dreamed.

She could have said "no."

Carly tugged on a pair of pink tights that had been washed so many times they were now the color of an anemic oyster. Her muscles twitched in anxious anticipation, like a dog seeing his master get the leash. Then she grabbed the first leotard she came to, a royal-blue tank with a run at the neckline from where she'd scrunched it into a V-neck with a safety pin.

She *should* have said no. Only then Libby wouldn't have been able to go to the dance, and she couldn't do that to the girl.

For three days, in between helping her father prioritize repairs to the house and more cleaning and continued, pointless searches for teaching positions, she'd been plowing the same damn ground, looking for God-knew-what. Justification? An out? A reason to be actually *happy* that now the entire town—not to mention all the surrounding hamlets—would immediately peg Sam and her as an item?

The house shuddered with the force of her father's taking a sledgehammer to the wall between the kitchen and the dining room. He usually disappeared after dinner, but apparently Ivy was attending a birth tonight, so here he was, merrily pulverizing eighty-year-old plaster and wooden laths. Carly dug out a loose, boatneck cotton pullover from an as-yet-unpacked bag, a pair of equally faded leg warmers—it would be cold as a witch's booty in the barn—then searched through a collection of ballet slippers and pointe shoes for her favorite pair of old, battered Freeds. The shoes tucked in her hand, she skipped down the concave stairs, waiting for a break in the plaster dust to call out to her father than she was heading for the barn, she'd be back in an hour or so.

The large, benign building beckoned to her like a favorite aunt as she hurried across the hundred or so feet separating it from the house; the gleaming expanse of floor seemed to smile a welcome when she threw the switch, flooding the space with light. She'd come the first time after Sam's impromptu invitation—although at that time, she hadn't yet figured out why.

Now, however, she knew.

With an economy of motion fine-honed after so many years, she shucked off her down coat and running shoes and quickly twisted up her hair, clamping it place with a single large metal barrette. The satin ribbons strangling the folded shoes rippled free; she slipped them on, securely crossing them over her high insteps, around her ankles, neatly tucking the tied ends back on themselves. She didn't need music—it pulsed through her blood, as integral to her makeup *as* that blood—simply the space to reclaim her soul. To reclaim as much of her world as she could, bum knee or no. Reclaiming whatever semblance of control she could from circumstances over which she had very little.

Using one of the support beams as a makeshift barre, she put herself through a knee-friendly version of the series of warm-up exercises any ballet dancer could do in her sleep: *demi-pliés, petit battements, grande battements, ronde de jambes.* Blackened by the night, the trio of floor-to-ceiling windows acted as mirrors, enabling her to critically observe every position, every move, to correct a sagging *port de bras,* ensure that her *arabesque* looked as sure as it felt. Sweat began to trickle down her back, between her breasts, as the discipline of making her body obey her mental commands began to melt at least some of the anxiety she'd been carting around for the past several weeks. She would never dance professionally again, but something far deeper than audience approval drove her now. As it always had, she thought, moving away from the beam, contemplating what she wanted to do next.

She moved slowly, carefully, deliberately, as her limbs loosened, responded, reclaiming the satisfaction and joy she'd always felt in the dance studio.

Tombe, pas de bourree, glissade, glissade…

She'd climbed up into the loft yesterday, could see it had already been altered into a living space, maybe for a sleeping area, that what had probably been a tack room downstairs had been roughed out for a small kitchen and bath…

Double *pirouette,* landing in fourth position…

A pair of faces, bug-eyed and eerily pale against a frame of blackness, peered through the window directly in front of her. Carly shrieked and jumped back, her hand landing on her pounding chest.

Then the faces grinned.

"Oh, for heaven's sake…" She tromped over to the door cut out of the same wall as the windows, the old barn door having been walled in, and yanked it open. "You two nearly gave me a heart attack," she said, her annoyance already losing steam at the sight of Sam's two oldest boys, both still grinning—and giggling—to beat the band.

"Don't think I ever saw anybody jump that high," said Mike, the oldest and the spitting image of his father with his flaxen hair and long, thin face.

Matt, dark like his sister, and already built like a four-by-four at eleven, giggled in agreement. "Last time I heard somebody holler like that was when Blair tried to milk Josephine and got hit in the head with a tail full of cow poop."

"Yeah, that'd do it," Carly said, then stood aside to let the pair in before they trampled her in the process, both boys already being taller than she by a couple of inches. They were almost identically attired in jeans and navy-blue hoodies, capped off by four of the dirtiest, biggest, off-brand sneakers she'd ever seen. Anybody in the market for a young, strapping farm lad need look no further: she could only imagine what these two would be like in a few years.

"So, like, what were you doing?" Mike asked, the strong overhead light nearly bleaching out his short blond hair as he scanned the empty room, seemingly baffled by what anybody could find to do in here.

"Dancing."

"Why?"

This from Matt, curiosity brimming in dark eyes.

"Because it makes me feel good. Haven't you guys ever danced?"

Words were inadequate to describe their horrified expressions.

"Dancing's for sissies," Mike pronounced with get-*her* raised eyebrows at his brother.

"Oh, yeah? So tell me something." Thoroughly enjoying

herself, Carly took a step closer, her arms folded across her middle. "Can you lift a hundred pounds over your head? And then walk fifty feet with it like that?"

"Well, no, but…"

"Can you spin on one foot eight times and not get dizzy? And without falling on your keyster?"

The boys glanced at each other, their brows knit, then back at her, clearly figuring something was up. Then, defeated, both shook their heads.

"You ever go to any of the Indian powwows? See the men dance?" They both nodded. "You think there's anything sissy about that?"

"Actually that kinda looks like fun," Matt said, and Mike punched him, and he glowered at his brother and said, "Well, it *does,* sheesh."

Carly laughed, then said, "Go back to my house and tell my dad I said to get my CD player and the case that should be right beside it. I want to show you something."

When the boys hadn't returned from their bike ride by eight-thirty—Sam never could fully relax when they went riding after dark—he went hunting. A very dusty, but cheerful, Lane had said they were over in the barn with Carly. Wondering *What on earth…?* he drove on over there, pulling up alongside the wall with all the windows. Considering the pounding salsa beat emanating from the building, he doubted they heard the truck, let alone that they noticed him.

He sat there, one hand still gripping the steering wheel, unable to do anything save gawk at the goings-on inside. Once the shock began to wear off, however, a chuckle rumbled up through his chest as he thought of the Maurice Sendak book Jeannie used to read to the kids when they were little, *Where the Wild Things Are,* where Max says, *"Let the wild rumpus start!"*

Arms flailed, feet stamped, butts wiggled—Sam nearly choked—and there was Carly, flailing and stamping and wiggling right along with them, albeit with a little more grace and dignity than his sons.

His sports-obsessed, car-obsessed, I-can-too-belch-louder-than-you sons.

He finally got out of the truck, silently pushing open the door to the barn. The throbbing beat nearly knocked him over, but now he could hear the laughter, too, the boys' as well as the woman's. She was wearing one of her God-awful outfits, some flour-sack of a top, what looked like triple-thick knee highs, bunched around her calves. But her long, trim thighs were sheathed in some dishwater-colored fabric that showed every muscle, and her face was flushed with both exertion and pleasure, haloed by a froth of…well, not exactly curls, but whatever they were, the overhead lights glinted off of them in a very interesting way.

Provoking some very interesting reactions in various parts of his anatomy.

"No, no," Carly said, laughing, as Matt launched into a series of moves like he'd sat on a hornet's nest. She planted her hands high on his hips and shoved to the right. "Like that…yeah, that's it!" Although from Sam's vantage point, it didn't look all that different, to be honest. Then his gaze slid over to Mike, staring at his pale-headed reflection in the darkened window as he concentrated on getting his big old feet going in what Sam presumed was the "right" direction.

Any second now, somebody was bound to notice his presence. Until then, he was content to simply watch his sons act like goofballs and Carly having the time of her life. Her interaction with the boys was completely natural, her laughter the most infectious he'd ever heard. So he stood in the shadows, hands in pockets, absorbing one of those rare, brilliant moments that makes a body just glad to be alive. And for some dad-blamed reason he got to thinking about how, every time Jeannie got pregnant, they'd wonder how they were going to fit another kid into their lives, only to be amazed at how each one had seemed, from that first newborn cry, to have always been there.

And it hit him that maybe this wasn't so much about wedging another person into his life, as it was about recognizing a gift when he saw it. Because if anybody already meshed with the absurdity that was Sam's life, it was Carly.

Whether she knew it or not.

"Dad!" Matt cried, his voice still firmly in squeaky-kid mode. "When'd you come in?"

"A few minutes ago," he said, his voice suddenly booming in the empty space when Carly turned off the CD player. "Looks to me like somebody was having a lot of fun."

"Uh, yeah, I guess." Sam could see his oldest son's blush from here, poor kid. But damned if his skinny chin didn't jut out. "Carly says dancing's a good way to work out your frustrations."

"Not to mention stomp out an anthill."

That got a pair of slightly embarrassed smiles. "We're not real good," Matt said, streaking a hand through his damp, dark hair.

"You are, too, good!" Carly said, and her vehemence cracked open his heart a little wider, letting in a few more possibilities. "Both of you."

Sam chuckled. "More natural talent than you know what to do with, looks like."

"Absolutely!" she said, her twinkling eyes hinting of warning, as well—*Don't mess with my kids.* Oh, she'd deny it from now to Easter, but Sam was far too well acquainted with possessiveness when it came to his kids not recognize it in somebody else.

"You think maybe we could come back again sometime?" Mike asked.

"I suppose that's up to Carly."

"Of course you can." She was pleased, Sam could tell. Real pleased. "Anytime. As long as you've got your homework and chores done. Because God knows—" she glanced over at him and all hell broke loose inside his head "—I do not want your father on my case."

Sam beat his brain cells back into submission enough to get out, "But now it's time to call it a night. Five-thirty's still gonna happen the same time it always does. You can toss your bikes in the back of the truck and I'll give you a ride."

Grumbling, the kids grabbed their abandoned sweatshirts off the floor and trooped outside. Sam peeked back at Carly, half to see if he'd imagined that scorching connection earlier. Apparently he hadn't.

"They didn't bother you, did they?"

She laughed, a low, soft sound that seemed caught in the back of her throat. "Once they realized I wasn't going to make them wear tutus, we got along just fine."

"I hate to tell you this, but you're really good with kids."

Her smile faltered. "So you caught me having an off moment."

"Bull. I've watched you with the others, too. You're a natural—"

"Sam…"

"Dammit, Carly," he said, sharp enough to get those brows shooting up. "Would you listen, for once? Nothing puts a kid off faster than a grown-up who tries too hard. But you don't 'try' at all. You're just yourself when you're around them, so they feel like they can be themselves, too. Do you even have a *clue* how extraordinary that makes you?"

"Sam, please…" Her eyes stayed trained on his, but it didn't take a genius to see how shaken up she was. "Don't read more into this than there is."

"Wouldn't dream of it," he said, swallowing down the trickle of irritation at the back of his throat, wondering why he wasn't making use of what any other man would have pegged as the perfect exit line.

Wondering why she wasn't walking him toward the door to throw him out on his can. Why he was scanning the room, frowning, unsure why he was even thinking what he was thinking. Getting "ideas," as his mother used to say.

"What is it?" she said, as if worried he'd seen something large and many-legged on the wall behind her.

He turned. "Why couldn't you start up a dance school right here, out of the barn?"

She flinched a little, like maybe he'd read her mind. "You're not serious?"

"Why not? There used to be a dance teacher here, up until seven or eight years ago, but she retired to Florida. I think some of the kids went to Claremore, or even Tulsa, but there's a whole new flock of little girls—or maybe even boys, if you taught 'em to dance the way you were teaching Matt and Mike... Now why are you shaking your head?"

"Sam, something tells me folks around here don't have a lot of money for frills like dance lessons. And I do have to eat, you know."

He frowned at that skinny body of hers, thinking, *Could've fooled me,* then said, "Oh, well. It was a thought."

"And a very nice one," she said gently. "Just not very practical." *Now* she walked him to the door. "The boys will be, um, wondering..."

"Yeah, I guess..."

Oh, for Pete's sake...now why was he ogling her mouth?

"Night, Sam," she said, gently pushing him outside, and the cold night air slapped him in the face, fast-freezing his overheated libido as he walked out to the truck and away from her scent, and her laughter, and the promise of things that only existed in his imagination.

Carly closed the door, then watched through the window as Sam walked back to his truck, taking with him his smile and his scent and the temptation to believe in something that barely even existed in her imagination. What was even worse, however, was that long after the brisk autumn night had swallowed up the sound of his truck's engine, she stood with her back to the windows, her hands on her hips, envisioning the room filled with dancing, laughing kids.

"Good Lord, Mama—" Hanging on to Max like he was a twenty pound sack of potatoes, Dawn shoved Ivy's back door shut with her hip, but not soon enough to keep out a good strong belt of late October wind. "Could you bang those pots around any louder?"

"Well, excuse me," Ivy said, not taking any pains to set the skillet quietly on the stove. "Last time I checked, there was no law against a woman banging her own pots in her own kitchen. But then, I wasn't expectin' company."

"Gee, I wasn't aware I needed an invitation to come by my own mother's house." Ivy guessed her daughter was not put off in the least by her bad mood. "We were just over at Ryan's for Max's six-month checkup, which kinda somehow slid over to seven months, and thought maybe you might enjoy a surprise visit. Clearly I was wrong."

Ivy *hmmphed* as Dawn planted herself on one of the kitchen chairs, immediately pushing everything on the table out of Max's chubby-fisted, gleeful reach. Needless to say, the baby let out a squawk, so Ivy hauled a box of graham crackers out of the cupboard and handed him one to gnaw. "So," Dawn said, flinging her own long braid over her shoulder, "you gonna tell me what's got your drawers inside out, or what?"

Wasn't her drawers that were inside out, Ivy thought. More like it was her whole damn life. She yanked open the spiffy two-door fridge Dawn had bought for her last year, then slammed a package of cube steak on the counter.

"Lane's comin' over for supper."

"Oh, yeah, I can see how that could be a problem."

"Don't you laugh, little girl," Ivy said, because Dawn was doing exactly that. "You have no idea what that man is doing to my blood pressure."

"Then why, might I ask, did you invite him to dinner?"

Ivy shot Dawn a look. Took a couple of seconds, but then a big grin spread across her daughter's face. "No kidding? You and he...?"

Ivy nodded. Miserably. Max chortled and waved the graham cracker around, then flashed his two bottom teeth at his grandmother. Dawn contemplated her son for a moment, then lifted her eyes to Ivy.

"Is he any good?"

Ivy thudded a wide-rimmed ceramic bowl onto the counter, dumped a cup of flour into it. "Yeah. He's good."

"And…?"

She really didn't want to talk about this. Especially with Dawn. Except there was a lot to be said for just fessin' up and getting the torture over with.

"And I think maybe I'm falling in love with him."

"Uh-oh," Dawn said in the way of a woman who understands all too well the pitfalls attendant to losing one's heart.

"Yeah. Uh-oh is right." Ivy slapped a piece of meat into the now seasoned flour mixture, pounding the flour into it with her fist. The chair scraped against the scuffed tile floor; Dawn's hand landed on her back, Max's garbled, graham-cracker-thickened coos a foot away.

"Doesn't he feel the same way about you?"

Ivy refused to meet her daughter's eyes, refused to give in to the frustrated tears that kept trying to make an appearance over the past week or so. She hadn't cried over a man in twenty years, and damned if she was going to start now. "Oh, I have no doubt the man thinks he's crazy about me."

"Sorry, but I'm not seeing the problem here."

"The problem is I'm not exactly thrilled about coming in second place, okay?" She pounded the meat some more. "Not again."

"What are you talking about?" Dawn said, dodging her son's sticky, grubby fingers as he tried to pat her face.

"I mean, if I have to hear about how perfect his wife was one more time, he's gonna find himself with a one-way ticket for a little reunion."

She could hear her daughter try to suppress a chuckle. Although not very well. "I don't suppose you've considered telling him this?"

"And sound like some insecure female who's jealous of a dead woman, for heaven's sake?"

"No, like a woman with the gumption to be honest about how

she feels. I'm sure in your shoes I'd feel exactly the same way—"

"Oh, Dawn…" On a heavy sigh, Ivy turned to her daughter. "I'm too damn old for this foolishness. No matter how you slice it, I'm still the first woman he's been with after his wife's death. What're the odds he's actually going to stick around, once the novelty wears off?"

"I don't know. But I would think it counts for something that the man moved here to be close to you."

Ivy felt her mouth thin. "I've had men who wanted to be close before. It's the stayin' part none of 'em seemed to have a handle on."

Dawn deposited the baby in the small play yard Ivy had set up in the corner of the kitchen, then turned back, concern beetling her brow. "So if this is upsetting you so much, break it off. Now. Before it gets any harder."

Ivy focused on her meat dredging. "You know," she said softly, "I'd almost forgotten what it was like, having a good man around. And twenty years is a damn long time to go without."

She felt her daughter's arm encircle her shoulders. Her daughter, who'd been so petrified of screwing up with Max's daddy, she'd nearly walked away from what even she would admit was the best thing that had ever happened to her. "Life's sure a bitch, isn't it?" she said, her breath warm on Ivy's cheek.

Ivy hugged her back, one-handed, leaving a floury splotch on Dawn's pretty little sweater.

A week later, the idea of setting up a dance school right in Haven still hadn't let go, despite Carly's doing everything she could think of to pry it loose. Even after ten-hour days of helping her father wrestle the startled old farmhouse into someplace livable, by every evening, the half renovated barn—nice and frosty now as fall inched steadily closer to winter—would draw her back like a mother hen her chick, where for an hour, maybe two if her knee cooperated, she would dance.

And mourn, a little, for the arabesque no longer quite as high as it used to be, the pirouettes that didn't always land as precisely as they once did. Since she'd never perform again, it didn't really matter, but still. She'd never been one to gracefully succumb to the inevitable. Yet, when the boys came, often enough that she'd begun to keep a hopeful ear out, she'd put on salsa or jazz or—if she could find any with lyrics that wouldn't get her in major trouble with their father—hip hop, and they'd *all* dance, and her mood would lift, and little *maybes*...and *why nots*...and *you knows*...would wriggle past the *no ways* and she'd think...*hmm*.

Sometimes Sam would come and watch, a relaxed grin spread across a face she'd begun to accept as comfortably familiar, and his low laugh would fill the empty space both around and inside her, and she'd think, irritably, unreasonably, *I can't do this*. Not that she was completely able, or ready, to face the *whys* of her resistance, but that didn't lessen the absoluteness of it one whit.

The heart-stopping fear.

It was like watching a thriller and being able to spot the setup for somebody getting blown up.

Oh, yeah, Carly thought that Friday night, watching Sam poke around the gutted tack room, all too aware that the warmth swirling through her had nothing to do with snuggling back inside her down coat, she'd had lots of practice in recognizing the signs of impending doom.

All his boys were standing in the middle of the room, seeing who could yell the loudest. Carly walked over to where Sam squatted, inspecting something jutting out of the wall. He'd yet to tell her why he was there, although she guessed it had something to do with all the poking and prodding he was doing.

"Libby finally recover from her party?" she asked.

Sam tossed her a weary grin. Since there'd been a teacher's meeting that day, Blair and several of Libby's other girlfriends had decided to throw her a surprise sleepover party last night at her house. The boys had spent the night at Lane and Carly's so they wouldn't be in the girls' hair. It had been an interesting experience, to put it mildly. Although judging from Sam's still slightly gray complexion, hosting a houseful of teenage girls hadn't done his constitution any favors, either.

"Yeah. Sure wish I had. Do you have any idea how much noise ten giggling teenage girls make?"

"Yeah. About half as much as four boys." He chuckled; she crouched beside him. "I know I'm going to regret asking…but what are you doing?"

He smiled at her, sending another, deceptively pleasant feeling through her, like the first bite of ice cream straight from the carton that would only lead to a bellyache if indulged. Except who thinks about the potential bellyache while that first—or second or third—bite is melting gloriously against one's tongue?

"I never got a good look at what the previous owners did. But it sure would appear—" he shifted his weight to his other leg, gesturing with a broad-brimmed cowboy hat that worked really well with all those angles in his face "—that this is pretty much ready to go. Plumbing seems to all be in place, just waiting for the fixtures and appliances. If, you know, you wanted to move in."

"Where they'd find me frozen to death one morning."

"Ductwork's all in, too. All you need is a furnace."

The boys tore outside; Carly sank crossed-legged onto the floor, covering her face with her hands. Sam reached over and peeled away enough fingers to look into her eyes.

"Let me guess. Putting in a furnace implies commitment."

"Damn. You're good."

"And you know you want to do this."

She dropped her hands. "Okay, so maybe I've been thinking about it. A little. But—"

"Your father's already said he'd pay for whatever you need. And between the two of us, we could get everything installed in no time."

"But how—"

"It's winter. Or just about. Not that there's not stuff to do, but things definitely ease up between now and March."

"But then Dad would be alone…oh," she said at Sam's funny expression.

He chuckled. "My guess is Lane would do just about anything to have you out from underfoot. And you gotta admit, this would be perfect."

Yes, it would.

She got to her feet and walked away, thinking.

"You're not saying 'no,'" Sam said behind her.

"Out loud."

He walked past her to the window, standing with his hands in his pockets, watching the boys running amok outside, his heavy chore coat bunched up behind him. "You got any idea what you're so scared of?"

Tears bit at her eyes. "All of this. The town, my options… You."

His head snapped around, his light brows crashed together over his nose. And she saw, in that instant, that her feelings were more than reciprocated. Except they weren't, not really, because if she knew nothing else, she knew that Sam would be coming at this from a totally different level, one Carly had never been anywhere near. For her, this was all about sex, as it always had been. Oh, yeah, she liked him—she liked him a lot—but there was a huge gap between the two she had no idea how to bridge.

"I don't suppose you'd care to explain that?" he said.

"I don't know that I can. It's just…this all seems so, so *real*. And I'm…" She met his gaze, sadly shaking her head. "Not."

Sam's face hardened. "That's crap, Carly."

"No, it's not! Sam…please, *please* don't start thinking you're seeing someone who doesn't really exist."

He withdrew his hands from his pockets, then took three or four slow, deliberate steps toward her. "Funny thing," he said, "but I think I've got a pretty good handle on the difference between illusion and reality. And far as I'm concerned, you are one of the most real women I've ever met. So deal with it." He slammed his hat back on his head and headed toward the door, only to turn back and say, "By the way, I'll be picking you up for the dance tomorrow night around seven. I'd appreciate it if you'd wear something to make every male in the room regret not being me."

Lane was watching TV in the newly-open-to-the-kitchen living room when Carly stormed through the house and up the stairs, after which he was treated to several minutes' worth of thudding and stomping around. He half thought of going up and asking what was wrong, but then reason returned. Besides, he had enough troubles of his own these days.

Not that he'd tell Carly, but Ivy had been acting strangely for most of the past week. As though she was keeping something bottled up inside that she was afraid to let out. On the surface, they still seemed to getting along just fine—in bed and out— but a man doesn't survive nearly four decades of marriage without learning to spot the clues when something was wrong. He wondered if Ivy was tiring of the relationship. After all, she'd never been married, and he surmised that she hadn't been alone for so long solely by chance. Maybe she was simply one of those women who for the most part preferred her own company, and she now felt that Lane was crowding her.

He clicked off the TV, plunging the room, and his mood, into darkness. If Ivy was pulling away…well. What a kick in the butt to discover he wasn't as prepared as he'd thought to deal with rejection. He wouldn't go so far as to say he'd fallen in love with Ivy, but he'd grown very fond of her, in large part because she was so different from his wife. Dena had certainly been a brick in her own way, but thinking back, he realized how wearing he'd often found her tendency to defer to him. Ironic that the very thing that attracted him to Ivy—her independence, her ability to deal with whatever life tossed in her path—could also be what eventually tore them apart.

However, there was little point in sitting here conjecturing, Lane thought as he pushed himself up out of his favorite arm-chair, carrying his empty hot chocolate mug to his disaster-area kitchen. Ivy was going to help him babysit for the boys while Sam and Carly went to the dance; but as soon as the boys were asleep, he and Ivy had some serious talking to do.

Whether she wanted to or not.

The morning of the dance, Main Street might as well have been the Wal-Mart parking lot on Christmas Eve, both from the number of cars clogging the streets and the number of yapping women in or surrounding them. Most of whom, Sam guessed as he and Travis carefully navigated bumpers plastered with political campaign stickers and assorted religious sentiment, were either on their way to or had recently left the Hair We Are. The bigger the event, the bigger the hair, was the philosophy around here.

The uncommon traffic congestion, not to mention Radar's incessant, cheerful barking at all the ladies desperately trying to shield their fresh do's from the raw wind, did nothing to ease his edgy mood. But at least parking wasn't a problem in front of Dawn's law office, where he needed to sign some paperwork for his brother. When he walked in, however, the woman seemed to be in almost as much of a state as he was.

"Coffeemaker broken?" he said, and she sort of growled at him. In her long denim skirt and boots, a sweater baggy enough to smuggle arms, she could have probably passed for her mother at about that age. "Just got a lot on my mind, is all," she said, her shiny brown hair streaming down her back as she walked over to a file cabinet to put something away. It was pretty enough hair, Sam supposed, but all it did was lie there, flat and smooth and kind of lifeless. These days, Sam had a thing for hair with a little more substance to it.

Which partially accounted for his state. What accounted for Dawn's, however, God alone knew.

She slammed shut the file cabinet, then turned, her face all scrunched up like she was fixing to ask him something, but hadn't yet decided whether she should or not. Out in the reception area, Travis was entertaining Dawn's secretary, Marybeth

Reese, by reciting the entire plot of *Finding Nemo*. Judging from the older woman's periodic "Uh-huhs" and "Isn't that nices?" they were getting on just fine.

He'd no sooner signed the paperwork than she said, "Got a minute?"

His insides did a little "uh-oh," but he said, "Sure, I guess. What's up?"

She shut the door and returned to her desk, where she sank into the big old leather chair that had belonged to Sherman Mosely before he retired. She indicated for him to take a seat, which he did, then said, "I'm not sure how to ask this delicately, so I won't even try. As a widower, do you think two years is too soon for a man to get serious about another woman?"

Sam didn't know Dawn real well, since she'd only moved back to Haven about a year ago after ten years in the East, but it didn't come as much of a surprise that she'd be as direct as her mother.

"Depends on the man, I suppose." Relieved this had nothing, apparently, to do with him personally, Sam relaxed in the old wing chair across from Dawn, crossing his booted ankle over his knee. "We talking about Lane and Ivy?"

"Do I look like a person with a death wish?"

Sam would have chuckled, except the gal looked really worried. "I thought they were getting along okay. This theoretical couple who aren't Lane and your mother."

"That's what I thought, too," she said, clearly giving up any and all pretense at speaking "theoretically." "Until Mama said something the other night that made me realize maybe this isn't as much of a good thing as I first thought. She's convinced—and so help me, if you breathe a word of this, we're both dead—that Lane's not over his wife yet. That he sees Mama as some sort of a way station. The first way station, no less."

"And...she's serious about him?"

"That's what she says."

Sam blew out a long, low whistle.

"Yeah. I know." Dawn leaned back, bouncing a pen on the

desk. "I've never seen her this worked up before. Or this afraid. Believe me, it's not pretty. I mean…" She huffed a sigh, tossing down the pen. "I know she's always gone out of her way to make everybody think she's this free thinker who doesn't need a man, what it all boils down to—once you get past all her b.s.—is that nobody's ever cared enough to stick around. To accept her just the way she is, attitude and all." Her mouth flattened. "To put her first. If Lane's only seeing her as a substitute…am I even making any sense?"

She had no idea her words were clanging around inside his skull loud enough to set off seismographs three states over. "Are you asking me if I think it's possible for him to really be in love with her?"

"Sorry," she said, waving her hands. "That wasn't fair, putting you on the spot like that…"

"No, no…it's okay. As long as you're okay with my answer."

"Which is…?"

"That I have no idea." He rose, his heart pounding. "But it's not like there's a rulebook for these things, you know. They're both good people. Who's to say it wouldn't work?"

"That's what I've tried to tell Mama. But…" Her hands lifted, a gesture equally annoyed and helpless.

Sam thought a moment, mostly about how he was probably the least qualified person to be giving advice right now, then said, "Seems to me they're the ones who need to be talking to each other, though. Not you and me."

She smirked. "Sure, piece of cake."

He laughed softly, then eased himself toward the door. Dawn thanked him—although for what, God only knew—they said their goodbyes, and Sam collected Travis and scooted out of there. But all the way back home, the conversation thunked and twanged inside his head, as a few things he hadn't fully understood until now started fitting in place.

Whether or not Lane was serious, or might one day be serious, about Ivy, Sam had no idea. By unspoken mutual consent,

Lane's love life wasn't something the two men discussed. But Sam meant what he'd said about not seeing any reason why it couldn't be possible, a man falling—and falling hard—for the first woman he'd ever felt anything for after losing his wife. Because that's exactly what was happening to Sam. Whether it made any sense or not, whether he wanted it to or not.

Funny how he hadn't even noticed the hairline crack in the mantra of self-reliance he'd hung on to since Jeannie's death, a crack now big enough to let a damn herd of elephants through.

Or at least to let one lonely, obviously confused woman in. Maybe.

He blew out a sigh sharp enough to bring both Travis's and Radar's heads around. There were still more obstacles to him and Carly's getting together than there were cheerleaders in Texas. But there was something more, something that went way beyond surface issues, that he had no idea how to reach, let alone help her deal with. From where he was sitting, frankly, the whole thing had "Dead End" written all over it.

Still, it was like his parents had always told him, and he and Jeannie had always drummed into their kids' heads—you don't love somebody because of what you might get back. You love 'em because they need to be loved, in the way they needed you to love 'em. And Carly Stewart was clearly somebody who needed to be loved. Just for who she was.

Except…who, exactly, was that?

And was she even remotely open to letting him find out?

And—here was the biggest question of all—was he totally out of his gourd for even thinking about any of this?

"Daddy?" Travis said beside him. "Why's your face all crumpled up?"

Sam looked over into his youngest's anxious blue eyes, forcing himself to smile. "No real reason," he said, reaching over to ruffle Travis's now shaggy hair and grin at the boy's relieved smile. "Just thinking."

Yeah. About how he'd looked away for a single second, and his sanity had gone toddling off.

Chapter 10

Butterflies in her stomach would have been bad—and absurd—enough. Pterodactyls, however, just went beyond all reason.

But there they were, Carly irritably mused as she checked her reflection for at least the hundredth time, fwomping around in there with their huge, pointy wings and those ugly cresty things on their heads. And the beaks! Let's not forget about the beaks, threatening to poke right through her gut any second now.

Dad had already left for Sam's. Worry filming his features like fine dust, he'd said something about Ivy joining him, since Dawn and Cal were leaving Max with their housekeeper, Ethel. Something was going on with that, something strange and not good, but Dad wasn't talking and Carly had enough on her mind with the pterodactyls and all that she'd decided to leave it for later.

The doorbell, which she realized she'd never heard before this very moment, ding-donged her right into a tizzy. More of a tizzy.

"Coming!" came out as a scrawny yelp. She stole one last glance—as if anything had changed in the last five seconds—before tripping downstairs in a pair of strappy bronze sandals she hadn't worn in about a million years, as layers of feathery, beaded chiffon took flight all around her. At the bottom of the stairs, she took yet another peek in the mirror over the hall table, immediately deciding she should have worn her hair up instead of going for the deranged voodoo doll look. Oh, God. She was going to throw up. The bell *dinged* again, sticking on the *dong,* which didn't release until she opened the door.

"Wow," she and Sam said at the same time, officially declaring themselves Lame Couple of the Night. But hell, she'd had no idea the man would clean up *this* well. Even if "cleaning up" in this part of the world meant pressed jeans, a suede blazer the color of a perfect pie crust and a shirt so white, it glowed against his sun-darkened skin.

Yeah, like she needed any more incentive to jump the man's bones.

Then she realized his grin for her had sort of frozen in place. He made a "turn around" motion with his finger. So she did, jostling the pterodactyls.

"You mind if I whistle?"

"Go for it."

So he did, and she grinned like a goon. "I did good?"

"Oh, honey, *good* doesn't even begin to cover it. That is *some* dress. What exactly do you call that color?"

"Red."

"Nope. I know red when I see it. Red is this color's poor relation."

Naturally, she turned back to the mirror to try to see herself through his eyes. The color did go beyond your average Crayola, she supposed, the multiple layers of glittering fabric hovering between fuchsia and sort of a persimmon. The neckline showed plenty of breastbone, but only a hint of breast (which was all she had, anyway); the uneven hemline offered glimpses of thigh even though the dress officially fell to midcalf. Feeling silly at feeling so pleased, she picked up her tiny beaded bag and cashmere shawl off the table and swept past him and out the door. Oh, boy, did he smell good.

"You're going to freeze," Sam said.

"That's why you're going to keep the heat on in the…what are we taking this evening?"

"I thought the Caddy would be nice."

Which would mean…yep. The van. The *empty* van.

"Where're the kids?"

"Libby swore she wasn't ready." His hand came to rest on the small of her back; Carly nearly bit her tongue. "Although she sure looked ready to me. I swear, if she's looked in the mirror once, she's looked in it a hundred times in the past half hour alone."

Carly laughed—a strange, sorta pterodactylly sound—as he held open the passenger side door for her to get in. The heater was already on. She wrapped her stole around her and let out a long, quivery sigh.

Sam got in, slammed shut his door, looked over at her. Then reached for her hand, lifting it to press a soft kiss against her knuckles. His lips were warm and smooth and his eyes were locked in hers and her mind went blank.

An almost hesitant smile pulling at his mouth, Sam let go of her hand to touch two fingers to her hair, as if it were something precious. As if *she* were something precious. "My mama used to wrap our Christmas gifts so pretty, my brother and I would spend hours lying on our stomachs in front of the tree, starin' at 'em. We were so fascinated with the glittery wrappings and the fancy bows we almost didn't even care what was inside. But next to you, honey, those presents might as well have been wrapped in newspaper and string."

Her eyes filled. *Dammit.* Blinking furiously, she turned around and said, "Thank you," and he said, "You're welcome," releasing the clutch to back out of her yard, and she felt like Alice peering over the edge to the rabbit hole.

Not good.

Not an extra ounce of fat anywhere on the woman, and she still made his mouth go dry. Jeannie had been soft and round and luscious, Sam's definition of beauty for more than twenty years. But Carly's delicacy, the way her skin seemed to glide over her bones like silk…you'd almost believe the light would shine straight through her if you caught her at the right angle. Or at least from her eyes, which had gotten all glittery when he complimented her. He wondered how long it had been since a man had made her feel treasured, instead of just wanted.

They opened the door to his house to find Libby having a hissy because Wade, who looked like he'd been wrestling the pigs, kept trying to give her a hug. "Get away from me!" she shrieked, trying to find a spot not already taken up with a brother or some animal or other, and Sam wondered at how a girl who encountered, without complaint, gross things on a regular basis could suddenly turn into such a priss. "Daddy! Make him stop!"

"Wade, cut it out," Sam said, except Libby had already moved on to gasping over Carly.

"Oh, wow! You look, like, *so* gorgeous!"

"You look pretty hot yourself, missy," Carly said with a grin, and Libby blushed. As well she should, having dragged Sam through what seemed like every store in Tulsa before she found the "right" dress, a shiny, changeable blue-green number with spaghetti straps and a full, short skirt. Her clunky heels killed the effect, in Sam's opinion—which clearly wasn't worth much—but with her hair all curly and loose, and the more subtle makeup Carly had shown her how to do, he had to admit she took his breath away.

As she clearly did Sean's, who, in khakis and a sport jacket he must've borrowed from his father, looked like somebody in sore need of the Heimlich maneuver. Still, Sam could feel the testosterone buzz clear over here. Although, come to think of it, he was probably generating a pretty good buzz of his own, so with any luck he and Sean would neutralize each other and both their dates would be safe. Lane came out of the kitchen with Travis clinging to him like a koala, a bowl of freshly popped corn in his hand, and over the bellows of swarming, hungry boys he sternly shooed them out of the house, but only after assuring Sam no less than three times that they'd all be fine.

On the way to the high school, Sam did his best to engage Sean in conversation, but gave up after five minutes of monosyllabic replies. "And by the way," he said, "don't think I can't see you back there, so don't get any ideas," which earned him a disgusted, "Daddy! Jeez!" from his daughter and a muffled snort from Carly. Who then touched his arm, giving him a tiny smile of understanding when he glanced over, a gesture which kept him warm all the way to the dance. And if that wasn't a comment on his sorry state of affairs, he didn't know what was.

The high school gym had been done up in your basic crepe paper streamers in harvest colors, shards of light from the spinning disco ball swimming frantically around the room in an—vain—attempt to camouflage the basketball court and bleachers, while paper-clothed tables with enough food to feed a whole 'nother state stretched across one end of the room. Around the perimeter stood clumps of girls, their grown-up-ness, like their shoes, painfully new; of boys, silently daring each other to be the first one to ask one of the girls to dance.

The band—a local group that Libby had given a thumbs-up to—had already launched into their first set, and the floor soon crawled with gyrating young bodies. Blair, looking about as tickled as Coop Hastings displaying that thirty-pound striped bass he'd snagged a couple years back, suddenly appeared in front of them, a tall young man with thick, dark hair and a shy smile in tow. After shouted introductions, the four kids disappeared into the crowd.

"What are you thinking?" Carly yelled up to him, the shiny wood floor seeming to breathe under their feet. She'd begun to sort of vibrate.

Sam slipped his fingers around hers, plugging into the vibrations, her warmth. One brow lifted, but she didn't pull away. "Just wondering when I stopped being one of the 'young people.'"

"Ain't that the truth." The vibrating started to get more serious, like she was one big itch. "Aren't you supposed to be working this thing?"

"Not until nine-thirty. Then the punch bowl's all mine for a half hour."

"People can't get their own punch?"

"It's not the getting that's the problem. It's the doctoring."

"Spoilsport."

"Kids gave me a mug last Christmas that said that very thing."

She laughed, then nodded toward the nearest clot of girls, so self-conscious in their fancy dresses. "They look like they're waiting to see the dentist, poor things."

"Just one of those rites of passage. We all went through it."

"Not all of us," she said after a moment. He frowned down at her, and she shrugged. "I never went to any of my school dances."

"You're kidding?"

"Nope."

"Nobody ever asked you?"

"I was a rebel, not a loser. Of course I got asked. I just refused to go. Even to my own prom."

The music suddenly stopped, leaving a pulsing, blissful silence in its place. But only for a couple of seconds. The lead singer mumbled something into the mike, it was hard to tell what, but laughter shuddered through the crowd. Then the band started up again, an old Bee Gees number, sounded like.

"Oh, my God! Fifth grade flashback! Oh, nononononono…"

Sam tugged her out onto the dance floor, where he immediately executed a rusty, but still serviceable, John Travolta move. Carly howled.

"I do not believe this!"

"Believe it. I saw *Saturday Night Fever* five times."

"And you're *admitting* this?"

"What can I say?" he yelled over the throb of the music. "I was a very weird kid."

"Who then grew up to be an even weirder adult."

"Says the woman with half a jewelry counter hanging off her earlobes."

"Okay, you asked for it, buster. Move over!"

A smarter man would have been intimidated to be on the dance floor at the same time with this woman, but Sam was too damn busy just trying to keep up—not to mention too fascinated with the interplay of soft fabric and lean muscle as she swayed and writhed and turned, every move as precise as a finely tuned engine. But keep up, he did, somehow. With a lot more enthusiasm than grace, God knew, but suddenly he realized they were the only ones dancing, like Jimmy Stewart and Donna Reed in the dance scene in *It's a Wonderful Life,* everybody ringed around them, clapping and letting out catcalls left and right. At one point he heard Libby call out, "Ohmigod, *Daddy!*" which got a huge laugh, but they kept on dancing.

Then the music changed to country—what the band lacked in technique, they more than made up for in versatility—a line dance, and it was Sam's turn to chuckle, watching her go at it with her turned-out feet in those strippy little shoes. But damned if she didn't give it her all, grinning up at him like one of his kids, and his heart turned over in his chest.

The music changed once again, this time to a ballad. Panting, flushed, Carly looked up at him, her eyes wide with questions, and he pulled her close so fast she stumbled slightly. He tucked her left hand against his chest, his other one settling nicely into that little hollow at the small of her back. The dress's filmy fabric snagged on his rough skin, bunched up against the slippery lining, both layers together no more a barrier to the woman underneath than a flimsy nightgown. Her perfume roared through his senses as her hand came to rest on his shoulder, so lightly he could barely feel it.

"You okay with this?" he whispered into her hair, his breath all that separated his lips from her temple.

"Depends how you define 'okay.'"

But she sure didn't seem to have anyplace else to go.

It had been a long time since he'd held another woman close, breathed in another woman's scent. But the expected pangs of guilt or regret or residual grief never came, much to his surprise. And relief. Instead, he pulled her a little closer, taking in the other couples in town sharing the floor with him—all the Logan men and their brides, Joe and Taylor, even the older couples like Ruby and her Jordy, huge and bald, the disco ball flashing off his dark pate, his gold tooth as he shared a joke with his wife.

He realized Carly had lifted her head, watching him with an expression he couldn't quite decipher. "What?" he said.

"This isn't real, you know."

He knew what she meant. Understood it, too. But no way was he going to let her fears ruin her night. Or his. So he smiled into her eyes and said, "Probably exactly what Cinderella was thinking, long about this time."

"Oh, Sam," she said on an exhaled breath, looking away, and he tucked a finger underneath her chin to bring her gaze back up to his.

"Hey. I would've thought if anybody knew how to live in the moment, it'd be you."

"But that's the problem," she said, and he thought, Well, hell—how do I get around *that?*

Carly's knee was killing her. But not nearly as much as her heart. Or at least, the space where her heart was rumored to be.

She sat on a metal folding chair, picking at an assortment of food she wasn't inclined to eat even when she was hungry, trying not to watch Sam standing a little way off, talking with a tall, good-looking blond guy with a mustache. Dr. Logan, she remembered. Ivy's daughter's brother-in-law. She smiled to herself, surreptitiously rubbing her knee—around here, you couldn't describe anybody without tacking on several apostrophe *s*'s.

She lowered her eyes to her plate, listlessly stabbing her plastic fork at something barbecued, wondering how she managed to get herself into these messes. The one thing she'd thought she'd been able to count on was Sam's unwillingness to get romantically involved. Not yet, at any rate. Not until she figured out what to do and got out of there.

So much for that. Because, unless she was further out of it than she'd thought, Sam Frazier was more than ready to move on. Which might have been cause for celebration if he hadn't been more than ready to move on with *her.* If he hadn't been the first really decent man to cross her path—whom she'd let cross her path—in a dog's age. If he hadn't been solid and sure and funny and kind and exuded an uncomplicated, meat-and-potatoes brand of sensuality that was driving her wild. Making love with him…she shut her eyes. There would be laughter, and tenderness, and surprises, and maybe a little awkwardness, but so much joy, it wouldn't matter.

In other words, nothing like her previous experiences.

And for his sake, an experience that would have to remain solely in her imagination.

Bummer.

The band, which had been on a break, started up again, something vaguely punk and brain-pulverizing. Kids swarmed back onto the floor like flies at a picnic; Carly watched them, half smiling, half thinking how nice it would be to turn back the clock, start over again….

"Carly?"

She turned to find herself bathed in the widest, dimpled smile she'd ever seen, crowned by an explosion of blond curls.

"I don't think we've met yet, I'm Faith Andrews? My husband fixed y'all's truck a while back?"

"Oh, yes! I've seen you with your kids in the Homeland, I think."

"Yeah, that's me, the crazy lady with the octopus in her cart." She pointed to a nearby chair. "You mind if I sit?"

Carly shook her head; the roundish young woman, around thirty or so, perched on the end of the chair, her hands folded on top of knees covered in some shiny fabric that might have been purple, it was hard to tell in this light.

"I've been sent as an emissary of sorts," she said, then

glanced behind her at a huddle of women of various ages, their expressions indicating an avid interest in the outcome of this conversation. "Word's out that you're a dance teacher?"

And there it was. Her destiny, all tied up in a bow. "I'm…thinking about it—"

"What kind of dance do you teach?"

"Well…I suppose I could manage pretty much anything. Classical ballet was my specialty. But jazz, modern, whatever. Even ballroom, if push came to shove. Why?"

"You think you could teach us to dance the way you were doing out on the floor?" She lifted her hands, shifting her rib cage from side to side. "All those fancy moves with your hips and all?"

Carly laughed. "Well, I suppose so, but—"

"Good. 'Cause some of us could definitely stand to lose a little postpartum weight—" she laid one hand on her poochy belly and grimaced "—and dancin' sure looks like a whole lot more fun than some of those godawful exercise videos! Not only that, but if you're interested in teaching kids, I bet we could scare up a few of those, too. Shoot, I've got three or four you can have for starters."

Now she noticed the other women had drifted closer, in a clump, their expressions every bit as eager and expectant as Faith's. And her vision of the barn, filled with laughing, bouncing kids—and adults, as well, apparently—came more clearly into focus. Became more real. More enticing.

"I…I don't know how long I'm staying," she said, and Faith's face fell.

"That mean you won't do it? Even if for only a little while?"

She caught all those hopeful faces a few feet away, and blew out a breath.

"Of course I'll do it. It'll be fun."

Faith let out a squeal and lurched forward to throw her arms around Carly's neck, as the rest of the women surrounded her, all talking at once. Faith let go, and Carly glanced up, catching Sam's smile, and happiness and dread collided in the pit of her stomach as she realized the whole damn town was railroading her into falling in love with…it.

From across the room, Libby saw Faith hug Carly, saw something unspoken and loaded with meaning between her father and Carly. She sipped her punch, feeling a tiny knot lodge between her brows. Lord, Dad and Carly had just about embarrassed her to death, out on the dance floor earlier. But at the same time, they'd both looked like they were having a real good time. Dad especially. A dark thought crossed her mind, which was that if Carly hurt her father, she'd never forgive her.

Sean's hand slipped into hers; she gave him a smile. He looked *so* hot tonight, her breath hitched every time she looked at him. And he'd been so sweet about everything, having to let Daddy drive them there and all.

"Let's get out of here," he whispered, his breath warm in her hair, sending a little shiver over her skin.

"We can't do that," she whispered, giggling. "Daddy'll be looking for me, you know he will."

"There's like a million people in here, he'll never know."

Biting her lip, she scanned the crush of bodies on the dance floor, then felt her cheeks warm with the daring of it all. "Okay, I guess. But where?"

Sean scouted out the other end of the room, to make sure Daddy wasn't watching, she presumed, then skimmed a finger down her cheek, his teeth flashing in the dim light in the gym. "You'll see. Come on."

The hall was completely empty when they slipped out the gym door; Sean grabbed her hand again and tugged her along behind him, their laughter and the hollow clicking sound of her heels against the tile floor reverberating tinnily off rows of lockers as they ran. Sean slammed down the metal bar to the door leading outside—*ka-chunk*—and the crisp night air enveloped them, heightening Libby's senses.

"Come here," he whispered, pushing her up against the brick wall, his hands framing her face as he lowered his mouth to hers and kissed her slowly, completely. His tongue touched hers, over and over, delicious and scary all at once; she felt powerful in a way she'd never felt before, even as tendrils of nervousness writhed in her stomach, competing with a tingly warmth spreading even lower. Then, carefully, he touched her breast through her dress and bra, and she jerked in response, stunned at the sensation.

"Do you like that?" he murmured into her mouth, but all she could manage was a groan of approval, deep in her throat. So he touched her some more, and kissed her a lot more, until she realized her back was freezing from being up against the frigid, rough brick.

"I'm cold," she whispered, and he immediately slipped out of his jacket and bundled her into it.

"I know where it's warmer."

"Yeah, let's go back to the dance—"

"No. Someplace better. Someplace where nobody's going to bother us."

A tiny alarm went off in her head. "Um, maybe that's not such a good idea…"

He silenced her protest with another kiss, then entwined their fingers. And smiled. "Trust me?"

"Sure, but—"

He placed a finger on her lips, then led her across the courtyard to the shop building. "I've got a key. And nobody will think to look for us here."

"Sean…?"

"It's okay, your dad will never know."

"Sean, I really want to go back…" But her words fell on deaf ears as he unlocked the shop door, guided her inside. Smells of grease and oil, the sharp tang of metal, assaulted her nose; moonlight filtering through the bank of windows along one side of the vast room glanced off any number of strange, hulking shapes. Shaking her head, Libby edged back out the door.

"I'm really not comfortable with this, okay?"

"Shh, baby, it's not gonna hurt, I promise. And I've got condoms, if that's what you're worried about."

Now panic screamed in her ears. "No, you're not listening, I don't want to do this. Not now." She glanced around the room. "And especially not *here*. Come on, let's go back—"

A yelp escaped from her throat when he caught her hand, then pressed it against the bulge in his pants. "This is what you do to me, baby, you can't leave me like this, you got me in this state, this is what you wanted, remember?"

"No!" she yelled, yanking her hand away. "I'm sorry, I didn't realize…" She tried to run, but he grabbed her from behind, his kisses sloppy and desperate, not like the ones he usually gave her, as she felt his hand slash up her thighs, underneath her dress.

"I know you're nervous—" came out in pants as she struggled against him "—but I'll make it good for you, you'll see…ow! *Dammit!*" His hand flew to his face where she'd slapped him; she gasped, then took off, wincing when she banged her hip against something hard and cold and unyielding as she ran.

"What the hell is wrong with you?" Sean yelled behind her.

But by now she was too far away to hear him. Her palm stung from slapping him, her hip throbbed, but those were the least of her worries. Her lungs screaming for air, she plowed through the only open door, the one nearest to the gym, before she realized she couldn't let anybody see her like this. Luckily the hall was empty, the ladies' room only a few feet away: she could duck inside and hide out in one of the stalls until she pulled herself together…

"Libby?" Blair said when they nearly collided in the bathroom doorway. "Ohmigod! Are you all right?"

One glimpse into her friend's worried eyes and she totally lost it.

Chapter 11

"S-Sam?"

In the midst of handing out what felt like his thousandth cup of punch, Sam looked up, his grin collapsing at Blair's distressed expression. He barely registered Carly's hand landing on his arm, barely heard his own, "What is it?"

"Oh, God, it's Libby," came out in a strangled whisper. "She's out in the hall with Jenna, I don't know what happened, she won't stop crying long enough to tell us…."

The punch geysered as Sam dropped the plastic ladle, then tore across the gym, Carly right behind him. Seconds later, Libby was in his arms, crying way too hard to make sense of anything she said. He nodded to Jenna, who led a protesting Blair away.

"Call me?" the other teen yelled back to Libby, but Sam wasn't even sure if Libby'd heard her.

The door to the gym swung open, letting out a group of teens who all glanced curiously over; Sam steered Libby down the hall to the unlocked teacher's lounge, each of his daughter's sobs a dagger through his heart. Libby almost never cried, not even when she'd been a baby.

"She needs another woman," Carly said, matter-of-factly, when they all sat down on the standard issue, metal-frame sofa, gently extracting Libby from Sam's nearly panicked grasp and wrapping her own long, slender arms around his child. Libby sagged against Carly, letting her rock her, stroke her messed-up hair out of her face, while Carly made all those soothing noises mothers have made throughout eternity for a hurting child. Except, when he tore his eyes away from his daughter long enough to glance at the woman comforting her, he caught a flash of anguish in her fine-boned face that rocked him all over again, producing an aftershock of suspicion, that Libby's pain was somehow her own.

Finally, in gasping fits and starts, Libby's story came out. Not in great detail, heaven knows, but enough to leave no doubt about what happened.

For the first time, Sam understood how an otherwise peaceful man could be driven to murder. He shot to his feet and began to pace the room, one hand braced on his hip, the other one streaking through his hair. If his heart pounded any harder, it'd come clean out of his chest.

"I'm so sorry, Daddy," Libby said behind him in a tiny, shaky voice.

Sam spun around. "For what?"

Although her sobs had trickled to hiccups, a new flood of tears crested on her lower lids. "For not listening, for thinking…" She blew her nose, then stared at her hands, knotted in her lap, before lifting red-rimmed eyes to Sam again. "For being stupid, for letting myself get in way over my head—"

"Hey," Carly said before Sam had a chance to. Her hands firmly on the girl's shoulders, she held her a little apart, looking her straight in the eye. "Don't you ever, ever let me hear you call yourself stupid, you got that? Sean had no right to try talking you into doing something you weren't ready for—"

"No, you don't understand—"

"We understand *plenty,* believe me," Sam roared, making

both females jump. "And so help me, the minute I catch him—"

"Daddy, *no!* Don't go after him, it wasn't his fault, I—I led him on, got him all worked up…oh, God, I'm sorry I said anything!"

"*Libby!*"

Carly's voice, low and feral, sliced through the tension vising the room. When she took Libby's face in her slender hands, fury such as Sam had never seen rolled in waves off her slight frame.

"*This is not your fault.* And don't you dare believe for a single moment that it is. A real man understands when a woman says 'no,' that doesn't somehow translate into 'try harder.' Honey, trust me," she said, more softly now, brushing tears off the girl's blotchy face, "just *seeing* a woman is enough to get some men 'worked up.' But no matter how turned on a guy is, or how he got that way, it never, ever gives him the right to force himself on you. Do you understand what I'm saying?"

After a moment, Libby nodded.

"And another thing," Carly said, rubbing Libby's upper arms. "Be proud of yourself for having the courage to tell your father." She hesitated, then added, "Believe me, this is one secret you don't want to keep."

Another shock wave coursed through Sam's already strained emotions. This time, he knew he wasn't imagining Carly's personal experience leaking through her words, her own emotions. But right now, he only had enough energy to focus on his daughter.

He crouched in front of Libby, taking her hand. The short-nailed, rough-skinned hand of a young lady who spent far more time in pigpens and chicken coops than she did in malls. "You got any idea where Sean is?" When she started up with the whimpering protests again, however, he said, "I promise I'm not gonna kill him. Although believe me, it's very tempting. But I can't let this go, Libby. I'd never be able to live with myself if I did."

She lowered her eyes, staring hard at her lap for several more seconds before she finally said, "I left him in the auto shop."

Sam squeezed her hand. "Will you be okay here with Carly for a bit?"

Another nod. Now he allowed himself a glance over at Carly, who'd again folded the girl into her arms. "Thanks," he mouthed over Libby's head.

"No problem," she mouthed back, but not even a blind man could miss the toll the evening's events had taken on her, too.

However, after a quick search of the school property, as well as any number of inquiries as to the boy's possible whereabouts, Sam realized the boy had fled, maybe hitching a ride with somebody else. Since the evening was clearly over for all of them, he found another warm body to take over his punch-pouring duties, then took Libby and Carly back home.

Lane came into the kitchen when they straggled in through the back door, took one look at Libby's tear-blotched face, and lifted questioning eyes to Sam. He put up a hand to stave off any questions; Lane got the hint.

"Boys all asleep?" he asked after Carly steered his wrung-out, devastated daughter back to her bedroom to put her to bed.

"Littlest ones, yeah. Big boys ended up at the Grangers, they said you'd already told them they could spend the night?" Sam nodded, although he'd plumb forgotten, actually. "They said to tell you they'd be back for church in the morning," Lane added, then gave him a look that said, *You gonna tell me what happened, or what?*

Sam leaned heavily against the counter, his hands braced against the edge. "Sean tried to pull a real fast one," he said in a low voice, swallowing past the burning sensation in the back of his throat. "I never did trust that boy."

"No," Lane said. "We never do." He pushed out a breath. "I'm sorry. Especially for that little girl. Is she going to be okay?"

"Knowing Libby?" Sam said with a tired smile. "Probably. She's real shaken right now, though."

"Almost as much as you, I imagine."

Sam looked over again, saw a shared commiseration in Carly's father's eyes, one that nearly pushed him to ask about Carly, what had happened to her. Except something told him if he wanted to know what was going on in her head, it didn't make much sense to go digging around in anybody else's. Then Sam realized Lane was alone.

"Ivy didn't come over?"

A cloud scudded across the older man's face. "No." He walked over to load several dishes into the dishwasher. "Guess she changed her mind." The dishwasher thunked closed; Lane looked around the kitchen, frowning, as if he'd forgotten something, then back at Sam. "Well. Since you're back…"

"Oh. Yeah. Go on. And thanks." He managed a tired smile. "Stayin' with my kids definitely goes beyond the call of neighborliness."

Lane chuckled. "They're just boys."

"My point exactly."

The older man slipped on his lightweight parka, clamped a hand on Sam's shoulder for a moment, then let himself out through the back door. Sam tiptoed upstairs to check on his three youngest, all sawing logs, tucking faded action-figure comforters around little flailed limbs and retrieving stuffed toys that had fallen overboard, his heart turning over in his chest for each one.

Back downstairs, he let cats out and dogs in, put on a pot of coffee, then carefully listened at the door to Libby's room, where he heard the two females talking softly. Half of him felt left out, the other half grateful; he decided he didn't have the wherewithal to dissect his thoughts any further than that. He poured himself a cup of coffee before finally wandering into his living room, loosening his tie one-handed as he set his mug of coffee on the end table, then collapsed with a soft groan onto the sofa. One booted foot automatically hooked the edge of the coffee table, a habit of his that had driven Jeannie to distraction. A habit he'd done his best to curb in the name of domestic harmony, until his wife's death rendered his good intentions moot.

One hand lifted to rub his aching eyeballs through his lids. Hell, his gut was churning enough acid to dissolve nails, and his temples threatened an all-out revolt. By rights, he should see Carly home, then hit the hay himself. But in a night that redefined the word "unsatisfying," he was determined that it was long past time Carly Stewart came clean about a few things. For all their sakes.

"Nice to see I'm not the only person who likes sitting in the dark." From the doorway, her voice flowed over him, soothing, arousing. Exhausted.

Unmoving, he said, "Jeannie used to swear I was a mole in a previous life."

"My mother used to say the same thing about me. Please tell me I'm not hallucinating the coffee smell."

"Nope," he said, not sure what to make of her apparently not being in any hurry to get home, either. "Help yourself."

He heard her footsteps recede, the tap-tap of her those delicate high heels on the pine floor, then return; sensed more than saw her settle into the dirt-old recliner that had been his father's. Then he heard a pair of soft thuds—her shoes falling onto the rug—followed by the groan of the recliner's mechanism as she let it fall back. Light leaked from the kitchen, two rooms away, mingling with the soft-silver glow of moonlight filtering through the windows. Sam sat forward just enough to tug loose the afghan from the back of the sofa, tossing it over to her.

"Heat doesn't go on again until morning. You'll freeze."

She laughed, the sound not so much soft as *worn*. Rustling sounds ensued, offset by the muffled squawks of the old recliner, as she tucked the afghan around her legs. "You're nothing if not gallant. Thanks."

"Anytime." He paused, his weight heavy in the sofa cushions, trying to make out her face in the low light. "How's Lib?"

"Stable. She said to tell you she loves you and she'll see you in the morning." He heard her take a sip of coffee. "We talked some more."

"Yeah. I heard. That you were talking," he quickly added.

"Not what you were saying." He hesitated, waiting for her to fill in the blank. When she didn't, he prodded, "So…I take it you were going over what happened?"

A pause. "More or less."

"I think that's what's known as a cagey reply," Sam said.

No comment.

"Carly," he said as gently as he knew how, "what happened tonight…am I correct in thinking it brought up a whole bunch of personal issues for you?"

He could barely make out her lifting her mug to her lips, almost hear the quiet clunk of her setting it back on the table next to the chair. "It's not something I talk about."

And unless he was sorely mistaken, they were inching closer to a secret cave she'd kept well hidden for a very long time. "I gathered as much."

"Are you going to bug me to death until I do?"

He thought about it for a moment, then let out a quiet, "No. But I get the feeling there's something going on inside your head that might help me better understand my daughter."

Her laugh was thin. Dry. "Nice try. But despite how it might look on the surface, believe me—Libby and I are nothing alike."

"And if things had gone different for her tonight," he forced himself to say, "would that still be true? If she…if she hadn't gotten away."

He heard her sharp intake of breath. Then: "Yes. It would still be true."

"Because…" Talk about stabbing blindly. "Because she came to me?"

Another long pause, during which Sam fully expected her to rocket from the chair and hightail it out of there. But when she didn't, not after five, ten, thirty seconds had passed, he got the feeling somebody was ready to let him peek inside that cave. Whether or not she let him all the way inside, however, remained to be seen.

"Nothing goes beyond these four walls," he said, encouraging her. "You can trust me on that."

He heard more shifting, rearranging, before she finally said, "It happened at performing arts camp. I was fourteen. Barely. I got a major crush on a senior in high school, who for some reason returned my interest. I was so dazzled by having this 'older' guy wanting to be with me, I had no clue where things were headed. Until one day, he managed to find a way for us to be alone." The silence seemed to scream between them. "He outweighed me by seventy-five pounds," she said softly. "I *didn't* get away."

The lack of emotion in her words lanced through Sam more than any outburst would have. "And you never told anybody?"

That got another dry laugh. "A therapist or two. Later. Much later. But at the time, I was so sure it was my fault, that I'd somehow done something to make it happen. And I was sure if Dad found out he'd yank me back home so fast my head would spin. God knew how long it would have been before he'd let me out on my own again, since he hadn't wanted me to go to begin with. But Mom and I had worn him down—this was my chance for two classes a day, six days a week, my idea of heaven. I wasn't about to risk losing that. So. I toughed it out. Faked cramps for a couple days, then went back to taking class, focusing all my energies on the one thing I knew I could trust, no matter what."

"So…this jerk got off scot-free?"

"Yes, basically." At his grunt of disgust, she said, "I was a kid, Sam. And a hardheaded one at that. And I guess he knew I'd never say anything. In any case, he lost interest, moved on to somebody else. An older girl, another actress."

"And you didn't warn her?"

"Like she would have listened to an eighth-grader? Besides, from what I gathered—mainly her own big mouth sounding off in the girls' cabin—she was more than willing to meet Reece halfway. Or rather, all the way. In any case, the minute I'd said anything, the cat would've been out of the bag. Not a chance I could take."

Sam felt like somebody'd fast-frozen his gut. "It makes me sick, thinking of you going through that by yourself."

"It was a long time ago. Although I still occasionally enter-
tain this fantasy involving Reece's family jewels and a swarm
of fire ants."

Sam turned his head, barely making out her profile in the
dark. "Your father still doesn't know, does he?"

"No."

"Why not?"

She paused, then said, "I actually worked through most of
the earlier mess, about it being my fault and all that. And I was
finally able to transfer my inappropriate anger with myself to
Reece, where it belonged. The whole fire-ant thing and all that.
The guy was a jerk of the first order, end of story. But Dad's big
thing was protecting me, you know? Always has been, always
will be, I imagine. It would kill him to find out he was right.
That, in his mind, he shouldn't have let me go, because ulti-
mately, he couldn't protect me."

"It could have happened anywhere, Carly," Sam said quietly.
"As hard as it might be for a father to accept, we can't protect
our kids around the clock. I think you're wrong to keep it from
him."

"I'm sure you do. But, you know, I think I've caused the man
enough pain for one lifetime. Now that things are finally on
somewhat of an even keel, what would be the point of coming
clean about something that happened more than twenty years
ago, something he couldn't have done anything about then any
more than he could now?" She unfolded herself from the recliner, shedding the afghan like a skin. "It's late. Mind taking
me home?"

"Are you pissed? That I brought up the subject?"

He could tell she was looking at him. "No. Just worn-out.
Besides, if I hadn't wanted to talk about it, I wouldn't have."

"Yeah," Sam said, getting up, as well, every muscle in his
body screaming in protest. "That much, I already figured out."

But during the short drive back to her place, questions still
swirled in his brain, the answers to which might—might—help
make sense of the enigma that was Carly Stewart. And once in .

front of her house, Sam cut the engine and shifted in his seat, one wrist on the steering wheel, looking at her. Again, she could have left any time she wanted, it wasn't as if he was holding her.

But she didn't.

"What?" she said, one eyebrow arched.

"I'm not sure. Except…all the stuff you led me to believe, about all your…boyfriends. You make that up?"

Carly let out a soft laugh through her nose. "No. Why do you think that?"

"Because, dammit, something doesn't feel right, here. After what happened, especially, why would you be so…pardon me, but I don't know how else to say this…indiscriminate?"

"But that's the thing. I've never been indiscriminate." Her earrings flashed when she twisted back to stare out into the darkness. "I've always chosen my partners very, very carefully."

"How do you figure that?"

Her chest rose with the force of her breath before she returned her gaze to his. "Okay, fine—you want the truth? After Reece, I made a promise to myself that I'd never give another man power over me, or my feelings. That I'd never let emotions cloud my ability to see exactly who he was. Or who I was. I used men for sexual release, my dancing for emotional release. A plan which worked extremely well for a damn long time."

"So what you're saying is, you've had a lot of sex, but not a whole lot of lovemaking?"

"A blunt way of putting it, but yeah. That pretty much covers it."

"And this made you happy?"

"It made me *safe*. And that's all that mattered."

"So when was the last time a man kissed you because he actually *cared* about you?"

"That I know of?" God, her defiance was as substantial as a mirage. And five times more aggravating. "Never."

"Then it's high time somebody rectified that," he said, cupping one hand at the back of her neck to bring their mouths together.

Chapter 12

The kiss was careful, but not at all hesitant, his mouth sure and strong on hers, and she opened to him—oh, boy, did she open to him!—her tongue welcoming his like a long lost friend. Her fingers curled into his shirt, encouraging him closer, as tingles of need shot here, there and everywhere, blasting her emotions—her resolve—to kingdom come. He tasted of strong, sweet coffee, smelled of suede and wood smoke, earthy scents, *real* scents, and her poor little old self went ballistic, wanting him on a level so deep, so basic, there were no words to describe it.

Sam's lips left hers, pulling from hers a tiny "oh!" of loss, and he smiled—a slight curve of his mouth, nothing more—and kissed her again, deeper this time, his tongue stroking hers as gently as his fingers now stroked her cheek. Rough fingers, *real* fingers, the fingers of a man who had nothing to prove, whose technique, Carly realized with a pang, had developed through the years with a woman he'd loved with all his heart. The old, familiar ache blossomed between her legs, her nipples greedy, desperate for attention; that she'd become aroused so quickly, so completely, she vaguely tossed off to six months of celibacy, the emotional drain of the evening.

Liar, a voice whispered.

She guided Sam's hand to her breast, the thin fabric of the dress, her sheer bra, little barrier to his skin on hers. She heard him sigh, a shuddering, soulful sound, heard her own soft moan of despair when he removed his hand. He touched his forehead to hers, shaking his head.

"We can't do this. Not until you understand it's not just about sex."

After a moment, she pulled away, hurt. Aching. "Then we can't do this at all. Not unless you're willing to accept it can *only* be about sex."

To her surprise, he lifted a hand, brushed back her hair. "Then this probably isn't a real good time to mention that I'm falling in love with you."

Her heart lodged in her windpipe. "Why?" she barely got out. "Of all the people…" She turned back around, her vision blurred. "Why?" she asked again.

"I have no idea. Just seems right."

"Right? How the hell could this possibly be *right?* Good God, Sam…" When she faced him again, his eyes shone in the moonlight, as calm and steady as the man himself. "This doesn't make a drop of sense."

"Can't argue with you there," he said, that damned inscrutable smile tugging at his lips. "Corny as it sounds, I never thought I'd feel this strongly about anybody else, ever again. I sure as hell didn't want to. And you better believe I tried to talk myself out of it, because this *doesn't* make sense." His smile gentled. "Didn't work. So, I figured I may as well let you know how things looked from over here. Because I can't see how it could hurt, letting you know you're loved."

"Oh, Sam…" She blew out a sigh, thinking, *Hurt doesn't even begin to cover it, buddy,* then pushed open the truck door. "You need to get back to the kids," she said, and he said, "Yeah,

I know," as the wind whipped around the yard, sending a couple of dry twigs skating across the windshield.

She got out of the truck, then turned back, still holding the door open. "I'm so sorry…"

"I wasn't expecting an echo, Carly," Sam said softly, releasing the clutch. "I just figured you needed to know that somebody cares. Somebody who doesn't give a damn about whatever you might have done in your past."

"But your kids—"

"This isn't about my kids, dammit. This is about you. About you needing to get used to the idea of being loved, so maybe you'll stop feeling so empty inside. Because, believe me, I know what that feels like, and it's a bitch." He looked out the window. "To be so lonely sometimes, you think you're gonna go crazy." When he returned his gaze to hers, one side of his mouth curved up. "So, okay, I guess it's about me, too. Because I finally realized, as much as I love my kids, it was like I had this empty room in my heart, just sitting there, waiting for somebody to come along and claim it." When she didn't say anything—what on earth *could* she say?—he added, "Now, I have no intention of pestering you about this. I've said my piece, and now I'm just going to love you, from near, from far, from wherever, until you get used to the idea. Once you do that…" His shoulders lifted, then dropped. "I suppose we'll go from there."

"You're insane," she said quietly.

"Tell me something I don't know," he said, then put the truck in gear and drove off into the night.

Well. That didn't go too badly, he didn't think, other than his being so turned on he was half tempted to go jump in the ice-cold pond, clothes and all. Man, he'd sure opened a can of worms with those kisses. And for all his nobleness about telling her they wouldn't make love unless and until she realized he wouldn't do it just for the sex, he hoped to hell she held to her end of the bargain. Because another couple of kisses like that, and it wouldn't much matter what she said, he'd have them both naked and panting in two seconds flat.

Although you better believe he wasn't going to tell her that.

The house was quiet when he got back, everybody asleep. He assumed Libby was asleep, anyway, since her light had been out when he pulled around back. He poured himself the last cup of coffee and went back out onto the porch to sit and ponder his foolishness, the moonlight so liquid he half expected the air to ripple if he reached out his hand.

Lane had taken a chance, driving into town to Ivy's. That she'd be awake, that she'd let him in. All her front lights were still on when he pulled up in front of her house, but he sat in the car for a few minutes, until, through her pulled blinds, he saw her shadow cross the room.

She was still dressed, in a sweater and one of her long skirts, when she opened to door to him. Judging from her lack of reaction, she wasn't all that surprised to see him standing there.

"We need to talk," he said.

She opened the door wider and let him inside.

Carly had been so stunned by Sam's declaration that she'd gone up to her bedroom, changed into her flannel jammies and robe, returned to the kitchen and was halfway through making herself a sandwich she then decided she didn't even want before it registered her father wasn't there. A realization that barely even blipped on the old radar screen before she sank like a stone back into the quagmire of her own tangled thoughts.

Where she still was, sitting on the sofa in the dark, when Dad returned some time later.

"How come you're still up?" he said from the doorway.

Oh, no special reason, other than having a man tell me something I have no earthly idea what to do with. "Couldn't sleep," she said.

Lane removed his coat and hung it on the coatrack, then came into the room, sitting in the wing chair. "Yeah, Sam told me about what happened to Libby tonight." Oh, right. Libby. Something else to drop into the morass. "Anybody hear from the boy yet?"

"Not that I know of. If the kid has a grain of sense, he's halfway to Canada by now."

Her father's chuckle sounded weary. "Not that anybody's asking me, but from what I saw of the boy, I wouldn't have pegged him as a monster. Maybe he just got his signals crossed?"

"He tried to rape her, Dad," Carly said, equally wearily, thinking, *And isn't* that *rich?* As if Dad wouldn't have strung Reece up by his gonads if he'd found out what happened. "That goes way past crossed signals."

Her father was quiet for several seconds, then said, "Trying to force somebody to do something they don't want to do is never right. Or that 'getting carried away' is a valid excuse. All I'm saying is it wouldn't hurt to hear his side of the story."

Carly's ears rang, even as she knew her father was right. She'd seen Sean with Libby enough over the past few weeks to get the feeling that, yeah, he was perpetually hot and horny, but he had seemed to genuinely care about her. She pushed out a sigh.

"Sex is such a pain in the butt," she said, forgetting this was her father she was talking to.

"Tell me about it."

She roused herself out of the quagmire long enough to realize where he must have been. "You were at Ivy's?"

"Yeah." She heard his fingers drumming against the arm of the chair. "I went over there to talk. So we talked."

"Is it me, or is this not sounding good?"

Another pause, then: "You think I mention your mother too much?"

"The two of you were married for like a million years," she said gently. "Of course you talk about her. It would be weird if you didn't."

"Ivy hates it."

A fierce protectiveness threaded through all the other junk inside Carly's head. "Well, for crying out loud—what does she expect? That you're simply going to forget about Mom, that she's never going to come up in the conversation again? That would be like…like me suddenly not thinking or talking about dancing, just because I'm no longer a professional dancer. It's been my life since I was ten years old—"

"And you're not ready to move on to something else, are you?"

"What?"

"I mean, it's still too much a part of who you are for you to even think about doing something else, isn't it?"

"It'll *always* be a part of who I am."

"Because it's your first love. And it's not that easy to let go of a first love, is it?"

"Dad? What are you saying?"

"I'm saying, that as well as Ivy and I get along, she made me realize that as long as your mother's still the first thing I think about when I wake up in the morning, I guess I'm not as ready for a new relationship as I thought. And she's right—that's not fair to her."

Carly finally realized what he was saying. "Ohmigod…you broke up?"

"Sounds a little high school, but I guess you could call it that."

"Oh, Dad…I'm so sorry." She squinted in the darkness, trying to make out his features. "You okay?"

"Yes, yes…" He got up, stretching out his back. "I'm fine. It's Ivy I feel bad for, though. I didn't mean…well. Guess none of this gets any easier as we get older, huh?"

Carly thought of Sam, his kisses, his confession, his bizarrely calm conviction that loving her was the right thing to do, and shook her head, tears stinging her eyes. "No, it sure doesn't."

"Guess I'll go on to bed, then," her father said. "Whaddya say we go over to Claremore tomorrow and pick up some appliances for the barn?"

She felt as though, somehow, her life had detached itself from *her*, and was speeding ahead, giving her the choice of getting the lead out in order to catch up, or getting left behind in the dust—

"Lee? Are you okay?"

How much effort she'd put into running from what she saw as the prison of her father's protectiveness for so many years. How strenuously she'd balked at any attempt on his part to simply do his job. How fiercely she'd resisted any relationship that ceded control of her feelings—of anything, really—to another human being.

"No," she said at last, on a long, ragged breath, then blinked when her father turned on a small table lamp nearby. "Sam says he's in love with me."

Her father's brows lifted, but when he crossed back to sit beside her, wrapping one strong arm around her shoulders, she could feel his understanding.

"That's quite a gift he's offering you," Lane said, his chin resting on top of her head.

"I know." She swiped at a tear trickling down her cheek.

"You know yet whether you want to keep it?"

His chin was sharp, roughened with beard stubble, when she shook her head.

"Well, does knowing this make you feel good? Or bad?"

"Would it make me sound like one messed up chick to say…both?"

"Nope. Not at all."

She wasn't sure if that made her feel better or not.

The next day, Carly and Lane hadn't been back from the Home Depot in Claremore more than ten minutes—there were now more appliances and bathroom fixtures than you could shake a stick at in the bed of Dad's truck—when she heard Sean's Eclipse wheeze up in front of the house.

Mildly annoyed at having to wait to play with her new toys, Carly glowered at the very stricken young man on her porch. A very stricken young man who looked for all the world as though he'd spent the night in a ditch somewhere. Carly crossed her arms, not inviting him in. The kid actually hung his head, peering up at her through his bangs.

"C'n I talk to you?"

"Why me? I'm not the one you—"

"I know, I know. It's just…Libby's always talkin' about you, about how cool you are and stuff, so I thought maybe…" The sentence ended in a shrug.

"There is no way I'm pleading your case, Sean," she said, as coldly as she could manage. "What you did was reprehensible."

That he didn't protest was a point in his favor. A tiny point, but a point. The kid stuffed his hands into his back pockets and glanced away, his breath frosting in front of his face. Behind him, dark, mean-looking clouds tumbled over one another, threatening to let loose at any moment. Obliquely, Carly remembered she now lived in Tornado Alley, then reassured herself that this was late October—tornado season was over.

Sean's gaze was once again trained on her face, the wind whipping his long, blond hair across his forehead. "I know what I did was wrong. I guess…things got out of hand, okay?"

"No, not okay. Not okay at all." She uncrossed her arms to cram her hands inside her hoodie's pouch. "Do you have *any* idea how frightened and upset and sick you made Libby?"

The boy's Adam's apple bobbed as he swallowed. Then he said, eyes lowered, "I really thought that's what she wanted."

"In the *auto shop?* For God's sake, Sean—what the *hell* kind of first time would that have been for her?"

To her shock, the boy's lower lip started to quiver, as two huge tears crested on his lower lids, and she silently swore, realizing, *Oh, hell*—Sean was only a kid himself. A stupid, overlibidoed kid who had very possibly just screwed up any possibility of Libby's ever talking to him again, but a kid, nonetheless.

She shut her eyes for a moment, reminding herself that this wasn't Reece. Reece, who'd never even given her a phony apol-

ogy, never admitted his culpability, never showed her, or anyone else, that he'd had even a sliver of regret for what he'd done.
Still, as much as she hated what Sean had tried to do, it wasn't
right to judge him for somebody else's sins.

"It's not up to me to run interference between you and Libby.
Or even to give you permission to see her, or talk to her. That's
up to her father."

Sean nodded, wiping his nose with the back of his hand. On
a sigh, Carly removed a wad of tissues from her pocket, peeled
off a clean one and gave it to him. "Well, come on, then," she
said, pushing past him to walk over to his car. "Might as well
get this over with."

She wrenched open the passenger side door; Sean scampered around to the other side and was in his seat with the car
started before she'd even gotten herself inside. "Thank you so
much, Miss Stewart—"

She held up one hand, stopping him. "You've got some major
groveling to do before I even think about removing you from
my S-list, buddy. If and when Libby says she's forgiven you,
then we'll talk."

The boy swallowed, nodded, and took off out of her yard so
fast her head bounced off the headrest.

"Daddy," Wade said, knee deep in pigs. "What's Sean doin'
here?"

Libby had ventured out of her room long enough to an-
nounce, "If Sean calls or shows up, tell him I died," which was
apparently enough to give her brothers the impression she didn't
like him anymore. So his appearance now, less than twenty-four
hours after the incident, was cause for some speculation.

His being with Carly—whose expression was that of one
mightily pissed woman—was cause for even more.

Sam stomped as much pig muck off his boots as he could,
then left the pen, turning his collar up against the biting cold.
"Go on," he heard Carly say, "you're not going to get anywhere
near Libby without getting past Sam first."

Sam's gaze touched Carly's for a second, then veered back to the sorry-looking—in more ways than one—boy in front of him. Wouldn't be long before the kid was taller than him, but that day hadn't arrived yet and Sam felt no qualms whatsoever about taking full advantage of that fact.

"Sean," he said, making his voice as low and menacing as possible. Out of the corner of his eye, he saw Carly bite down on her lip to keep from smiling, so he threw a warning glare her way. She bit down harder, then turned away altogether. "What are you doing here?"

"I—I came to apologize. F-for my behavior last night."

Sam slipped his hands into his front pockets and glared some more. "You come to apologize to me? Or Libby?"

"Anybody who'll listen, I suppose."

Now it was Sam who had to fight to keep a straight face. Not that his anger had abated any, far from it—Libby had spent far too much time in her room crying her eyes out for that—but it'd been a long time since he'd seen anyone that miserable. Gave a whole new meaning to the word "hangdog." Wade had gone back inside; now Sam could sense assorted sets of eyes at assorted windows, glued to the scene. He doubted Libby's were among them, however.

"You know," he said, "right now I can't quite decide if your coming out here is one of the bravest or one of the dumbest things I've ever witnessed."

Sean peered up at Sam, a weak smile, like a flickering lightbulb, playing around his mouth. "Me, neither. Sir."

"Daddy?"

The boy went rigid, like he'd been struck by lightning. Sam turned to see Libby standing at the door, half in, half out, her arms tightly folded across her middle. "Sean says he's here to apologize," he shouted over to her.

"Oh. Well, I guess that'd be okay," she yelled back after a moment over the whistling wind. "Long as it doesn't mean I'm obligated to forgive him."

The boy winced as Carly shouted over, "Absolutely not."

Sean stepped around Sam—a courageous move on his part, Sam thought—and said, "I just wanna talk, Lib." He paused, then said, "I was an idiot, okay?" and Libby said, "You got that right," and Carly's soft chuckle mingled with the relief washing over him that Libby was probably gonna be fine.

Nobody said anything for a minute or two; then Libby disappeared inside the house, letting the screen door slam behind her. Sean seemed to deflate, until she reappeared a couple seconds later, wearing her heavy chore coat over her sweater and jeans. And some sparkly pink lipstick, Sam noticed. She trooped down the steps and over to where they all stood, saying to Sean, "I got stuff to do in the barn, you can talk to me there if you want," then kept going, her long hair bouncing against her back, gleaming dully in the thick, gray light.

Sean looked back at Sam, hopeful.

"Go on," he said. "But so help me—"

"I won't touch her," the boy said, hands raised in surrender. "I swear."

"Smart man," Sam said, and the kid spun around and took off, nearly tripping over himself in his split to catch up to Libby, who could make tracks like nobody's business when she was mad.

Sam turned back to find Carly looking inordinately pleased with herself.

"You put the fear of God in that boy or what?" Sam asked.

"From what I could tell, that was pretty much already there when he landed on my doorstep. I just tightened the screws a bit." She jerked her head toward the barn. "You sure you're okay with leaving them alone?"

"Not much he can try on a girl with a pitchfork in her hand," he said, and Carly laughed. Then she sobered, her eyes steady in his, her hands shoved in her pockets of her flimsy sweatshirt. It occurred to Sam she must be freezing.

"Just so you know," she said, "I don't think I slept five minutes all night."

"Was it something I said?"

"Yeah, as a matter of fact."

The boys came shooting out of the house like bullets from a six-shooter. Which pretty much described the sound of the screen door *whapping* shut behind each of them in turn. Travis wandered over to Sam to wrap around his leg, but the rest took turns diving headfirst into a pile of leaves that Sam fully intended to toss into the compost heap, one of these days. He watched Carly's attempts at not flinching every time one of the guys let loose with a bellowed, "Carly! Watch what I can do!" or "Carly! Did you see that?"

Her eyes lifted to his. "You, um, wouldn't by any chance be having second thoughts? About what you said last night?"

"'Fraid not."

"Just checking."

Travis let go of Sam's leg to sidle over to Carly; woman and child stared silently at each other for several seconds, then resumed their observation of the goings-on in the yard. When Travis slipped his hand into Carly's, her head snapped to Sam's, panic huge in her eyes.

Sam chuckled. "I had a pup once, when I was a kid, who'd cornered one of the barn cats one day and got popped on the nose for his efforts. From then on, every time he saw that cat, he got pretty much the same look on his face you're wearing right now."

That earned him another smirk, but her shoulders did seem to relax some. She glanced down at Travis, who'd plugged his thumb into his mouth, then sighed. "I don't know how to do this. Any of it."

"Let you in on a secret—neither does anybody else."

"Is that supposed to make me feel better?"

"Is this you tellin' me that maybe there's a reason you're worryin' about any of this?"

After a long moment, she said, "Maybe."

He nudged her arm with his elbow, bringing her eyes back to his. He winked. "This mean you like me?"

She angled her head toward Travis, who grinned up at her

around his thumb. Pulling Trav's and her linked hands inside her kangaroo pouch to keep it warm, she again focused on the rest of his rowdy boys. "Yeah, S-Sam," she said, shivering. "I l-like you."

He lifted one hand to massage the tight muscles at the base of her neck, savoring the tiny thrill of victory when she let him.

Chapter 13

"Ladies and gentlemen..." Carly caught Sam's grin as he twisted the thermostat dial, then executed an exaggerated courtly flourish. "We have heat!"

Her applause echoed off the rafters. Amazing what two men—and whichever friends they could hoodwink to help—could accomplish in a week. But the barn was now fit for human habitation, with appliances and running water and heat, which, with three south-facing windows, she'd only need on cloudy days. Like this past week, when a series of storms sweeping across the state had kept things damp and bone-chillingly cold.

But at least she had a place of her own, now. And, much to her amazement, she thought, skimming her palm across the top of the double barre her father had helped her install against the one wall, a *business* of her own. God knew she wouldn't be turning out a string of candidates for the Joffrey or New York City Ballet, but by the time Faith Andrews—and Faith's mother Didi (there was a lot to be said for being a pastor's wife), and Ruby at the diner and about a half dozen other ladies Carly wasn't even sure she'd met yet—had gotten through spreading the word, she had a fairly sizable dance-exercise class for the women, a couple "movement" classes for the kids, including something for the teenagers, and maybe even a real ballet class or two for some of the girls. Faith had helped her come up with a fee structure she thought most folks could afford, although she said Carly might want to consider trading goods or services from time to time for those folks who might be short on cash. Carly thought that sounded perfectly fair to her.

Of course, whether or not she actually made a go of this, she couldn't predict. Sure, everybody was enthusiastic now, but she hadn't fallen off the turnip truck in the last ten minutes. People got busy, got bored, got tired. Except she knew all too well how much dancing fed something basic inside most human beings. So maybe, just maybe, this would take. Even here.

And if she found even one jewel, one child with the potential to go all the way…well. That would be the icing on the cake.

"My grandma used to call what you're doing woolgathering," Sam said behind her, startling her.

She turned, smiling. "You know, if anybody'd told me three months ago I was going to open a dance school in a tiny town in Oklahoma, I would have said they were off their nut."

He squatted to check out something with the heating gizmo. "Yep. Funny how often things work out in ways we could never have dreamed of."

Her gaze lingered on his back, muscled and lean underneath layers of cotton and flannel. He liked to wear plaid or denim shirts over T-shirts or Henleys, and they always smelled like a combination of smoke and the outdoors and animal and some scent that was uniquely Sam.

And she was getting more and more desperate to smell the uniquely Sam part without all the rest.

But he'd been true to his word, about not pushing, not crowding, giving her time and space to absorb his feelings for her with no pressure to return them. Still, simply knowing how he felt should have sent her shrieking in the other direction, should have annoyed her, or terrified her. Something. But somehow, as long as he left things in her control—that nothing would happen unless and until she wanted it to—she was okay. Borderline, some days, but still…okay.

That they would eventually sleep together wasn't even a question, she doubted in Sam's mind any more than it was in hers. What *was* in question was an indefinable something that went to the core of who she'd always thought she was. The old Carly would have been content enough to wait it out, to play along, letting him think he was in charge of the hows and whens. The old Carly wouldn't have thought twice about manipulating the situation, maybe even conning him into thinking her feelings had changed, just so he'd take her to bed.

Unfortunately this new pain-in-the-butt Carly apparently had a conscience. The new Carly couldn't deny that, even if she wasn't sure how strong her feelings were for the man, she still cared for him, and about him, and respected him far much too much to ever deceive him. However, she could tell this arm's length business was killing Sam as much as it was her. All the scruples and good intentions in the world couldn't disguise the heat in his eyes when he looked at her. Especially considering this was a man whose entire life was defined by a palpable, physical connection to his environment. So from where she stood, the issue wasn't "if"—the issue was who would crack first.

And Carly's money—all buck-fifty of it—was on Sam.

He could feel her eyes on his back, could pretty much figure what she was thinking. And boy, it would be so easy to give in to the clawing, brutal hunger that had more or less poleaxed him these past few days, a hunger intensified tenfold every time she looked at him with those crystal-clear eyes of hers, eyes that all but begged him to take her.

Sam got to his feet, nodding in approval at his own handiwork. "Long as you keep the overhead fans on, you should be able to keep the heat from settling up in the rafters. At least the guy insulated before he put on the new roof."

"Just in time," she said. "The moms are coming for their first class tomorrow."

By some sort of unspoken understanding, there'd been no more talk about his feelings for her, or what anybody was going to do about them, since Sean's visit the other day. Sam knew his confession had rattled Carly—which had been his intention—but he'd kept his promise about not pestering her. Anybody listening in to their conversations over the past week would have thought they were simply neighbors, nothing more.

If they weren't listening real closely, that is.

"Well, I better get going. Polls close in an hour."

"Oh, that's right! Since Dad and I aren't residents yet, I can't vote." Sam wondered if she even realized she'd said "yet"—a pretty strong word for somebody who still held to the notion that she might not stick around. "You think Ivy'll get the job?"

"Oh, I'd say she's got a pretty good shot, but there's lots of folks, older ones, mostly, who still haven't gotten over her having the nerve to raise an out-of-wedlock child right under their noses."

Carly's gaze tangled with his for a moment before she walked back to her little kitchen, twisting on the burner to stare at the dancing blue flame. "Wow. I can cook and everything. If I cooked, that is."

"Okay, what's eatin' at you now?"

She flicked off the burner, then faced him, her arms crossed over a sweater big enough for a cow. "Good Lord, Sam— Dawn's, what, in her early thirties? And you're telling me people are *still* bent out of shape about Ivy not being married when she had her?"

"Some people. Not everybody. Not anywhere near everybody."

"Yeah, well, what's gonna happen if *some* people find out about the new dance teacher's past, huh? How do you think they're going to react if they discover I was in rehab at twenty?" Her mouth thinned. "And again at twenty-three?"

He flashed back to their first conversation at his kitchen

table, all those weeks ago. How uneasy she'd seemed when she'd talked about her career, like she'd been leaving out certain parts that at the time she'd clearly felt were none of his business. And no wonder, he thought as an unseen fist reached inside his chest and squeezed his heart near to breaking.

"First off," he said softly, "unless you go around tellin' 'em, I'm not sure how they'd find out. And secondly, it's really beginning to tick me off, the way you keeping putting yourself down all the time."

"I'm not putting myself down! I had to overcome a helluva lot to kick that monkey off my back, and I'm damn proud that it's been fifteen years since I've even been tempted to look down that road, let alone *go* down it. But I also know that the past has a nasty way of coming back to bite a person in the butt. All I'm saying is…" She pushed out a sigh. "*Some* people might have a problem with sending their children to somebody like me."

"What? You think this town is some Utopia, where nobody ever does anything bad, or stupid, or has a secret they don't want gettin' out?"

"No, of course not. But—"

"But nothing. There's girls around here who don't know the fathers of their babies, folks who think nobody knows there's alcoholism in their families, guys who've done time for things they should've known better than to do to begin with. I swear, sometimes I think you carry your past around like it's some kind of damn crown or something, as if nobody's ever done anything wrong except you."

"What the hell would you know about it, Sam? For crying out loud, you're like the most perfect human being on the freakin' planet! What have you ever done to be sorry for?"

"Believe me, I could give you a list that'd make your eyeballs fall out of your head. But for starters, how about takin' up with another woman less than a week after my wife's death? Would that do it for you?"

His words hung between them like thick, acrid smoke.

"You're making that up."

Sam's laugh, if you could call it that, scraped his throat on the way out. "Oh, believe me, I'm not making it up."

For several seconds, the only sounds were the fans' soft whirr, the periodic hum of the heater cycling on and off. Then she closed the few feet between them to thread her arms around his waist, laying her head against his chest. Eventually Sam returned the favor, enveloping her. Wishing he could somehow absorb her. "What's this for?" he asked.

"For being human," she said, then tilted her face up to his, her eyes reflecting his old pain. "What happened?"

So he told her the whole sad story, a story he'd never told another living soul, about how, after Jeannie's funeral, he'd been so overcome with grief and confusion he was afraid to be around the kids, that he couldn't be the pillar they needed him to be.

"So I got Didi and Chuck Meyerhauser—Faith's parents— to stay with them after they'd gone to bed, and I took the truck and just...drove. Ended up in Vinita, ran into some gal Jeannie and I went to school with. Katrina Nichols. She hadn't heard about Jeannie, and when I told her, she was real...sympathetic." He leaned back to meet Carly's eyes. "Can you tell where this is goin', or are you gonna make me go into the gory details?"

"No, I think I've got the general idea. Except...why?"

"Because the only way I could think to make the hurt go away was by making myself hurt even more."

On a soft moan, Carly nestled against him again. "Was it just the one time?"

Sam shut his eyes. "No." Then, on a released breath, he opened them again. "Until I realized what an ass I was being, that I was only putting off the inevitable. So I called it off after a couple weeks. Took a while longer, though, before I stopped hating myself."

"And Katrina?"

"Understood what was going on inside my head a helluva

lot better than I did. Last I heard, she moved to Oklahoma City, got married, had a kid. Far as I know, she never told anybody about the time I'd lost my mind."

After a moment, Carly slipped out of his arms, linked their hands, then stood on tiptoe to kiss him on the cheek.

"Go vote," she said quietly, steering him toward the door.

By the time Ivy finished up delivering Angel Clearwater's newest grandson up near Bushyhead, made sure mother and baby were stable and got back to Dawn's and Cal's, where everybody was waiting to hear whether she'd won or not, the polls had been closed for a good two hours already. She'd been too busy earlier to think about it much, but now, seeing so many cars and trucks parked every-which-way across the front yard, knowing all these people were here for her, her stomach felt like a herd of buffalo was stampeding through it.

Which, believe it or not, was better than how she'd been feeling for the past week, ever since she and Lane parted ways.

She had to park her old Ford pickup a good fifty feet from the house, which gave her ample time to collect herself before facing everybody. Telling Lane she couldn't see him anymore had ranked right up there with the top five or so hardest things she'd ever had to do in her life. Had she been younger—much younger—she'd probably have let things ride, enjoyed the relationship for whatever she could get out of it. What a kick in the butt to discover, at this point in her life, when pickings were about as pitiful as they could get, malewise, that her tolerance level for men who couldn't make up their minds was a big, fat zero.

But, oh, how she missed him, she thought as she trudged up the porch steps, smiling at the laughter spilling from inside, laughter from her family, all those friends who'd stood by her through the years. That wife of his had been one lucky woman, that was for sure. Too bad she cast such a big shadow.

"There's our next mayor!" Dawn shouted when Ivy opened the door, and a roar went up from the crowd.

Ivy clucked, setting down her delivery bag on a table next to the door and unwrapping herself from her poncho. "Aren't y'all bein' a little premature?"

Ruby Kennedy, all decked out in what Ivy assumed was the fanciest dress the woman owned, a brocade number dating back to a time before Ruby's breasts had reached their current impressive proportions, let out a loud laugh. "You know how I was conducting that exit poll the other day? Askin' folks who they were gonna vote for as they left the diner? It was runnin' close, I won't lie to you, but by the end of the day, you were still ahead."

"Right," Ivy said, laughing. "Like folks were gonna be straight with you, seeings as they know you're my friend, for one thing. And for another, who'd be fool enough to risk getting cut off from Jordy's barbecued ribs?"

"Well, you might have a point at that," the black woman admitted, which got everyone to laughing. The dining table was loaded with just about every goody imaginable, and as Ivy loaded her plate—birthing gave her almost as much of an appetite as it did her mothers—she could really feel Mary's and Hank Logan, Sr.'s presence in the ranch house where they'd raised their three sons. Mary had been her first friend when she'd landed in town thirty years ago, and along with her husband had been there for her when she decided to stay, even after discovering she was pregnant by a man who couldn't have married her, even if she'd wanted him to. So it seemed more than fitting that they should be here, in a way, to see how far she'd come.

Of course, if she only got—she counted heads—twenty-two votes, then it was all moot, she supposed.

"Mama!" Dawn hollered. "Your cell's ringing, but I can't find it!"

"Oh, my word…" She shuffled across the floor as quickly as she could, careful not to upend her full plate. "It's in my purse, honey…you got it?"

Three people shouted, "There it is," and Dawn pounced on

the bag, tearing the big leather contraption open and fishing out the phone, which she slammed to her ear. "No, Beverly Ann, it's Dawn. But Mama's right here, hold on!"

Somebody took the plate from Ivy's hands as Dawn handed her the phone. Beverly Ann was about a hundred and fifty and had been tallying votes in Haven since Truman was in office. A hush fell across the room, but Ivy could still barely hear Beverly Ann—who never spoke above a whisper, anyway—for all the rushing in her ears. Something about being really close, they had to do a recount….

"But you're sure now?"

"Oh, yes, honey. We're just having them post it up on the Git-n-Go sign now. And congratulations—'bout time we had some fresh ideas around here!"

Ivy clicked off her phone, then stood there with it clutched to her chest.

"Well, for pity's sake, girl," said Luralene, her magenta lipstick a nice contrast to the orange hair. "Don't keep us in suspense! Didja win or not?"

Ivy scanned the room, all those expectant, loving faces…and nodded.

"I did," she said, still disbelieving. "You're lookin' at your new mayor."

There were shouts and screams and hugs and kisses and an off-key chorus of "For she's a jolly good fellow," and in the midst of it all, the doorbell rang. Well, she assumed the doorbell rang, because suddenly the crowd parted right down the middle so she had a straight shot at the open door.

Where Lane stood, with a huge smile on his face and the biggest damn bunch of flowers Ivy'd ever seen.

Lane could tell, he'd caught Ivy off guard. Well, good. Because even if he couldn't give her anything else—like his whole heart, undivided—he could at least give her a few minutes of whatever she was feeling right now. Surprise. Delight. The knowledge that he really did care about her, even if not as much as she needed.

She'd barely had a chance to snag that blanket thing she wore before he dragged her out onto the porch. Then he shut the door on everyone's bug-eyed staring so he could take her by the shoulders and kiss her, flowers squashed between them and all.

She blinked those big, brown eyes that drove him crazy. "B-but, how'd you know I won?"

"I didn't. Not until I got here and heard the cheer. But I figured you could use the flowers, either way. That if you didn't win, maybe you could use some cheering up."

She didn't say anything for a long time after that, just stood staring at the bouquet as though she'd never seen flowers before. Then she finally said, "You know, it would make this mess a whole lot easier if you weren't so damn *nice*."

"Yeah, I know. It's a curse."

She snorted a laugh through her nose, lifted her face to his. "Thank you."

"You're welcome. And congratulations, Ms. Mayor. Now go back inside and enjoy your victory party."

She waved the flowers toward the door. "You're welcome to join us…."

"Let's not complicate things any more than they already are." He kissed her again, a short peck on her lips, then went down the porch steps, his head bent against the obnoxious wind.

"Lane?" she called, and he turned back. "This goes against everything I've ever believed in as a woman…but—"

"No buts, Ivy. And no compromises. That wouldn't be fair to either one of us, would it?"

Hugging the flowers, she finally said, "No, you're right. Still, I don't mind tellin' you that you've just made my little triumph a whole lot sweeter."

He blew her a kiss, then walked away from what he knew had been his only shot at a second chance.

While rinsing off the dinner dishes before she put them into the dishwasher, Libby could smell Mike and Matt before she saw them.

"Eww," she said, shielding her nose with the back of her hand. "Both of you have got to take showers tonight, you stink to high heaven! When was the last time y'all cleaned out the chicken coop anyway?"

"This afternoon," Mike said. "Which is why we stink." He took the dish out of her hand to stack it in the dishwasher, and Libby stared at him. Then at Matt, who was staring at her. Then she noticed Wade and Frankie were sitting at the kitchen table, staring at her, instead of out in the living room, staring at the TV. She did not have a good feeling about this.

"Okay. Who did what?"

"Nothin'," Mike said, holding up his hands when she gave him a "Yeah, right" look. "I swear. It's just Matt and me think we should have a family conference."

"Well, yeah, okay. As soon as Daddy's finished giving Trav his bath—"

"Without Daddy," Matt said, his expression about as serious as she'd ever seen it.

She glanced around the room, from brother to brother, then finally back at Mike, who, while nearly three years younger than she was, had passed her in height some time ago. "Okay, I guess. What about?"

The boys looked at each other. Then Matt said, "Carly."

"Okay, guys," Carly called out to the group of panting, sweaty teens. "Time's up." This was met with assorted "Aw, man's" and groans that swelled her heart, she had to admit. All girls in this group, dressed in everything from sweats to bicycle pants and tees, some barefoot, some in sneakers. The last thing Carly expected was for them, or their parents, to shell out for real dancewear. And Mike's and Matt's enthusiasm notwithstanding, she hadn't expected boys to show up, not in this age group, although she still entertained hopes of pulling a Jacques d'Amboise with the younger kids one day, filling the room with both genders.

"Hey, Carly," one girl called out, a tall blond cheerleader type named Billie. "You think you could show us how to dance like that chick in *Chicago?* The dark-haired one, I mean, not Renee whatshername."

"Yeah, that'd be so cool!"

"Can you, Carly? Can you?"

She laughed. Bob Fosse was probably spinning in his grave. "We can try, I guess. I'll rewatch the movie between now and then, see what I think."

With a chorus of "All rights!" and "Bye, nows!" they all filed out into the raw, gray day. Libby, however, stayed behind, slipping a sweatshirt on over a double layer of tank tops in turquoise and lime-green.

"Hey, Lib, what's up? Want some hot chocolate? I finally found a sugar-free brand that doesn't taste like poison."

"Uh, yeah. Sure." She followed Carly into the kitchenette, but there was no place to sit, so she stood, shifting from foot to foot.

"Haven't seen you around much."

"Dad's been substituting all week, so I've had to watch the boys more, do more around the farm. You know."

Carly stuck two water-filled mugs into the microwave, doing her level best to appear calm when she felt anything but. Whatever was on the girl's mind, she had a strong feeling she didn't want to hear it. Not now, at any rate.

For the past three days, ever since Sam's telling her his little secret, Carly's brain had felt like a gerbil on an exercise wheel. Not because of the secret itself—even though her heart still ached at how horribly he must have been suffering, to be driven to do something that out of character—but because he'd entrusted her with it. That had rocked her far more, even, than his telling her he loved her. That he found her trust*worthy*…well. There was a role no one had ever bestowed upon her before. Or that she'd let anyone bestow upon her.

And annoying as it was, understanding that fact had wedged open her heart a little more.

"Carly?" Libby said. "The microwave dinged?"

"What? Oh, sorry...drifted off, there." She retrieved the mugs, stirred hot chocolate mix into them, then handed one to the girl. "Let's go sit," she said, leading Libby back out to the studio, where she'd arranged a cluster of chairs and a sofa for parents to sit and watch, if they wanted to. Her sleeping loft was basically a mattress on the floor, a chest of drawers and an iron pipe across the tops of two ladders to hang her clothes, and she was as content as if she'd been given one of those eye-popping mansions they used on those dating reality shows.

"What's doing with you and Sean?" Carly asked, pulling her feet up under her on the chair-and-a-half, while Libby piled onto the sofa.

She took a cautious sip of her hot chocolate, then peered up at Carly. "Other than me feeling like an idiot?"

"Why would you think that?"

Eye-roll time. Then: "I don't get it, Carly. How could I be so sure I thought I knew I wanted it one minute, then totally change my mind the next?"

She could almost feel her own ambivalence about Sam whisper *Yeah, I can't wait to hear how you answer* this *one.* "Well...maybe because the reality of the situation didn't exactly meet your expectations?"

Libby seemed to think this over for a second, then let out a breathy, "I guess."

"Sweetie...changing your mind doesn't make you an idiot. Especially not about something like this. Yes, really," Carly added when the girl smirked.

"It's just...God, I hated feeling so out of control, you know? Like my body had totally left my brain behind somewhere." She carefully skootched back farther into the cushions, then skimmed her index finger around and around the mug's rim. "Sean and I talked for a long time that day he came over to apologize. And I believe him, that he's really sorry, but...I think we're kinda cooling it for a while."

"Oh, honey...I'm sorry."

"No, it's okay. I realized I'm not as ready for a steady boyfriend as I thought I was. And I know a lot of the kids just 'hook up' with each other, for like, sex and stuff, but…" She flipped her long hair over her shoulder. "I don't dare say this to any of my friends, 'cause they'll think I'm like this big throwback or something, but some of the stuff they say they do…it really grosses me out. I mean, maybe I'm missing something here, but how is that being in charge of your body? Doin' stuff that maybe you don't really want to do, just so everybody will think you're cool?"

A chill scampered down Carly's spine, one she decided had little to do with her cooling off after the class. Did she have a sign stamped on her forehead—*Go ahead, you can trust me with your secrets?* And what a kick in the head to discover that, after years of being convinced that being "in control" meant keeping herself emotionally distanced from her encounters, some fifteen-year-old-girl had more of a handle on the issue than Carly had ever dreamed of. "Maybe you should tell your friends exactly what you just told me," she said. "I'll bet some of them are grossed out, too, but they're scared, like you, to say anything."

Libby shrugged, the classic okay-maybe-but-God-forbid-I-admit-you-might-be-right gesture.

Carly sipped her chocolate, then asked carefully, "Are you afraid of sex?"

Libby thought for a moment, then said, "I think it's more that I'm afraid of messin' it up by having it before I'm supposed to. Or something. I mean, it really is better when you're in love with the other person, right?"

Great. How the hell was she supposed to answer that? "It's definitely better when you're sure you want it," she hedged. "Instead of doing it just because you think you should."

"Anyway," Libby said, setting her empty mug on the floor by her feet, then sitting up again. "That's not why I wanted to talk to you."

The chill made an encore appearance. "Oh?"

Libby scrutinized her for several seconds, then said, "What's really going on between you and Daddy?"

Oh, boy. "I don't know," she finally said. "And I know that sounds like an avoidance tactic, but it's the truth."

"Do you at least *like* him?"

"Oh, honey," Carly let out on a breath, "what I feel goes way beyond *liking* him. That much, I can say. I've never met anybody like your father."

"You think he could make you happy?"

"That's not the issue."

"Then what is?"

"Whether I could make *him* happy."

The girl's topazy eyes stayed fixed on hers for another several beats, before something on her sock grabbed her attention. "At first, I was so sure you weren't right for him. I mean, sure, you're cool and all, but…"

"You don't have to explain, I completely understand."

"No, I don't think you do. You know what Daddy does? We'll be out feeding the cows or whatever, and I'll catch him staring over here with this goony look on his face. Or one of the boys'll start talking about you, and it's like Daddy freezes, gawking at whoever said your name. You know how I knew I wasn't in love with Sean? Because I look at Daddy, and I know what I feel for Sean doesn't even come close to how he feels about you." She swallowed. "How he felt about Mama."

"Libby, I—"

"It's us, isn't it? You're scared of getting involved with him because there's so many of us?"

Carly's knee began to ache; she stretched out her leg, massaging it. "I won't lie to you, that's a big part of it." And at least this part, she could talk about. As opposed to everything else, which she couldn't even define. "Libby," she said when the girl made a face, "I know nothing about taking care of kids. I mean, you guys are great, but honestly? I don't think I'd make a real good mother. It's a huge responsibility. Which has never been my strong suit, unfortunately."

"But that's the thing, we don't need a mother, not really." Libby leaned forward, her eyes huge and importunate. "I mean, not the kind who cooks and cleans and does laundry and all that stuff. We can do all that by ourselves. Well, except for Travis, maybe, and even he knows how to help keep his room clean and throw his dirty clothes in the basket. After Mama died, Daddy told us that there was no reason to let everything go to pot just because she wasn't there anymore. Not that anybody likes doing all that stuff—housework is the pits—and Daddy's all the time on our cases when we get lazy, but we manage okay. And nobody expects you to suddenly start riding the tractor or cleanin' up after the pigs and stuff, if that's what you're afraid of. I mean, just because we get off on the whole farming thing doesn't mean we'd expect you to."

Then her eyes got all shiny, and Carly felt a sympathetic knot lodge in her throat as well. "You have no idea how huge this is. Daddy liking you, I mean. It means he's admitting that maybe he needs something besides us and the farm. But what worries me—and the boys, too—is that, if he's lonely, and you say 'no'…well, we don't even want to think about who else he might end up with."

Carly's sip of cocoa went down the wrong way; her coughing fit, however, didn't stop Libby from continuing.

"I mean, maybe you could spend a lot of time over here, anyway, so you wouldn't even feel like you were living with us…"

"Libby, Libby…" *Do not laugh, do* not *laugh.* "I get the point. And, believe me, I really appreciate all the concessions you guys seem willing to make, here. But—"

"Oh, come *on,* Carly! You admitted you liked him! And excuse me, but somehow I can't see you living over here all by yourself for the rest of your life. I mean, jeez, how boring is that? So I don't get it—what've you got to lose?"

She didn't—couldn't—answer at first. Instead, she got up, carting her empty mug back to the kitchenette. Living alone, knowing she had a someplace to retreat when things got too close, too pointless, had always been her safety valve. *Boring* had never been an issue—when you're content with the status quo, why would it be?

But then she remembered an ancient Russian-trained dance teacher she'd once had, early on, who'd admonish Carly whenever she balked at trying a new step. "*Vat are you afraid of?*" Madame Propoviova would bark. "*You can only fall as far as the floor! So you fall, you get up, you try again. Is no big deal.*"

Yeah, well. This wasn't about attempting a triple pirouette en pointe. Which did result in her falling. Repeatedly. Until eventually she got it. This was about letting herself admit to the possibility that maybe—something that felt like an electric shock zapped through her midsection—she was actually interested in seeing how far this could go. That maybe, with the right person, you might be willing to consider doing something you'd never thought you'd want to before.

That maybe it was okay to change your mind.

She turned around. Libby was sitting with her elbows on her knees, watching her. Waiting.

"Got any ideas how I should go about this?"

The girl grinned, then clambered off the sofa. "You and your dad could come over for supper tonight, to start. I mean, how're you gonna get used to us if you're never around us?"

Kid had a point.

"I don't suppose your father has a clue about any of this?"

"You're kidding, right?"

Huh. If nothing else, the look on Sam's face alone might make this worthwhile. "Okay."

"Okay? You'll come?"

Carly nodded away the "*What have I done?*" demons screaming inside her, as Libby said, "What don't you eat?"

"Bad carbs and fat."

"Oh. That doesn't leave much, does it?"

Carly laughed. "Don't worry about it, I'll adapt. Dad eats anything on his plate, though."

"Okay, I'll think of something." Libby shoved her feet back into her sneakers, then tromped across the room to get her coat off the long rack that Dad had put up for her. Before she left, however, she turned back and gave Carly a long, assessing perusal.

"Um, don't take this the wrong way, okay? But maybe you should think about fixing yourself up or something?"

Carly barely got the door shut behind the girl before she burst out laughing.

Chapter 14

Sam's first clue that something was up was when he came in from milking and spotted candles, and the good dishes, on the table.

The dining table, not the kitchen table.

He stepped into the room to make sure his eyes weren't playing tricks on him, couldn't help but notice there were nine place settings.

Back in the kitchen, Libby was humming up a storm as she cooked—two roast chickens, sweet potatoes, broccoli, a huge salad. "So, what are *we* gonna eat?" Matt said on a moan, which was pretty much Sam's take on the situation.

"Don't worry, I'm makin' macaroni and cheese for the rest of you. Travis, Frankie—go wash your hands! And your faces! And change those grody shirts, too!" Then she gave Sam the same *ewww* face. "Daddy! Honestly!"

Sam glanced down at himself, half expecting to find his fly open, then met his daughter's eyes. "What's going on, Lib?"

"Nothing. I invited Carly and Lane to come to supper, is all.

So you might want to think about changing. Maybe a quick shower? We've got time, they won't be here until six-thirty."

Now his gaze swept the room. Several sets of eyes, including a few of the not–human being variety, met his, all innocence. Sam crossed his arms. "Y'all wouldn't be tryin' to fix me up, now, would you?"

"Nooo," Libby said in exasperated teen mode, as the boys all solemnly shook their heads. She set about transferring the chickens to the big turkey platter, then arranging the sweet potatoes around them. "I just thought it'd be fun to have them over, that's all." She tossed an oh-so-sweet smile in his direction.

"Yeah," Wade said, "'specially since we all got tired of waitin' for *you* to make a move on the woman!"

"Wade!" everybody said, except for Travis who frowned, like he'd been left out of the loop.

Sam opened his mouth to expound on the foolhardiness of their mission, only to realize, well, hell, maybe they were right. Maybe this business about giving Carly space wasn't the way to go about things, after all. Maybe she needed a little push.

Right over the edge, with this bunch.

"Guys…"

Libby waved the salad tongs at him. "Don't *even* try to tell us you don't like her."

"Well, no, I suppose it's pretty obvious that I do, but—"

"I know, I know," Libby said, on a sigh, dousing olive oil on the salad. "We're a handful. And being a farmer's wife might not have exactly been in her plans. It's okay, Daddy—we've already got it covered."

Sam decided maybe it was best not to know what that meant.

He grabbed his daughter's chin, tilting it toward him. "You changed your mind?"

"No," she said. "*You* changed my mind."

Feeling slightly dazed, he dropped his hand. "Okay, fine. Just…don't expect miracles from one dinner."

They all grinned at each other. Sam let out a sigh himself, then went upstairs to take a shower. Wasn't until he'd scrubbed most of the barn smell off that it hit him that, his daughter's persuasive abilities notwithstanding, Carly wouldn't have accepted the invitation unless she'd wanted to.

That was worth digging out his best shirt for.

In the end, despite Carly's pleas, Lane had refused to go, clearly more down about the whole Ivy thing than he was letting on. Instead, he kissed her on top of her head and pushed her out the door with some gibberish about her needing to face this on her own, anyway.

So here she was. Facing this. *Them.*

All of them. Not including Henry, the old tom, who kept staring at her with a judgmental gleam in his rheumy yellow eyes.

Not that the boys weren't being perfect angels—Mike and Matt had nearly collided in their zeal to both pull out her chair for her, and every time she glanced over and caught Wade's serious expression over one of his father's ties, looped around a scrawny neck jutting out from a Shrek T-shirt, the funniest, sweetest feeling shot through her—but she wondered how long they had before the kids exploded.

She wondered how long before *she* would.

Oh, God, this was torture, all this politeness, watching the big ones glower at the little ones if they so much as looked like they might be thinking of acting like, you know, normal kids. Carly complimented Libby on the meal, which really was delicious, and the girl beamed, which was spontaneous and real, but other than that, the tension at the table was congealing faster than the chicken juices on the rapidly cooling platter in the center of it.

To make matters worse, Libby had insisted on seating Carly at right angles to Sam, at the head of the table, a position from which there was no escaping the occasional graze of his knee against hers.

Or the hot, dripping-with-meaning eye contact that resulted. Hot, dripping-with-meaning eye contact that did not escape the attention of any of the Stepford children having dinner with them.

"Wade," Mike asked, "would you please pass the macaroni and cheese?"

"Frankie, would you like me to pour you another glass of milk…?"

"No, it's okay, Matt—you c'n have the last roll, if you want it, I don't mind."

Yeah, right.

Carly leaned over to Sam, took note of how extraordinarily good he smelled, and whispered, "Who are these kids, anyway?"

"Beats me," Sam whispered back, cutting his chicken. "Never seen 'em before in my life."

"Daddy," Libby said, and Carly chuckled.

"Okay, guys?" she said. "You're really giving me the creeps. I've seen you in action, remember? So please…drop the act. It's too weird."

"That does not mean, however," Sam said mildly, "that the sanction against food fights has been lifted."

"Damn," Mike muttered under his breath, and Carly pressed her napkin to her mouth to cover her laugh.

But things relaxed after that. Not enough to degenerate into chaos, exactly, but when one of the bigger dogs snatched a chicken bone off Frankie's plate and made off with it, and four boys went after him, all yelling their heads off, and Libby rolled her eyes and Sam just shook his head—and kept on eating— she began to understand how people did this.

And maybe even why.

A thought that she later shared with Sam, when she was getting ready to leave and Sam—and a dog or two—had walked her out to her car.

"Not that I've changed my mind about wanting any of my own," she said, clutching the collar to her fake—*faux*—mink jacket closed at her neck, figuring she might as well be up front about that part of things.

"Not to worry," Sam said. "I think six pretty much does it for me. Teachin' six teenagers to drive…" He shook his head, and she laughed, only to breathe in sharply when his hands slid inside her coat, tugging her closer.

"What are you doing?"

"Let's go with keeping us warm. You got any objections?"

"Nope, don't think so."

"Good," he said, sort of sandwiching her between her car and his body, which, all things considered, was not a bad place to be.

She angled her head back at the house. "You think they're watching?"

"Oh, I think you can pretty much count on it. So. You and your father gonna come for Thanksgiving?"

"Do we have a choice?"

He grinned. "No."

His chest was so solid under her hands. "I've never been courted before, you know. Especially by six kids."

"I wouldn't exactly call what they're doing 'courting.' Railroading's probably more the word you had in mind." She laughed. "So…they don't scare you anymore?"

"Don't kid yourself. Kids—your kids, *any* kids—will always scare me. All I have to do is think back to the hell I put my own parents through…"

"But you think maybe you're closer to being able to deal with them?"

Well, that's why she was here, wasn't she?

She lifted her eyes to Sam's. "For you, I'd be willing to deal with almost anything. Or at least try."

Underneath her hands, even his heartbeat seemed to still. "What are you sayin', Carly?"

"I'm saying…you're making me want to try things I never dared to before now. I see you with your kids, and I think…" She focused on her hands on his chest, then back up at him. "I think, more than anything in the world, I want to be like that. Care like that."

"Oh, honey," he said, the tenderness in his expression wreaking havoc on her ability to stand, only then his hands lifted to cradle her face, and his mouth found hers, and her legs said, *You have* got *to be kidding!* "But don't you see?" he whispered when he'd done kissing her (way too soon, in her opinion). "You already do care like that. And I suspect you always have."

That's when she finally understood what it felt like to be loved. *Really* loved, not just the hot stuff that burns out, but the warm stuff that makes you go around with a stupid smile on your face for, oh, fifty years or so.

Not that there was anything wrong with the hot stuff. The evidence of which was getting trickier to ignore by the moment.

She shifted against him. "Is this you, um, courting me?"

"No, apparently that's me tryin' to seduce you." He glowered down at where their bodies were happily getting acquainted. "Although the timing sucks. I mean, it's not like we can…you know…" He nodded back toward the house.

"No, I didn't think so." A tiny crease lodged between her brows. "Did…I just pass some kind of test?"

"Either that, or I just royally flunked."

She buried her face in his shirt to muffle her laughter, only to have a sonic-boom-size *Ohmigod!* go off in her head. For a moment—if that—she longed for the good old days of no-strings, no emotions, no-hard-feelings-when-it's-over sex, only to realize it was like trying to remember someone you hadn't seen in a hundred years. Then she heard herself say, "Even if we do sleep together…"

Even if? said the voice inside her head.

"You still want to take things slowly," Sam finished for her, and she nodded like a little kid asked if she wants ice cream, and he shrugged and said, "Not a problem. I'm not going anywhere."

"And if it doesn't work…?"

"Then it doesn't work."

"But the kids…"

"I'll have a talk with them. Or better yet, you have a talk with 'em. Best chance we have of getting through this is if we're both straight with them. Because if anybody understands that things don't always go the way you hoped, it's my kids."

Tears stung her eyes. "You, too?"

"Yeah. Me, too." Then he kissed her again—how could she have ever thought kissing was the boring part?—and held her in his arms long enough to reevaluate her long-held opinions on hugging, too, and dropped the hint that he'd started taking Travis to Didi Meyerhauser's preschool on Tuesdays and Thursdays so he'd have kids his own age to play with while his siblings were in school.

"I'll keep that in mind," she said, and got into her car.

She was a good half mile away before she realized she was shaking.

"Well?" Libby said the instant he walked back inside.

"Anybody ever clue you guys in to the concept of some things being personal?"

"Seems to me," Mike said, from where he was sprawled on the sofa, "if you end up marrying Carly, that would make it pretty personal for us, too."

"And how, may I ask, do you get from having her over for dinner to us getting married?"

"You took her to the dance, too," Matt, ever helpful, put in.

"Uh-huh. Two dates. Neither of them alone. I think it's safe to say it's early yet. Besides, your mother and I dated for six years before we got married."

"Yeah, but you were young then," Mike said, scratching his pale head. "Time's no longer on your side."

Sam scowled at his oldest son for a second or two, but no comeback, brilliant or otherwise, came to mind. Then he thought about Carly's obvious nervousness about all of this and let out a sigh.

"Okay, everybody—listen up. If it were up to me, yeah, I guess I'd get things moving a lot more quickly than Carly wants to. But that's my point—she's not in the same place I am. Or, apparently, you all are. Frankly I don't think any of you realize how much of a coup it was gettin' her over here tonight to begin with. But that only means she's willing to put her toe in the water, not that she's ready to jump in. And you know what? It might not work out between her and me. We might get to know each other better and decide, nope, not what we want. So don't go getting yourselves all worked up about something that might not ever happen. Okay? Now. It's past most of your bedtimes. So come on—" he clapped his hands "—teeth and pj's, now."

Grumbling, the boys all trooped upstairs to get ready for bed. Libby, however, hung back, waiting.

"She needs us, you know," she said, then took off for her room.

Maybe so, Sam thought, sinking into the sofa for a minute before heading upstairs to do the nightly tucking-in. But that was one conclusion the gal was going to have to arrive at all on her own.

And that, heaven knew, was anything but a given.

Why Carly drove into town, she had no idea. By eight-thirty, there was virtually nothing open. But she couldn't face either her father and his moroseness or the emptiness of her place, so she parked at an angle in front of the hardware store and got out to walk up Main Street. All three blocks of it. It was freezing, the wind cruelly assaulting her practically bare knees between her hemline and the tops of her boots; she huddled inside her jacket as she peered into store windows filled with Western clothing and fishing gear, the drug store running specials on Maybelline and Metamucil; at the Hair We Are, she chuckled at the faded color posters of ladies in hair styles that were outmoded thirty years ago. Life in Haven might not have been exciting, by popular definition, but there was a lot to be said for the comfort of tradition, of predictability in an uncertain world.

Although Ruby's neon sign was turned off, the lights over the counter still glanced off Jordy's gleaming head as he scrubbed down the grill; one of the waitresses, her bilious pink uniform sagging around her thin frame, filled salt shakers, while in a corner booth, Ruby sat with a cup of coffee clamped between both dark hands, deep in conversation with the brunette seated across from her.

Dawn, she realized. Ivy's daughter.

Carly backed away, but not fast enough.

"Come on in," she made out from behind the glass. "Coffee's still on, no charge."

Despite hand signals meant to convey, *No, it's okay, I need to get going,* Ruby hustled over to the door, holding it open for her, as if knowing she'd never be able to resist the lure of French fry–scented heat. "Get yourself in here, out of the cold. Although the weatherman says we're supposed to have unseasonably warm temperatures in a few days. Can you believe it? Cold enough to freeze the you-know-whats off a brass monkey now, back up in the seventies three days from now. Craziest damn weather I ever did see…"

Carly had no reason to feel uncomfortable around Dawn, really. Well, other than the whole thing between her mom and Carly's dad. But that had nothing to do with either of them, did it?

She slipped into the vinyl-upholstered booth across from her, nodding her thanks as Ruby set a mug of coffee in front of her, vanishing to see what Jordy was goin' on about.

Dawn smiled at her over her mug of coffee. "Considering how often I considered driving out to your place and giving your father a piece of my mind, it's funny we've never really met before now."

Carly mumbled something and sipped her own coffee, which was strong and scalding and would undoubtedly keep her awake all night. Not that she needed caffeine to accomplish that, but still. Then she raised her eyes to Dawn and asked, "So why didn't you? Come out and read my father the riot act?"

"Probably for the same reason you never confronted my mother."

"Because it was between the two of them, you mean?"

The brunette lifted her mug, confirming. Then she said, "But what would you have said? To Mama?"

"That if she hurt my father, there'd be hell to pay."

Dawn laughed, deep in her throat. "Same here." Then she set

down her cup and asked, "Your dad really loved your mother, didn't he?"

"Yeah. He did."

"See, nobody ever loved mine. Not really. That's why she called it off, because she didn't want somebody's leftovers. But you know what I think?" Carly shook her head. "I think what she's really afraid of, is screwing it up. That she won't be able to make Lane as happy as your mother did."

Carly fingered her mug for a moment, then said, "For what it's worth, Dad's been miserable since they broke up. If you want my opinion, he's got it for your mother bad. Real bad. But maybe, I don't know…maybe he doesn't think he'll be enough for her, either?"

Dawn seemed to study her for a long moment, then finished off her coffee. "Could be. I mean, your father certainly doesn't seem the type to just fool around for the heck of it."

"There's an understatement," Carly said, and Dawn chuckled.

From the kitchen, Ruby fussed at Jordy, who fussed back at her; a second later, they were both laughing their heads off, making both women smile. Then Dawn sighed and said, "Falling in love is so damn scary, you know? Having to trust somebody else. Hell, having to trust *yourself,* that you're not going to make a fool of yourself, mess everything up…" She glanced at her watch, then scooted out of the booth. "Lord, I had no idea it was so late—there's a pair of guys at home probably both wondering what the heck happened to me…"

She shrugged into a voluminous cape, her expression suddenly turning puzzled. "It's funny," she said. "I had a late client, which is why I was in town late to begin with. But normally I would have gone straight home. Why I decided to stop here first, finagle a cup of coffee from Ruby before I drove home…" She shook her head. "Strange, the way things happen, isn't it?"

After Dawn left, Carly sat in the booth, sipping her coffee in the half-light, listening to the Kennedys' good-natured bickering, thinking *strange* didn't even begin to cover it.

* * *

Over the next week, the weather warmed up considerably, pushing up near eighty in the afternoons. Since everything indicated it was going to hold out—which meant Thanksgiving, now just two days away, was going to feel more like Easter—Sam decided he might as well scrape and repaint the barn, a chore he'd been putting off since before Travis's birth. And one he'd hoped to take his mind off all the Travis-free days that had passed, days when Sam would rush back from leaving Trav in Didi's capable hands to change the sheets on his bed, days when he'd keep an ear out for Carly's Saturn or the sound of his doorbell, days when he found himself getting more despondent than he had any right to be.

Craziness, is what this was, he thought, attacking the leprous-looking paint up near the eaves. Pure out-and-out craziness. Especially since it wasn't as if she hadn't been around at all. In fact, she'd come over for dinner again, and played video games with the boys, and even tried her hand at milking Bernadette (with little success). She just didn't seem to be in any big hurry to test out those freshly washed sheets. Which was her prerogative, after all. No point in getting his drawers in a knot about something he'd agreed to, for crying out loud. So he'd best get over it, and get on with his life, and stop worrying over things that might not even happen. So when Carly called out, "Having fun?" he nearly fell off the ladder.

He looked down at her, standing there in some lacy little white top that fluttered around her midriff and a pair of those potato-sack pants she was so partial to, and his spirits lifted. Among other things.

"Don't you have a class or something?" he called down to her, thinking maybe she wasn't quite as skinny as she had been, although you'd still have to put three of her together to make one normal-size woman.

"Everybody's too busy with the holiday. So they're mostly cancelled until next week." He started down the ladder. "But don't let me interrupt you if you're in the middle of something—"

"I've been putting off this job for five years. I somehow doubt a few minutes longer is gonna matter a whole lot one way or the other."

One eyebrow lifted. "A few *minutes?*"

He'd closed the space between them to where he could see wisps of hesitancy clinging to the boldness, to get a whiff of coconut and flowers. Tropical paradise, right here in Oklahoma. "Hours, I meant. Days. Weeks. Your call."

She smiled the smile of a woman who knows she's about to get what she wants, and alarm spiked through him, that he might not be able to give her whatever that was.

"I'd pretty much decided you'd changed your mind," he said.

"Oh, I did. At least six times."

"And?"

"And I suggest you quit yakking and get my clothes off before I change it again."

He tossed down the scraper, very nearly pegging one of the dogs, then hauled her by the hand into the house.

Chapter 15

"No," he said when she reached out to him, barely two minutes later. Completely naked, Sam reached over to hoist his blinds, watching sunlight streak Carly's slender body as she lay on her side, her skin rich as caramel against the white sheets. A slightly puzzled smile teasing her lips, she stretched in the swath of white-gold light gilding her high, small breasts, glancing off her flat stomach, glistening in the darkness between her legs. He threw open the window, letting in an unseasonably warm breeze tinged with the rich tang of leaf-mold and sun-warmed hay, then turned around to indulge in a little visual feasting.

Her head in her hand, she grinned up at him, the earrings glistening. Beckoning. "Are you planning on just standing there all day, staring at me?"

"Not all day, no. But this is one image I definitely want embedded in my memory."

Her eyes lowered. "I know what you mean," she said, and Sam laughed and climbed into bed beside her, close enough to touch, if he had a mind to. And boy, did he have a mind to. But he hadn't driven himself crazy all these weeks to have it all over and done with in thirty seconds flat.

So he continued to look, then look some more, smiling smugly at the flush of arousal that followed in the wake of his lazy perusal. Her nipples hardened; he swallowed in anticipation of how they were going to feel against his tongue. Eventually. Again, she reached out to touch him; he grabbed her hand, said, "Uh-uh-uh," and she gave up an annoyed sigh.

"Just out of curiosity," she said, "will there be any kissing or touching anytime soon?"

Sam pretended to consider this for a moment or too, then nodded. "Yeah. I think that's a safe assumption."

"How soon?"

"Impatient little thing, aren't you?"

"So sue me. Well?"

"Betcha you were one of those kids who ripped open all your Christmas presents in five minutes flat without even bothering to look at 'em, weren't you?"

Her eyes snapped to his as a flush that had nothing to do with sexual arousal, he didn't think, surged across her cheeks. "As a matter of fact, I was."

"Well, remember how I told you about how pretty my presents were when I was a kid? About how I loved lookin' at 'em as much as opening them? Then, when I did…" He leaned over to brush his lips across hers, barely enough to make contact, barely enough to count, really. "I opened them carefully…" Another kiss, this one slightly more substantial. "Slowly…" And another. "Savoring every…single…moment." He touched her lips with his tongue, pulling away before hers had a chance to figure out what was going on. "Making the most wonderful morning of the year last…as long…as I could…"

He rolled her onto her back, straddling her, pinning her hands over her head, careful to keep the nitro well away from the glycerin. No mean feat when she kept thrusting her hips up like that.

"Slooow, honey. We're gonna take this slow."

She glared at him. "I was thinking more along the lines of hard and hot and fast."

"Well, that's fun, too, no doubt about it. And believe me, with all these kids, I know all about hard and hot and fast. But the thing is, see, opportunities for nice, slow, leisurely lovemaking don't come along too often, and seeings as this is one of those times, I intend to make the most of it." She writhed some more, he hardened some more, and saw a few teeth-gritting minutes in his future. Then he caught something else in her expression, a fierce determination to gain control of the situation. That he was equally determined to wrest that control from her should make the next little while highly entertaining, to say the least.

He held her wrists a little tighter and lanced her gaze with his. "This isn't about sex, Carly," he whispered, placing lots of kisses all over that pissed little face of hers. "It's about me loving you. Now why don't you relax and let me do just that?"

"Fine," she finally pushed out. "But I'm warning you…I am one *really* primed chick. If you expect me to hold back…"

"I don't expect you to do anything except have a good time. Although I'm beginning to see how maybe you could use a little something to take the edge off…."

So he kissed her. But probably not where she was expecting to be kissed, judging from her gasp…and then her moans…and then her shriek of release as he took the edge off, all right, but with anything but a *little* something.

She was in trouble now, boy. Because with each kiss, each touch, each smile into her eyes, Sam was pulling her deeper and deeper into a place she'd never let herself get anywhere near before, a place that had always scared the hell out of her.

As if soothing an overexcited child, he'd continued to press gentle kisses into her until the pulsing subsided, then had taken those exquisite, in-no-hurry kisses on a road trip, across her hips—lingering over the small tattoo on her hipbone—her belly, her ribs, her breasts, where he toyed and nuzzled and nibbled until she heard herself say something about being ready again, and he dipped a finger inside her, working magic circles with his thumb, and she shut her eyes and arched, aching, wanting, and then he whispered, "Look at me," and she saw such love in his eyes that tears sprang to hers because she realized she was lost, that she'd let him take her down a path from which there was no return...

...unless she turned back now.

Her second climax rippled through her, his touch the pebble disturbing the still waters of who she thought she was, what she thought she wanted, and she tried, desperately, to tell herself it was just sex, nothing more than an involuntary stimulus-response, except she clung to him afterward, trembling, still needy, unable to untangle the joy from the terror.

The old Carly—who had never been a cuddler—would have gotten out of his bed, would have gotten the hell out of there. But this crazy person who'd taken her place took Sam's face in her hands and kissed him back, kissed him as though she would die if she didn't, even though she briefly considered that death would be preferable to feeling this lost, this out of control. Because she was out of control, out of her mind, her mouth moving over him as if she wanted to devour him.

Desperate to avoid the emotional equivalent of a head-on collision, she took him into her mouth, wanting to drive him at least as crazy as he was driving her. But he apparently read her mind, something at which he was becoming far too proficient for her comfort level, and lifted her off, rolling her onto her back before reaching into his nightstand for a condom, ripping the foil, sliding it down over his erection. An action she'd witnessed more times than she wanted to admit, an action from which she'd thought the eroticism had faded a long time ago.

She opened to him, helpless, yearning, hearing a whimper of delight and despair, both, when he slid into her, filling her, terrifying her, sweeping her away in a torrent of emotion as he began to rock inside her, and she wanted more than anything in the world to not want this so much, even as she wanted nothing more than to be able to simply *let go*.

To trust that what she was feeling right now was as true and sure and solid as what she had no doubt, none, that Sam was feeling.

Sam's climax burst within her, around her, like the proverbial fireworks. For a second, she thought about faking one of her own, only to decide Sam deserved better than that. Besides, something told her this man wouldn't be so easily fooled as some whose egos were more than willing to believe what they wanted to believe.

He frowned down at her, smoothing a knuckle down her temple. "Did I lose you?"

She did everything in her power to keep the tears at bay, afraid he'd misinterpret them. "Guess two's my limit."

"Not on my watch, sweetheart. Hold on," he said, rolling away to dispose of the condom.

"No, Sam, really…I'm fine."

He stilled, then twisted back. "You're anything but fine. And I'm guessing your mood has nothing to do with how many orgasms you had. Or didn't have."

"I'm so sorry," she whispered, reaching out.

But her fingertips glanced off his arms as he sprang from the bed and yanked on his jeans, muttering a swear word under his breath she'd never heard him use before.

"Okay, you win," she finally said, scrambling for her underwear on the floor. "But at least know that this has nothing to do with how things went in bed—"

"Oh, for God's sake, Carly—my ego's not *that* fragile!"

"I didn't think it was, or I wouldn't be here! But there's no comparison between my previous…experience and what we just shared. So you were right." She pulled on her pants, punched her arms through the sleeves of her blouse, swearing when one of the rings snagged on the lace. She yanked it free, fumbling with the pearl buttons as she pushed out, "There's a huge difference when there's love involved. Happy now?"

His eyes were like cut glass. "I might be if it weren't for the huge, silent 'but' tagged onto the end of that sentence."

"Sam…you can't love me into being who you want me to be. Or think I am. And this has nothing to do with anything I've done in my past. But it does have to do with who my past has made me. How it's shaped me. Or maybe it isn't even that, maybe it's just…my nature. I mean, I had wonderful parents, who had a solid, loving marriage. Yet I still went off the deep end, didn't I? Maybe I don't do the things I used to do, but that's because I finally realized how self-destructive I was being, that there was a difference between being a rebel and being stupid. But even though I've changed in some ways, deep down I'm still the same person who did those stupid things, the same person who's never been in love and who has no idea how to trust if what I feel for you is real or not. God *knows* I'd love nothing more than to see where things lead." She swallowed. "But the longer I do that, the more I risk hurting you, and your kids, if I run true to form and this wears off after a few months."

"And I told you, that's a risk I'm more than willing to take."

"I know you are. But I'm not. I *can't*. And you have no idea how much it's killing me to say that." .

His expression ripped her apart. "Actually, I think I do."

"Then think of how much more it would hurt if we let this go on."

Sam grabbed his blue shirt off the chair where he'd thrown it, jerking it on. "You're right," he said, buttoning it, glaring at her. "I don't get it. I don't get why a woman as generous and loving as you are can't accept the simple fact that she *is* generous and loving, why you seem to think what you've got to offer isn't somehow good enough for me, for my kids. But for sure I can't crawl inside your head and fix whatever's got your brain so clogged up. I'd hoped loving you would be enough, but obviously it isn't."

"You have no idea how much your love means to me!"

"Even if you can't return it."

"But I do return it! Oh, God, Sam—I love you so much, it hurts! My loving you isn't the issue!"

"Then what the hell *is?*"

"That I don't know if it's real!" Much to her aggravation, tears streamed down her cheeks. "How can I possibly trust something I don't understand? That I've never felt before?"

Sam glowered at her for another several seconds before blowing out a huge breath. "You know, I knew full well there was a real strong chance you'd say exactly what you just said. I guess I'd hoped maybe you'd give this more of a shot."

Her eyes burned. "I didn't realize I'd be *this* scared."

"Then I guess you've made the only decision you can."

"Sam…"

He held up his hands. "Just go, okay?"

She grabbed her sandals, then stumbled out of the room and ran down the stairs, flinching when something struck the wall over her head.

Chapter 16

There were times when being old, and maybe at least somewhat wise, Lane thought when Carly walked into her kitchenette, letting out a little "oh" of not-exactly-thrilled surprise at finding him there, was a definite liability. Like now. Didn't take a genius to figure out where she'd been. Or what she'd been up to. Or—and here was the hardest part—that she wasn't exactly glowing with happiness about it.

Damn. She'd never stop being his little girl, would she? Would he ever stop wanting to protect her? Or get a clue how he was supposed to do that when she'd never let him?

She opened her small fridge, removing a bottle of fancy water. "How come you're here?"

"Ran out of coffee," he said, holding up the can. At least she drank plain old Maxwell House like a normal person. "Isn't this weather crazy?" he said, more or less for something to say until he could better gauge her mood. "Up near eighty today and tomorrow, with thunderstorms predicted for both days. Then back down into the thirties for Thanksgiving."

She grunted, only half listening, then took a sip of her water.

"Did I tell you, I picked up two new clients off the Web site today?"

"That's great," she said, and burst into tears.

Lane dumped the coffee on the minuscule counter and wrapped his arms around her, leading her out to the sofa in her studio. Before he even had a chance to ask her if she wanted to talk about it, chunks of the story began to tumble out of her mouth, interspersed with lots of gasping sobs and nose blowing. Frankly, he wasn't really following most of it—he'd always found female logic hard enough to decipher without hysteria mucking it up even more—but one thing, he did figure out.

"It finally happened, didn't it? You're in love."

She nodded.

"So what's the problem?"

"Other than the fact that I have no idea if what I'm feeling has the shelf-life of a banana? And that I'm terrified of hurting him?"

"How on earth could you do that?"

"Well, for starters, by not being there as completely for him as he certainly seems to be for me."

"That's ridiculous."

"You didn't think so when you decided to break it off with Ivy."

Touché.

Carly rose and plodded over to the window, the pale gold light haloing her frail-looking silhouette, and it occurred to Lane that maybe it was better to simply sit still, keep his trap shut, and give her room to figure this out on her own. Especially since he obviously didn't have any answers, anyway.

"Sam's love…I don't know. It's so…*bottomless.* I'm used to limits, to being able to see the boundaries. But there aren't any boundaries to this." She turned back, her mouth pulled into a flat, humorless smile. "Not for him, anyway. The man just gives, and gives, and gives…" She stopped, her fingers touching her mouth. "What if he's sees me as…a challenge?"

"What do you mean?"

"I'm not entirely sure. But from what I know of Sam, he

thrives on doing things the hard way. Being a farmer, raising all those kids…" She shook her head, then let out a long breath. "You've seen his house, how hard he works at keeping things orderly. Under control. What if…when I admitted I'd never been in love before, he saw it as a gauntlet being thrown down? Something out of order than needed to be straightened out?"

"Or conquered?"

"Whatever."

"So you think he set out to make you fall in love with him, just to prove he could?"

Her brows nearly met over her nose. Then she laughed, a harsh, dry sound. "Okay, so maybe that's a stretch."

"You said it, not me."

She returned to flop down in the chair across from the sofa, as vulnerable and confused as the rebellious twelve-year-old who used to drive him crazy. "Which only proves how messed up I am."

Lane shook his head. "Confused, maybe. Headstrong, definitely. Although maybe not as much as you used to be. But messed up?" He shrugged. "No worse than any of the rest of us."

"Meaning, how you feel about Ivy?"

"Among other things."

She wriggled into a more comfortable position, her arms crossed. "*Do* you love her?"

"Yes. But like you, I'm not sure it's enough. For her, at any rate."

She gave him a long, speculative look, then said, "So where was this wise, patient person when I was going through all my teenage traumas?"

"Right where I've always been. Even if you never felt you could trust me."

"Had nothing to do with trust," she said, her words tripping over his. "I was afraid…"

"Of what?"

Her slender fingers raked the velveteen on the arm of the

chair for a second before she said, "Not *of*. *For*. For you. That you'd find out how little you could really protect me."

"I drove you to rehab, Carly. Twice. I was well aware of how little I'd been able to protect you." Lane studied her profile, half listening to the gentle whirr of the fans overhead, then said softly, "And I'd been aware of how little I could protect for some time before that, believe me."

Her eyes slowly lifted to his, and he knew the exact moment when the penny dropped. "Ohmigod," she breathed. "You *knew*? About—"

"That summer in camp?" She nodded. "Not the details. Only that something had happened."

Tears shined in her eyes. "But how…?"

"About halfway in, we got a call from the director, telling us the teachers and counselors had noticed a huge change in you. That you'd suddenly become almost rabidly focused on your dancing, that you'd withdrawn from many of your friendships. They wanted to know if anything had happened on our end that might have affected you so profoundly."

"I never knew about that call."

"No, we didn't figure you did."

"So why didn't anyone say anything? To me, I mean?"

"They did. We did. Remember, Mom and I came out to visit, to see for ourselves what might be going on? And the staff told us they'd done everything they could think of to draw you out. But every time anyone gave you an opening, you clammed up. Since you seemed to be okay otherwise, though…" He blew out a breath. "We all decided that you'd simply become obsessed with your dancing, which wasn't uncommon to kids your age, and had tuned everything else out. Except…except deep down inside, I'm not sure I ever fully believed that. I couldn't help feeling I'd failed you in some way."

"Oh, Dad…" She got up and sat beside him, weaving her arms around his middle. "You've never failed me. Ever. If anything, I've failed myself. But…"

Lane waited, his blood moving like sludge through his veins.

"But not that time," she said. He felt her take a deep breath. "I was raped," she said quietly, "by some idiot boy I was dating. I thought it was my fault at first, but not for long."

Lane shut his eyes against the stab of pain, the overwhelming feelings of helplessness and rage for something that had happened more than twenty years earlier. When he felt he could trust his voice, he said, "And you were afraid to tell us because *I* might be hurt?"

"Actually, at the time I was more concerned that you'd yank me out of camp. Which you know you would have done, so don't try to deny it. The whole afraid-to-hurt you thing came later."

"So you toughed it out."

"Yeah, basically."

"Which is what you've been doing ever since, isn't it? Toughing it out, living your life on your own terms. To avoid the pain."

"This isn't a newsflash, Dad. I'm well aware of what I've been doing."

"Because you never felt you could trust anybody, is that it? You couldn't trust your mother and me to be reasonable about letting you stay if that's what you wanted, so you didn't tell us what had happened, you wouldn't let us be parents. Then you decided it would be easier to have a string of half-assed relationships, rather than trusting that maybe not every guy is a jerk like the one who hurt you. Now you've got this first-rate man in love with you, and you're afraid to trust…who? Him? Yourself? Fate? *What?*"

Before Carly could answer, however, Lane bounced to his feet and charged to the middle of the room, rounding on her with, "But who am I to talk? Me, with this second chance I never in my wildest dreams thought I'd have right in my lap, and I'm afraid of *her* fears?"

Okay…clearly the conversation had taken a sharp right. Carly gawked at her father, feeling as though someone had turned her brain upside down.

"But how do you *know?*" she said, and her father blinked, looking slightly lost. Yeah, well, join the club, she wanted to say. She leaned forward, her hands out. "How do you *know* if it's enough? If you're really in love?"

Dad seemed to consider this for a moment, then said, "When you feel as though you've been clobbered with a two-by-four…"

"Oh."

"Or sometimes, it's like something warm washing over you, and you hear 'oh, yeah' inside your head. Like, who was it in the Bible? Elijah? Elisha? The one who heard the still, small voice in the wind."

Carly laughed. Her Sunday School memories were dim at best, but she thought she remembered this one. "Wasn't it that God *wasn't* in the wind?"

"Maybe you're right. But my point is, no matter what else is going on inside your head, or around you—"

"You just *know*. Yeah, yeah, I get it." Only she didn't. Not at all.

"Sorry, baby. But the thing is—" Dad strode back into her kitchen and picked up her coffee can, tucking it up under his arm like a football "—when one of the best things to ever happen to you comes your way, you can't let anything get in the way of accepting it. Especially yourself."

Seconds later she stood at the window, watching her father make off with her only readily available source of caffeine, leaving her with an inverted brain and spilled guts all over the damn place. And this stupid weather, jeez! She cranked open the window, only to grimace at the muggy, gritty, unfall-like breeze that elbowed its way inside.

A free spirit? Who was she kidding? Now she was Alice *after* she'd taken the plunge, tumbling down the rabbit hole, having no idea where—or if—she'd land, clutching frantically at the nothingness whizzing past her ears in the vain hope of latching onto something familiar and solid instead of reveling in the thrill of possible adventure, the sensation of floating, *flying,* weightless and unencumbered. Irritation swamped her, not only because her life, her feelings, even her body were spiraling out of control, but that she'd *kill* for even the smallest clue as to how, precisely, one learned to go with the flow.

And through the angry helplessness threaded a sadness, heavy and thick as mud, that if she hadn't heard the little voice, or felt that two-by-four, while making love with Sam Frazier, she never would.

The breeze snatched up her sob, sucking it out the window to blend with the howl of the wind.

"You're changing your sheets *again?*" Libby asked the next morning as she stooped to gather up her backpack. "Isn't this like the fourth time in two weeks?"

Sam jammed the last pillowcase into the washer and let the lid crash closed. He was hardly going to tell his daughter that he'd gotten basically no sleep the night before because his sheets smelled like coconut and flowers and sex. That every time he moved, he got hard. And depressed. "Since when are you keeping track of how often I do my laundry?"

Straightening to swing her backpack up onto her shoulder, Libby gave him a strange look. "Jeez, what's eating you?"

"Nothing." He twisted the dial like he was wringing a chicken's neck. "I'd just like to be able to go about my business without getting the third degree, if that's okay with you."

"Whatever. But maybe you should get another cup of coffee or something before you inflict your mood on the rest of the world. So you're gonna go into Claremore to pick up the rest of the stuff I need for dinner tomorrow, right?"

Tomorrow. Thanksgiving. Oh, yeah, like he was feeling so thankful right now. What he was feeling, was like an ass. You know, one of those dumb beasts with a real long learning curve?

"Yeah, this afternoon, I've got stuff to do around the place first."

"And Carly and Lane are coming, right?"

"As far as I know," came out with surprising aplomb, considering Carly had been a little preoccupied with explaining why she couldn't stick this out to formally accept, or decline, the invitation. Whether she showed up or not, it wouldn't surprise him.

Hell, at this point, *nothing* would surprise him.

Libby left to catch the high school bus, which came earlier than the boys', leaving Sam, Travis, and a dog or two to ride herd for the next several minutes until, finally, they all tumbled out of the house and down the steps. Standing on the porch, Radar sitting on his hip nearby with a satisfied doggy grin, Sam watched the motley collection of too-long legs and arms in denim and cotton jersey make its disorganized way down the drive, the still, oddly warm air occasionally punctuated by a yell, a laugh, some rude noise or other. Humidity filmed Sam's skin, plumped up smells normally kept more or less at bay due to his father's having laid out the farm to take advantage of the seasonal wind direction.

Travis poked Sam's thigh, then pointed east. "Look over there, Daddy. At the clouds."

Sam squinted out toward the horizon, taking note of the thunderheads just beginning to build over the mountains, tinged peach from the early morning sun.

"They're pretty, huh?" Trav said.

"Yeah. They are. Means we're probably gonna get rain later."

"Yeah?" The boy snuggled up next to him; Sam cupped his head, his fingers lingering on the smooth skin below his hairline. "I don't remember—do we get presents on Thanksgiving?"

Sam chuckled. "No presents, short stuff. Just food. Good food. Pumpkin pie and mashed potatoes and turkey."

"Oh. Do I like pumpkin pie?"

"You sure seemed to last year."

"Okay." Apparently satisfied that the day wasn't going to totally blow, Travis went back inside, holding open the door to let Radar in before him. Sam's gaze, however, slid back over to those clouds, getting bigger and more bodacious by the second.

Thunderstorms the day before Thanksgiving…yeah, that

sounded about right, considering how screwy and unpredictable everything else felt these days. Still, he thought as they went back inside, at least he didn't have to worry about the storm messin' up his crops, this time of year.

Something to be grateful for, he supposed.

"I can't tell you how much this means to me," Faith Andrews said to Carly, the blonde's dimpled smile as effervescent as her oldest daughter's was shy. "To us, I guess I should say," she added with a one-armed hug for the eleven-year-old blonde pulling up her jeans over a lime-green one-piece swimsuit. "You really, really think Heather shows promise?"

"I really, really do," Carly said with a smile of her own for the coltish adolescent with the long limbs, high instep and straight back of a dancer's body. Even completely untrained, the girl already showed a natural ability that blew Carly away. She crossed the floor to crank closed the window—the wind had picked up after lunch, blowing a fine layer of dust all over everything. "And thanks for coming out today! I can't imagine how busy you must be with Thanksgiving tomorrow."

"Oh, Mama's doin' most of the cooking this year, all I'm bringin' are the green bean casserole and mashed potatoes, and I can do those in my sleep." Carly waited out the twinge of envy, even though she knew how hellish holidays could be for many families. Most of the ones around here, though, seemed to have things figured out. She still hadn't decided whether or not to go to the Fraziers, although she didn't want to disappoint Libby and the boys.

"So...I guess this means you're plannin' on sticking around?" Faith said.

With a smile that felt more than a little forced, Carly turned around. "For a while, anyway. It all depends on...a lot of things, actually."

On how she and Sam could pull off pretending everything was fine when basically nothing was even remotely fine.

However, here was something to be grateful for, in the form

of a willowy eleven-year-old girl with amazing potential, and the drive to go with it, from what Carly could tell from working with her this morning. She and Faith had already discussed the demands and sacrifices that went hand in hand with being a dancer, that while it was way too early to push the girl too hard, not starting lessons until eleven could put Heather at a disadvantage if she was later to compete with other girls her age who'd started at six or seven. Both mother and daughter seemed to understand, and both were more than ready to give it a shot.

"She'll need real practice clothes, though—a couple of leotards, pink tights, pink ballet shoes." Just as the studio now needed a real mirror.

Mother's and daughter's eyes both went wide. "You mean, those toe shoes they all wear?" Faith asked.

Carly smiled. "No, not yet. Sorry, sweetie," she added when Heather's face fell. "You won't be ready to go *en pointe* for another year, maybe two. Just regular ballet shoes. It'll mean a trip to Tulsa, most likely."

"Oh, I think we can manage that," Faith said with a giggle.

"And I'd like to work with her privately, since she's going to quickly outgrow the other class."

A tiny wrinkle settled between Faith's neatly arched eyebrows; a cloud scurried across her daughter's face. "Mama...?"

"How much would that cost?"

"Tell you what," Carly said, walking them to the door. "Why don't you go home and talk it over with Darryl, see what might fit with your budget. I'm sure we can work something out."

"Oh, no, I don't want your charity—"

"Every dance school in the country gives scholarships, Faith," Carly said gently. "And if Heather really wants to do this..." She met the girl's eager, bright blue eyes and got an eager, dimpled nod in response, and Carly felt a little fireworks shower go off in her chest, warm and bright and sparkly. Grinning, she faced the girl's mother. "I cannot tell you how excited I got when Heather walked into class the other day. This is as much for me as it is for her, believe me. So we'll make it happen, okay?"

"Well…" Faith gnawed on her bottom lip for a moment, then nodded so hard her curls blurred. "Okay. I guess we've got a deal."

The girl squealed and clapped her hands, then—with as much exuberance as her mother—threw her arms around Carly's neck. And Carly heard the little *This is right, this is how it's supposed to be,* which at least reassured her that she could hear the voices, even if the one she most wanted to hear remained stubbornly silent.

Over Trav's protests that he was too big to ride in the baby seat, Sam swung the boy back up into the shopping cart and squinted out over the jam-packed parking lot, trying to remember where he'd parked the damn truck.

"Too many cars, short stuff," he said, his hair whipping around his face in the wind. "Besides, we're runnin' real late— I thought we'd be home long before this! At this rate, Libby and the boys'll get there before we do."

He made a mental note to never, ever again go to Wal-Mart the day before Thanksgiving. Lord, every female residing in a hundred mile radius must've been there today, half of 'em in his line. He'd begun to wonder if he was gonna die there.

They made it to the truck without major incident, Sam secured Trav in his booster seat in the back, then he jumped in, slicking his hair off his forehead. If traffic wasn't too bad between here and Haven, they'd just make it. Not that Libby couldn't handle her brothers for a few minutes, but she'd made it very clear she intended to start on the pies as soon as she got home.

Once out on the highway, a light rain misted the windshield from a cloud apparently directly overhead, since the sky was clear as a bell for miles in front of him, the sun drenching spent, golden fields. The storm clouds had come and gone all day, enough to make Sam periodically check the weather report to make sure there was nothing serious in the offing. Thirty percent chance of showers, was all they'd said. So he guessed—

things were getting blurry enough to warrant turning on the windshield wipers for a second—this was it.

He'd calmed down some about Carly, at least enough to start thinking rationally again. Like she said, he couldn't love her into being somebody she wasn't. Or in her case, had convinced herself she wasn't. So maybe it was for the best, their getting it over with now.

And maybe if he kept telling himself that for another decade or so, he might actually believe it.

"Are we gonna get home soon?" came from the back. "I gotta pee."

"Oh, for Pete's sake, Trav—why didn't you say something back at the store?"

"I didn't have to go then. Daddy?"

"Yeah?"

"Why's the sky all split in two like that? No, over on my side."

Grateful for the distraction from the having-to-go crisis, Sam took a gander out the passenger side window…and his insides turned to stone.

"Holy—!"

The rest of his curse was swallowed by a roar as the funnel dropped down out of the cloud and started cheerfully chewing up the countryside.

The weatherman had blown it this time, boy. Big-time.

Carly's phone rang at the precise moment the siren began to wail. The sound not registering at first, she picked up the phone, barely getting out "Hello," before Libby's frantic "Dad's not over there by any chance, is he?" trampled all over it.

"No, he's not…Libby?"

"He was supposed to be back by now, and that's the tornado siren goin' off, which means he's out there somewhere, with Trav, I'm guessing…."

Carly's hand instantly fused to the phone as her brain processed only the salient points of the girl's message, *tornado* shooting to the top of the list, followed quickly by *Sam and Travis out there somewhere.* She hurried over to the window: the wind had definitely picked up, hurling dirt and leaves against the glass, but from here the sky was still clear. "I'm sure he'll back in a minute, sweetie—"

"They just said on the news that one twister t-touched down right outside Claremore a few m-minutes ago!" Carly could tell the poor thing was on the verge of meltdown. "Daddy'd gone to the Wal-Mart to get some stuff for d-dinner tomorrow, and now…"

"Libby, honey—are the other boys all with you?"

"Yeah, they're asking where Daddy is, too, and I need to get them down to the basement, but…"

"But, nothing." Carly grabbed her purse and a sweater. Not that she had a clue what she was supposed to do, but no way was she leaving Libby to deal with this on her own. "You get everybody in the basement, I'll be there in a sec, okay?"

She ran outside, the wind snatching at her hair and clothes like a crazed groupie a rock star, grinding grit into her eyes and mouth. She hopped into her car, first checking to make sure no funnel cloud was snaking out of the putrid gray-green sky behind her.

"Come on, come *on*," she urged the recalcitrant engine, which finally turned over as thunder cracked open the clouds, rendering her wipers useless against the river of water sluicing across the windshield. Like witches' fingers, broken branches pelted the car as she peeled out of the yard and sped as fast as she dared past her father's house, her heart sinking when she noticed his car wasn't in the driveway. Yeah, he had a storm cellar, too, but fat lot of good it was going to do him if he wasn't there. She dug her cell out of her purse and called him, but no answer.

Swallowing down her fear for her father, for Sam, for Travis, she fishtailed into the Fraziers' driveway and jumped out of the car, taking the porch steps two at a time. The kids—and whichever dogs and cats they could corral—were already in the basement; Frankie and Wade nearly knocked Carly down with hugs when she got to the bottom of the steps.

"It's okay, it's okay," she whispered, wondering where the hell this flood of protectiveness was coming from as she hugged the little boys, taking in the valiant attempts at bravery from the other three, all of whom were calm, but trembling.

"You ever been through a tornado before?" Mike asked her.

"They have them in Ohio, but I've never seen one, no. I imagine you guys are old hands at it though, huh?"

They all shook their heads. "We get warnings all the time," Libby said, crouched next to one wall, hugging her knees, "but one's never touched down in Haven proper." Her eyes filled with tears. "I really wish Daddy and Trav were here."

"Yeah. So do I," Carly said, forcing down another surge of panic. "Come on, guys, let's sit real close to each other."

They lowered themselves to the floor by one of the freezers, propping their backs against the cold, damp wall. Wade and Frankie grafted themselves to her sides; Carly wrapped her arms around them and thought, *Okay...now what?*

"Now we wait," Libby said. "Until the sirens sound the all clear."

Even in the basement, they could hear the storm brutally pounding the house, the groans and scratches of tree branches scraping the walls, the dulled thunder of hail hammering the roof two stories above their heads. The electricity flickered, held, went out; Libby clicked on a battery-powered lantern, its light dim and eerie in the blackness. Nobody talked about the possibilities, that they might lose the house, the livestock. Or worse. The young ones huddled closer and Carly kissed their hair, the gesture so instinctive she didn't at first realize she'd done it.

"You guys ever see *The Sound of Music?*"

"Some of us," Libby said. "It was Mama's favorite movie."

"You know the part where Maria sings to the children when they're scared of the storm?" The teenager nodded. "Yeah, well, I don't do that," she said, which got little laughs out of the older ones, at least.

Then, as if someone had turned off a radio, dead silence swallowed up the wailing, the battering.

"Is it over?" Wade asked.

"I don't think so," Libby said, barely above a whisper, and Mike said something about almost wishing he could go outside and see what was going on and Libby said, "Don't be an idiot," and lifted her eyes to the ceiling, tucking her hair behind her ear. "Listen…"

The silence seemed to thicken, until Carly felt as though she couldn't get her breath. Then it started, that freight-train roar she'd always heard about, as if they were all lying right in its path, tied to the tracks. She heard Libby muffle a scream, saw the older boys inch closer to each other. Now Carly swallowed back a hot-cold sick feeling as sweat beaded on her forehead. Frankie tugged on her shirt; when she looked down, he whispered, "You think this'd be a good time to pray?"

"It sure as hell couldn't hurt," she whispered back, and the roar grew louder, and louder still, the howl of a ravenous monster desperate for something to devour, and she shut her eyes as well as she could, prayed for her father and these children and the farm and everyone in town, and the man she suddenly knew beyond a shadow of a doubt she loved with all her heart.

Overhead, threaded through the roar, she heard the faint, almost musical tinkle of shattering glass, then an earsplitting crack she couldn't identify. She held her breath, anticipating the sense of helpless terror…but it never came. Instead, even in the midst the most out-of-control situation she'd ever been in, a deep sense of peace washed over her. That she could let go and trust in something she couldn't see, and certainly didn't understand.

And if that wasn't weird, she didn't know what was. But since it felt pretty damn good, she figured maybe this praying stuff was working, so she hugged the boys more tightly to her and got back to it.

"*Now* it's over," Libby said.

Carly opened her eyes, realizing the roar was gone. Seconds later, the all-clear sounded, and they scrambled to their feet and cautiously climbed the cellar steps that led directly outside. For a moment or two, Carly was tempted to think it'd all been a dream: The air was cool and dry, the sun shining serenely in a cloudless blue sky.

Then she did a slow turn, slamming her palm over her mouth to stifle her gasp. Oh, everything major was still standing, thank God, but there was debris and mud and shingles *everywhere.* She glanced back at the house, saw that the dining room window was missing, broken glass glittering like diamonds on the mud. Shielding her eyes from the ridiculously bright sun, she squinted toward her father's house, her barn-slash-studio-slash-home, saw they were both still there, too. The worry that had been fisted in her chest for the past half hour eased, but until she knew that Sam and Travis and her father were safe, there was no way she could relax completely.

"Oh, *hell,*" Libby yelled. "The pigs are out!"

Sure enough, the swamplike yard swarmed with porkers, none of whom were the least bit interested in anyone's attempts to herd them back into the one pen that hadn't been damaged—

Carly nearly jumped out of her skin when her cell phone buzzed in her pocket. All five kids went stock-still, their eyes locked on hers while pigs cavorted and squealed with the glee of the newly liberated as she fumbled to get the phone out, nearly dropping it twice before finally getting it to her ear.

"Thank God," her father said when she answered, and tears stung her eyes.

"It's Lane," she told the kids, her heart breaking at their attempts to hide their disappointment.

"Is he okay?" Libby asked, almost as an afterthought, and Carly nodded over her father's, "Is that Libby? You're over at Sam's? Is everything all right?"

"Basically, yeah. A few shingles, a broken window, pigs everywhere…"

"Where's Sam?"

She turned away, so the kids wouldn't hear, which is when she noticed there seemed to be a lot more sky from this angle than she remembered. Probably because there was a lot less tree, specifically the huge old oak that had once shaded the far side of the barn. "We don't…exactly know. He and Trav had gone to Claremore, they're not…" Her voice caught. "They're not back yet."

"It's gonna be okay, baby," her father said quietly.

"Yeah. I know. It's just…" She sucked in a huge breath, shoving her hair off her face. "So. Where are you?"

"In town. I rode it out in the cellar underneath Ruby's. But right now…" She heard his sigh over the phone. "I'm standing in front of Ivy's house. What's left of it, anyway."

"Ohmigod—is she okay?"

There was a pause. "I don't know yet."

"Ivy's a tough old bird," Carly said, trying to smile. "I'm sure she's fine."

"You keep thinking that, sweetheart. I'll call you when I know something."

"Me, too," she said, stuffing her phone back into her pants just in time to be sprayed with mud, courtesy of an amazingly fleet-of-foot hundred and fifty pound pig, a bellowing pair of boys hot on its hooves. Then she looked over and saw that Libby had gone catatonic, hugging herself as she stared toward the road.

Carly sloshed through the muck to take the girl in her arms, where they both held on to each other for dear life in a desperate attempt to keep the dread at bay.

Sprung from the Town Hall basement (which was more than could be said for Hootch Atkins, who was sleeping off a bender in one of the two cells that passed for Haven's jail), Ivy hauled ass around the corner of her block, only to come to a dead stop. She'd heard about the small twister that had decided to dance around town for five minutes or so; what she hadn't known was that it had seen fit to uproot the fifty-foot mulberry at the back of her house, which now bore a striking resemblance to Baby Bear's chair after Goldilocks had planted her big fat butt on it. With a wailed curse that no doubt singed ears clear out to Cal's place, she sank onto the curb, only vaguely aware of Hazel Dinwiddy wandering onto her porch, a male voice calling her name.

"My house, my house," was all she could say, and then Lane's arms closed around her, his masculine scent swirling through her battered senses. Her inclination was to resist, except something inside her said, *Don't be an idiot,* especially when she realized, through her shock and grief, how tightly he was holding on.

Like a man who'd had the bejesus scared out of him.

"When I saw the house—" he got out through what Ivy suspected was a convulsing throat "—and thought you might still be inside…"

She heard Hazel mutter something about leaving them to it, then.

"Well, I wasn't," she said, wiping her eyes—oh, Lord, she'd been crying?—before daring to peek back across the street. The houses on either side of her were untouched, praise the Lord. But hers… "Everything I own is—was—in that house. My gorgeous refrigerator," she moaned, and Lane bracketed her face in his hands and forced their eyes to meet, and she thought, *Oh, my.*

"Refrigerators can be replaced," he said, his voice rough with emotion. "So can houses. *You* can't."

A good three or four seconds floated by before she got up the nerve to ask, "What are you sayin', Lane Stewart?"

His eyes were like hot ice. "That you're not a substitute for Dena, and you never have been. You're the real thing, Ivy Gardner. You started to heal my heart from the moment I laid eyes on you. And if you'll let me, I intend to love you like nobody's ever loved you before." He kissed her, then stroked her hair off her face. "Like nobody's ever going to love you again. And before you jump to any conclusions about this being a crisis-inspired revelation..." Now he kissed her knuckles, his expression downright beseeching. "It isn't. I was on my way over when the damn sirens went off."

"Oh," she said. "I wasn't home."

He smiled. "I know."

Well. That sure took the edge off of having her house smashed to smithereens. As it apparently took the edge off *her,* since she realized she couldn't think of a single smart-assed comeback. In fact, all she said was, "Okay," which she guessed did the trick, judging from the huge smile Lane gave her in return. Then he helped her to her feet, linked their fingers together, and lead her across the street to face yet another crisis in her life.

Only this one, she didn't have to face alone.

"Daddy's back!"

Even the pigs seemed to squeal with glee at the sight of one very dirty pickup bumping up the road to the house. Carly hung back, her chest feeling way too small for her thudding heart as five kids swarmed around the truck before Sam even had a chance to cut the engine. Libby scooped a grinning, filthy Travis out of his booster seat as Sam—as mud-caked as his truck—tried to hug all four boys at once, his deep laugh reverberating over their high-pitched chatter.

"Everybody's okay?" she heard him ask, his head swiveling to take in the house, the barn, clearly reassuring himself that everything was still more or less intact. Then his gaze landed on her, and held, his brows lifting with questions, his grin somehow softening and expanding at the same time.

"What happened?" somebody said, and Sam steadied himself, as though fully realizing what he'd been through.

"Twister touched down right outside Claremore, only thing to do was get out and throw ourselves in a ditch." He hitched Travis up into his arms. "And pray like I've never prayed before."

"Yeah," Travis said, "an' I couldn't hardly breathe for Daddy layin' on top of me," and they all laughed, nervously, and Mike said, "How close did it get?" and Sam said, "A lot closer than I liked," and everybody got real quiet.

"We lost that big old oak," Matt said.

Sam squeezed his shoulder. "Yeah. I saw. Guess we won't be runnin' out of firewood for a while, huh?"

That got another round of laughter, stronger this time. Then Sam's gaze returned to Carly's, the love in his eyes washing away the last wispy remnants of doubt, leaving her finally free to take this man up on an offer she'd never believed possible. Because apparently her voice *did* come in the wind.

But it came. And that's all that counted.

Libby's dark hair glinted in the sun as she glanced over at Carly, then back at her father.

"Come on, Trav," she said, "let's get you in the tub…guys? I think we need to go inside…"

The screen door banged behind her—*bam! bam! bambambam!*—and then it was just Sam and her and a pig or two, contentedly rooting in the mud at the base of the house. Carly started toward him, her pace quickening in response to his smile, and then she flew into his outstretched arms, crying and laughing with joy and relief and more love than she'd ever thought possible.

"Ohmigod, ohmigod, ohmigod," she sobbed into his neck when he lifted her, and she never wanted to let him go, evereverever. Except when he eventually set her down, she slugged him in the arm as tears streamed down her cheeks. "Don't you *ever* scare me like that again!"

He smiled.

And kissed her.

For a very long time.

When he finished he bent down to take her mud-splattered face in his hands, his expression full of wonder. "You came over to be with the kids?"

"Yeah, well, when you weren't here, Libby called… and…and I couldn't have left them to go through that alone for the world." She laughed, the sound a little frantic. "I guess that means I love them, huh?"

"That would be my take on it—"

"Which is pretty damned convenient seeing as I'm also head over heels in love with their father. And yes, I've never been more sure of anything in my life."

His grin would be her undoing. "Oh, yeah?"

"Yeah," she said on shaky sigh. "Go figure."

"You're not just sayin' that 'cause you thought maybe I'd gotten blown into the next county?"

"Don't *say* that!" she said, slugging him again, only when he laughed, she added, "And anyway, no. I'm saying that because, somehow, you managed to blow everything I thought I knew about myself all to hell."

"Hmm," he said, encircling her waist with his hands, sending a nice little shiver of desire skipping along her skin. "You know, the only other woman who ever told me she loved me ended up being my wife."

"I see." Shielding her eyes from the sun, she said, "I don't suppose there are any other options?"

"Not from where I'm standing."

Her smile started in the vicinity of her heart and kept on going. "I was hoping you'd say that," she said, and this time, she kissed *him,* a kiss of promise sweeter than any she'd ever known.

"What's goin' on—"

"Move over, dork, I can't see…"

"Shh," Libby said, her brothers all crammed around her as they stood at Daddy's window, overlooking the yard. "They'll hear you!" Of course, what she really meant was that she wouldn't be able to hear *them,* which was the whole point of eavesdropping, after all.

Frankie poked her in her arm. "I couldn't hear…did Daddy just ask Carly to marry him?"

Libby wrapped an arm around her brother. "He sure did."

"What'd she say?" asked Wade.

"I said 'yes'," Carly shouted up at them, laughing, and Daddy gave them all a thumbs-up, with a special wink for Libby. Who thought her face would crack in two, she was grinning so hard.

And when she looked over at her mother's photo on her desk, she could have sworn she saw Mama wink, too.

Imagine that.

* * * * *

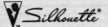

SPECIAL EDITION™

presents the next three books
in the continuity

MONTANA MAVERICKS

GOLD RUSH GROOMS

Lucky in love—and striking it rich—
beneath the big skies of Montana!

THEIR UNEXPECTED FAMILY
by **Judy Duarte**
SE #1676, on sale April 2005

CABIN FEVER
by **Karen Rose Smith**
SE #1682, on sale May 2005

And the exciting conclusion

MILLION-DOLLAR MAKEOVER
by **Cheryl St.John**
SE #1688, on sale June 2005

**Don't miss these thrilling stories—
only from Silhouette Books.**

Available at your favorite retail outlet.

If you enjoyed what you just read,
then we've got an offer you can't resist!

Take 2 bestselling love stories FREE!

Plus get a FREE surprise gift!

eHARLEQUIN.com

The Ultimate Destination for Women's Fiction

For **FREE online reading,** visit
www.eHarlequin.com now and enjoy:

Online Reads
Read **Daily** and **Weekly** chapters from
our Internet-exclusive stories by your
favorite authors.

Interactive Novels
Cast your vote to help decide how these
stories unfold...then stay tuned!

Quick Reads
For shorter romantic reads, try our
collection of Poems, Toasts, & More!

Online Read Library
Miss one of our online reads?
Come here to catch up!

Reading Groups
Discuss, share and rave with other
community members!

For great reading online,
visit www.eHarlequin.com today!

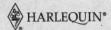

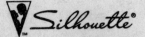

COMING NEXT MONTH

SIMCNM0405